SHORTING THE UNDEAD AND OTHER HORRORS

A MENAGERIE OF MACABRE MINI-FICTION

ALSO AVAILABLE
BY
SAUL TANPEPPER

‡ ‡

A Thing for Zombies

Flawless: a Claire Fontaine novella

‡ ‡ ‡

SHORTING THE UNDEAD AND OTHER HORRORS

A MENAGERIE OF MACABRE MINI-FICTION

‡ ‡ ‡

by
Saul Tanpepper

BRINESTONE PRESS
San Martin, CA

SHORTING THE UNDEAD AND OTHER HORRORS
A MENAGERIE OF MACABRE MINI-FICTION

‡ ‡ ‡

‡

Brinestone Press
http://www.brinestonepress.com

‡

For more information, contact Brinestone Press or the author at:

editor@brinestonepress.com

authorsaultanpepper@gmail.com

ISBN-13: 978-0-615-58048-7 (soft cover)
ISBN-10: 0-615-58048-3 (soft cover)

To Cheryl
who haunts me every day (in the best possible way)

Contents

Introduction

I'm frequently asked, usually by an old colleague from my former life as a molecular geneticist, "How does a person go from studying science *fact* to writing science *fiction*?" And I have to chuckle to myself before answering because I know that what they really mean is: "Are you freaking crazy or something?"

What they really want to know isn't *how*, but *why*. The *how* of it is easy to understand—or at least to explain: You wake up one day and decide, "I'm tired of talking about real stuff, the nitty gritty, itty bitty detail stuff. I'm going to start making shit up. And not just random shit but the craziest kind of shit you can imagine." Well, science tends to frown on that sort of thinking.

Which, I guess, explains why my decision eludes so many of the people I knew from that past life. Hell, the *why* sometimes even eludes me.

But I'll give it a shot:

For me, the world of science and fact has always been too routine, too sciency and factual, too dry. No, really. When's the last time you heard someone shriek "*Eureka!*" and mean it? There are no more of those moments anymore, no great leaps forward in scientific understanding. Every new discovery is an incremental step beyond the place where we stood just a moment before. Imagine walking Interstate-90—all thirty-one hundred miles of it—heel to toe. The scenery changes very little over time, and the horizon continues to dangle just out of reach. Oh, there are huge differences in the landscape overall, but you can only see them from very high up. Science on an individual level is like that. It's a long, slow walk. I just don't have the patience for it.

That's not to say that I don't appreciate science and technology and development and all that. I do. These are all worthwhile ventures, and I certainly made my own contributions to them. The real world can be fascinating at times. But for me, it just wasn't enough. It wasn't fast enough or steady enough or new enough. My mind craves freshness at levels and speeds unattainable by my individual technological endeavors. I wanted to explore regions heretofore only dreamed of in the wildest imaginations of the craziest minds. And then go beyond.

I want to make real what *isn't*, as much as I wanted to unearth what is. Maybe even more so.

But, you know, all fantasy has its roots in fact. That's what makes it so compelling, so...believable. Science and fiction.

Science. Fiction.

To be accurate, though, I guess I should explain that I don't write science fiction, *per se*. At least not what most people associate with the genre (think spaceships and robots and ray guns and inter-dimensional wormholes). What I write stretches beyond the boundaries of genre and into the wider realm of *speculative* fiction (or *specfic*, as some call it). And this is where things really start to get messy, because the kind of *specfic* I like to write, the kind you're holding in your hands, isn't just the fantastical, but the horrifying. The only wormholes you'll find in these stories are the sort often associated with corpses.

Speaking of the Dead, they're among my newest best friends. Oh, I still keep tabs on the old ones, but they're just not as interesting as the Undead and the Unliving. I find these new friends of mine so much more fascinating. They have the most interesting stories to tell. I believe every word they tell me. And so should you.

Inside this collection of eight short stories and novellas, you'll find many of my new acquaintances. The Undead are well represented (*The Headhunter, Outsourced, Golgotha*), as are the Unliving (*Mr. November, Nocturne*), people who have forgotten the how to live. In some of my stories (*Open Wide, Occupied, The Object of Her Obsession*), I leave it to you to decide from which side of the grave they come.

Just remember: there is horror in both fact and fiction.

See you on one side or the other.

Saul
San Francisco, CA
December 10, 2011

SHORTING THE UNDEAD AND OTHER HORRORS

A MENAGERIE OF MACABRE MINI-FICTION

‡ ‡ ‡

Occupied

IT WAS NINE-THIRTY at night and I was already sitting on a razor's edge waiting for the LA-bound redeye out of Hamilton, when I first noticed the fat guy standing over by the boarding gate. What had drawn my attention to him wasn't the thinning, greasy black hair on his head or the briny sweat stains spreading from underneath his armpits, though they certainly added to the overall effect. He had this guarded look about him, a way of standing and glancing furtively about that suggested his appearance was just that: an illusion. There was an intensity in his eyes. He looked like someone waiting to explode. All it would take was the smallest spark to set him off.

It felt like I was looking in the mirror.

Not that I'm fat and sloppy-looking or would ever dress anything like that. At least until my crash down in Australia six months ago, I'd been pretty fit and trim. I still was, for the most part, though I'd gotten a bit soft. It couldn't be helped.

No, I meant the stuff going on inside the guy's head. And mine.

He was pacing. He'd cleared a tiny space for himself at the front of the queue and he was careful not to stray too far from it. I figured what was going through his mind was someone trying sneak in front of him. He kept glaring at the people behind him, as if he thought they might try.

Way to go, Frank, I thought, sighing down at my chest as I sat on the unforgiving seats of the airport terminal. This is supposed to help calm me down?

Frank Gorme, my shrink back in LA. Make that former shrink. He'd come up with the idea about a month ago, suggesting that if I studied how other people acted under situations that I found stressful, maybe it'd help calm me down. Problem with that theory was, you gather enough folks together in one place at one time—like an airport terminal in Bermuda, for example—then one of those people is bound to be bordering on the edge of psychotic.

And, naturally, one's attention always tends to gravitate toward such people, doesn't it?

Not that I thought of myself as crazy. I had issues, true. A few irrational fears. Some...let's call them obsessive notions. I consciously avoided participating in any activities that carried with them any risk of injury, death. Like racing motorcycles.

Why motorcycles? Because I'd been a supermoto champion, before the

(engine failed)

wipeout on the double-S curve at Philip Island. After that, just the thought of riding a bike gave me the shits and made me want to puke. Airplanes were just as bad.

So this was to be my first flight in six months. Well, second, actually. I'd pretty much slept through the inbound flight here ten days ago, thanks to a combination of drugs, both legal and otherwise, which my agent Harry Bigelow was more than happy to provide. But now I was stone-cold sober and regretting the fact that I'd ever hired the guy in the first place. So that's why I was barely managing to hold myself together as I waited to board my flight home.

And why watching someone like the guy standing at the gate was almost definitely not the best thing to be doing.

Harry's been with me for over ten years now, so it's not like I'm going to fire him now, even though he promised the trip would help me exorcise the demons inside my head. He's a hell of an agent, but even he doesn't know everything about what makes a person tick. That's why I have Frank—*had* Frank.

I wonder if Harry's getting a percentage of what I was paying that scumbag shrink. Who knows? It's all about the money—what I make, what I *could* make. What I'm losing by not racing. I'm sure it was driving him nuts, each day I refused to get back

(into the cockpit)

on a bike. He probably had a running total inside his head of how much money he was losing with each race I didn't enter. Right down to the last penny. This little vacay was supposed to fast-track my recovery so he could go on living the life he'd become accustomed to.

"A little time away to gather your thoughts, Stack," he'd told me. "Time to remember who you are."

"I haven't forgotten who I am," I'd snapped back at him. "I'm Stack Miller, supermoto champion."

"*Riiiight*," he countered, frowning and shaking his head. "Supersofa champion is more like it."

"Fuck off."

"Hey, I got kids to support."

"Does your wife know that?"

He laughed. He never takes what I say personally, not unless it has to do with money.

"I just don't see how going somewhere else is supposed to help," I complained. "I can relax here at home." In all my travels, I'd never made it to Bermuda, but it hadn't been a great loss: I'd been to a ton of other places, many of them much more exotic.

"You're not just going somewhere, you're going somewhere in an airplane. Besides, you need to get out more. You've become a hermit. It's not healthy."

If you didn't count the trips to Gorme's downtown office, I'd barely stepped foot outside of my Malibu home in six months. I even had the physical therapist go there to work on my knee.

"Once we get you on that plane, Stack, you'll be fine. Everything'll work itself out, just you wait and see if it don't."

"I. Don't. Want to. Fly."

Harry didn't hear. I suppose that's what good agents do.

It actually turned out to be a lot easier than I'd thought it would be, getting on the plane and coming down here to Bermuda. I don't even remember the flight at all. Harry had gotten me nice and sloppy before the cab came to take us to LAX, got me to pop whatever tranq-du-jour he could get his hands on, then washed it down with a quarter bottle of tequila he'd shoved into my hands when I opened the door to my house at eight o'clock that sunny Friday morning. "Just loosening things up," he'd said as he dumped his bag into the trunk of the cab and guided my body into the backseat. Looking at me, the poor driver probably thought he'd have to clean the backseat after that trip, but I behaved myself. I don't think I threw up until after we landed in Hamilton ten hours later.

After I sobered up that night, I swore I would never go back to that shit-for-brains shrink again. I told Harry he was on notice, too. And Harry, being good old Harry, cajoled and placated me until I calmed down again. He always took good care of me.

Then, after three days on the island, he slipped off without telling me. Next thing I know, he's back in LA and calling me on my cell phone saying, "It's time you came back, Stack." He'd abandoned me.

I begged for him to come back; he refused.

So I finally got up the nerve to make the damn reservation. After procrastinating for another week, I'd gotten my nerve up to fly again. Gone were the drugs. And alcohol just wasn't cutting it anymore, especially not after last night's trippy escapade. In fact, just the thought of alcohol gave me the sweats.

The flight was supposed to have boarded at five that evening, but there'd been delays, storms or something coming up from Cuba. Four and a half hours later I'd chewed my nails down to the quick. My fingertips were pale and wrinkly and they throbbed like hell, so I was ready for something else to distract me.

I started drawing shit on my jeans with a cheap ballpoint pen I'd lifted from the bedside table in my bungalow. Before I realized it, I'd ripped a hole in the knee—not the one with the nasty scar on it, but the right knee. I kept thinking I should just get up and walk right on out of there, just go back and spend the rest of my life on the island—I had the money; I could do it—but then what? The only thing I knew how to do was

(fly)

race motorcycles. It was the only thing I was ever really good at.

I tried to sleep, but the plastic seats in the waiting area were rock hard and sort of greasy so that I kept sliding down and having to push myself up again. Besides, I didn't want to miss the announcement. I lost count of the number of flights that had been cancelled or delayed. It looked to be a good two dozen by how packed they had us in the terminal. The place was like a cattle yard.

The latest update over the loudspeaker had the LA flight departing after ten, but at twenty minutes till we still hadn't started boarding, so I doubted we'd make that time. I hoped for it nonetheless. If I could just manage to get on the plane without having a panic attack first, I might just make it all the way back to LA without too much problem.

I caught a whiff of cigarette smoke mingling with fryer fat, and my stomach responded by grumbling quite unhappily. I hoped I wasn't coming down with traveler's diarrhea

People were fanning themselves. The air was oppressive, hot and full of an oily kind of humidity, carrying an undertone of something not quite rotten, but close. I'd gotten a whiff of it upon first arriving on the island, but then quickly forgot about it. But now I could smell it again. It reminded me of meat that was on the verge of going bad.

Like the fat guy.

I tilted my head and stared at the ceiling. The fans were on but they were useless. The blades were turning way too slow to have any effect. Flies were landing on them just to catch a breeze. Thinking that, I started to chuckle and then choked on my tongue, making a strangling noise. A couple people looked over. I pretended it hadn't been me.

I couldn't sit still. I got up again and walked around this time. I even considered hiding in the bathroom—small, confined spaces calmed me—but decided against it. Sat down again. Messed with the hole in my jeans again. Drew some nonsense on the other knee without realizing I was doing it. Saw that it was a plane going down in flames and rubbed it out. Started drawing something else. Letters: *CHR*— Crossed them out. Finally, I just gave up and started watching the fat guy again.

I knew my restlessness wasn't entirely mental. Some of it was at least partially due to the half bottle of Benadryl that was coursing through my veins. I'd overheard a couple conspiring to knock out their kid with the stuff so they could sleep during the flight. I thought I'd give it a try. But all they'd had in the airport gift shop was a dusty old box of the children's formula that was probably expired. It tasted like cherry-flavored shit, and I can't stand cherries. I'd managed to down half the bottle before throwing the rest in the trash. Now my tongue felt like somebody had replaced it with a pelt of dryer lint, and there was this strange clicking sound in my ears. I couldn't tell if it was coming from my mouth or my nose, so I kept swallowing and sniffling, but it kept right on clicking.

The boy whose parents had tried to dope up was lying on the floor, still wide awake and eating a chocolate bar I'd seen him swipe from his mother's purse. Thanks to him, every time I closed my eyes, my head filled up with horrific images: the plane plastered against the side of some mountain, the plane falling apart in mid-flight, the plane sinking into the ocean, the plane disappearing. He'd informed those of us unfortunate enough to be sitting within hearing distance that our flight path took us directly over the Bermuda Triangle. Except he'd called it something else. What the hell was it? Devil's Triangle, something like that. Or Triangle of Death. I whispered over to him that he should shut up. I mean, really? His parents were sound asleep.

Triangle of Death. What the fuck is that about?

The boy looked over. I held up the phone and gave him a weak smile. "You mind?" I said, realizing I might have said that out loud. "I'm talking to

(myself)

someone." Then, as if to prove it, I added a cheerful, "Bye, honey. See you when I get home. Kisses."

The kid looked away, neither impressed nor disgusted, just blank, dead. It was this damn heat. It was turning us all into zombies.

Last night's binder came back to me, the part when I was in the bar. I was finishing my fifth drink. Or maybe it was my seventh. Doesn't matter. I remember the bartender was telling me

(nothing)

this strange local bullshit lore about the walking dead. Or undead. What the hell was it? Something about leaving and the undead were coming. The island was full of voodoo hoodoo crap. I'd laughed and asked him what the fuck he was talking about. And he'd answered: *Zooombies, mon. Dey are reel, awright. Seen dem mahself. Done let nobody tell you uddahwise.*

I remember I hadn't quite understood what he was saying at the time—not because of the accent, but because he was talking pure bullshit. Of course, it was also possible that I'd reached some sort of critical brain-alcohol threshold that was really screwing with the old brain cells. *Don't Worry, Be Happy* was playing in the background and it was all just so flipping strange that I might even have agreed with him, just to get him to stop talking.

But I was sober now, and the reference seemed even more arcane than it had last night. I recalled the look he'd given me, the shadows thrown onto his face by the flickering of the tiki torches surrounding the thatch hut that served as a bar. That stare he'd given me. The whiteness of his teeth against the darkness of his skin. He licked his chapped lips with a tongue that was so pale and blue and thick that it looked like it belonged to a dog. *Yoo tink I'm jokin', my fren', but Bair-moo-da is where da dead come aliiive.*

He'd pointed his finger at me and touched me on my forehead, just beneath my hairline, like he was anointing me. He'd held my gaze for a moment the way a mesmerist might, and then he suddenly broke out in a long, rumbling laugh—I could still hear it in my head, even now, could still feel the spot where he'd touched me, which was now itching and beginning to scab over—and I'd laughed reflexively along with him, even though what he'd said had struck me as a hell of lot more frightful than funny. In fact, it hadn't been funny at all.

I'd woken this morning with a hangover, but even the pounding headache hadn't been able to mask this new fear blooming up inside me, inchoate and terrifying and spreading like ink in still water, like something horrible was about to happen.

The fat guy over by the gate was still pacing, still waving his hands about, still talking to himself.

Another of Frank's useless ideas was to try and guess things about people I saw. I'd figured Fat Guy to be a comic book writer. He was in his mid-fifties. Probably unmarried. He sure looked the type, like he spent the bulk of his time in some dark attic or cellar somewhere, drawing comics with one hand while getting himself off with the other. He had an almost obscene look to him. He made me uncomfortable just looking at him.

But I kept watching him anyway.

I saw him reach into his pocket and extract a cell phone and start talking into it. The terminal was noisy, so I couldn't hear what he was saying, but it was obvious from the redness creeping up his neck that it wasn't a happy conversation. The dark bib of sweat beneath his shirt collar quickly began to spread. Before long, it covered the top half of his chest.

He started shouting, just a few words at first, incoherent. But then the shouting became louder and longer. It began to draw other people's attention. Then, just as I'd expected, he exploded:

"Listen, you fucking moron! I don't give a rat's ass what you think!" The terminal went nearly silent then. I could sense the alarm level rising. The guy didn't notice the attention he was attracting. "Get your goddamn Jew-ass down to those boys in the newsroom and tell them what I just told you! And in case you missed it the first time, you tell them to shove that other fucking story back up their tight little asses and start working on the background for mine. I want this piece to be on the cover when it hits the stands on Wednesday. I'll be on the ground in…" He checked his watch. "In nine hours—six-thirty local, if the airline ever gets their collective heads out of their collective asses—and the first thing I'm going to do is find you, Harvey, and I will personally drill you a new one if you don't have a packet ready for me to review!"

Editor, I realized, not comic book writer. Or maybe roving reporter, although, by the looks of things, the only place he spent much time roving around was the line at the local all-you-could-eat buffet.

But the guy wasn't finished: "You tell that shithead Perkins he better— What? That's right, you tell him I'm the one who told you to say it. Do I need to spell it out for you, you dumb fuck? Tell him if he doesn't run my story as the lead, I'm going to sue his goddamn fat ass for sending me down here to this third world shithole in the first place. He knows I've got a bad ticker and can't tolerate the humidity." He clutched his chest, as if he was going to drop dead right there, but he just kept right on shouting. "And if Perkins doesn't do as I say, you tell him that I'll sell the zombie story to the highest bidder… I bet I could get two million for it."

Zombie story?

The laughing bartender inside my head suddenly got a smug look in his eyes. What had been the guy's name? Peter, I think. Peter the Bartender. It didn't matter; the guy had just been messing around with me. But it did seem like a strange coincidence.

So the fat guy wasn't an editor, either, but a tabloid reporter.

(Scum of the earth. Bet he writes for the Orange County Juice.*)*

The *Juice* was a third-rate tabloid that published out of Anaheim. Not even worth the space on the supermarket discount rack. They probably had a readership of less than half a million.

(Except you happen to be quite familiar with it, aren't you?)

They'd run a story about Christie breaking up with me, and then her disappearing after the accident, dropping out of sight. It was this big mystery. Except, there was nothing mysterious about it. The girl had stayed with me for my money. Once I stopped racing, she bailed.

I had to chuckle, even if it was mostly out of spite. Two million for a zombie story. Made me wonder how much the writer of that fiction about me and Christie had gotten, how much they must've paid her parents to dish on me. Just didn't seem right. Two million was more than I'd earned all of last year racing on the circuit.

I watched as one of the TropicAir people went over and told the guy he needed to quiet down. He was furious, especially when a bunch of people started applauding. He turned and gave them a withering stare, and they quickly stopped, but he did quiet down.

A few minutes later they announced that they were starting the boarding process for LA, and so my entertainment for the evening went on his merry way, disappearing down the gangway with the first class passengers, and leaving me once again with nothing to distract me. Not that I was going to miss him. In fact, I was glad for once that Harry had booked me in economy class. "You go with the commoners until you get your head on straight," he'd said, half teasing, half serious. Fat Guy was now the problem of the first class passengers and crew.

Or so I thought.

Fifteen minutes later I was shuffling down the aisle looking for seat twenty-one F, and who should show up again? There he was, in twenty-one E, and he was fast asleep. There was no way I could get to my seat.

I considered climbing over him. Heck, six months ago, I would have. I'd have gone right up and over the top of the guy without giving it a second thought. But then again, six months ago was another lifetime and I had been a different person. Six months ago I didn't have a plastic

(spine)

kneecap. And I certainly didn't have a catalogue of fears as long as Santa's naughty list.

It had been down in Melbourne, during the Superstock 600 on Phillip Island last spring. Besides the shattered knee, I'd suffered a hell of a concussion. I still had days when I couldn't remember the simplest things, like the name of my favorite cereal or my mom's phone number. But remembering those sorts of details had never really been a priority for me before, so why should they be now?

PTSD. That's what Frank told me I was suffering from. Post traumatic stress disorder. "Your first brush with death, Gary." Like it was some kind of benchmark I'd been striving for or something, like a bar mitzvah. Woo hoo! Time to celebrate my first date with the Grim Reaper.

"I've told you at least a half dozen times to call me Stack," I told him.

"Stack's what your fans used to call you," he'd replied. "But I'm not a fan of quitters."

Christ, he could be as much of a prick as Harry sometimes.

I looked around me, wondering what the hell I was going to do about getting to my seat. The woman standing behind me scowled. For some reason, she reminded me of my great Aunt Rhoda. Maybe it was because both women had the same pinched look to their mouths, like somebody had sewn drawstrings into their lips. But this woman took it to the extreme, like someone had planted their foot on her face and yanked on it as hard as they could. She also had this hot red gloss on her lips and her mascara was on a bit too thick. Maybe she was trying to compensate for something. Her hair was flat black and straight, except for at the part, where a few kinky, gray strands and some dandruff showed. And she couldn't have been any taller than four-six. Yet, despite all that, she looked

(respectable)

strangely appealing.

Her eyes dropped and she stared at my belt buckle for a moment. It was the one I'd gotten for taking the Supermoto in Rio when I was nineteen. Twelve years, I realized with a start. Twelve damn years and what had I accomplished in all that time? Not a damn thing except, literally, spin my wheels and go in circles. I supposed it was as an apt a metaphor for my life as any other.

The buckle had always been my favorite. It had been my first big win and got me that first huge contract. Who the hell had it been with?

(Red Bull.)

Honda bikes. When Kawasaki countered the offer is when Harry came on board; he negotiated them to almost twice what Honda had offered. Did I say he was good?

Anyway, the chicks always dug the buckle. God knows why.

The woman looked up and her face shifted and I thought for a second that she was going to smile. "Motorcycles," she said, sneering, as if anyone who rode one—or even smelled like they rode one—had to be a contributing member of the Hell's Angels and therefore was scum of the earth. I took an awkward step backward and nearly stumbled over someone's feet.

"Sorry," I muttered, then repeated the apology to the woman. "I guess I should wake him."

She didn't answer, yet, incredibly, the drawstring lips pulled even tighter.

"Listen, why don't you go on ahead?" I gestured and squeezed up against the opposite seat, but if there was any hope that she'd nudge the guy awake passing him, it was quickly lost. She obviously didn't want to touch him any more than I did. She squeezed right up against me and her jacket caught on the buckle. After I unhooked her, she practically took out my knee with her carry-on. It didn't hurt, but it was irritating, and she didn't even apologize.

"You're welcome."

I sighed, shook my head, and checked my boarding pass again, hoping that somehow my seat assignment had magically changed. It hadn't.

I went over to the guy and bent down and said in a fairly loud voice, "Excuse me. *Sir?*"

A strong moldy smell wafted into my face and I recoiled in disgust, coughing, my skin crawling. Maybe it was the oppressive heat coming off of him, made worse by the thick air inside the airplane. Maybe it was the way he looked, bloated and shiny and overinflated, like if I were to touch him he'd pop. Like his skin would break open at the point of contact and shrink away and all his bodily fluids would come spraying out. Like watching a water balloon pop in super slow motion.

Suddenly, sitting next to this guy just went from about a zero on my list of things I wanted to do to negative one hundred.

"Come on!" someone complained. "What's the hold up?"

I nudged the man's foot with my toe and his mouth dropped open. A snore rolled out, but he still didn't wake up.

My stomach gave a tremendous lurch right then, and I was pretty sure I was going to lose whatever food I'd managed to hold down for the past twelve hours. The plane was suddenly much hotter and stuffier than it had been just a moment ago, dryer and more caustic on my eyes and lungs.

And where the hell were the flight attendants?

"Why don't you go around?"

It was the short woman with the purse strings mouth. She was seated two rows back and across the aisle next to the window. I hadn't seen her sit down. She was tapping the armrest with her long, white fingernails, looking like my indecision was somehow inconveniencing her.

"Go around," she repeated, and she thrust her thumb toward the other side of the plane. But the other aisle was just as packed as this one was, and in order to get there I'd have to go against the flow of the traffic.

I gave my seat a last desperate glance, then mumbled, "Thanks," and headed down the aisle. I felt her eyes following me. Or maybe it was my buckle she was watching.

When I got to the galley, the attendants were busy stocking supplies. We weren't even off the ground yet, eight hours of flying time still ahead of us, and they already looked wiped out, like the heat and humidity and too many people asking them for the stupidest things had worn them down to nothing. And here I was about to ask one of them to wake some guy up so I could get to my seat.

"Can I help you?" The attendant looked to be in her early thirties, slim and attractive but starting to fray a bit around the edges. The first worry lines were beginning to show up around her eyes and mouth. A smoker, I decided. The whites of her eyes had a jaundiced tinge to them. I felt sorry for her. Redeyes were a bitch on passengers, but I'd sure hate to be an attendant on one.

"I was hoping to…to pass through to the other side."

She looked over at the line of people marching past the galley. They all looked as weary as she did.

"What's your seat number?" she asked. A plastic grin was plastered to her brittle face.

"Twenty-one F."

She frowned and pointed back the way I came. "A through F on the port side. Left. You passed it."

With that, she went back to stocking her Styrofoam cups, while the voice inside my head just made a noise of utter self-loathing.

I'd met Frank Gorme through Harry, who introduced us at dinner one evening at Vosco's—one of the few nights he'd convinced me to leave the house after the accident, after Christie's sudden departure from my life. Harry had been worried about me, naturally, and at his urging I'd invited Frank over to the house 'just to shoot the breeze.' Our conversations soon became a regular thing, and they quickly moved on to subjects deeper than the weather.

After a couple of sessions, Frank announced he'd made a breakthrough: he deduced that the root of my problem wasn't the crash or my inglorious fall from my perch at the top of my field, but actually from Christie leaving me. He said it turned everything inside-out and upside-down for me. Instead of me being all fearless and crap, I'd become vulnerable. It made me afraid to ever do anything that might yield a similar outcome.

"What the hell does that mean?" I'd demanded.

"It means you've never developed the tools to recover from failure."

"Gosh, that's…brilliant."

"That's right."

Apparently, he didn't get sarcasm.

"Gary," he went on, "you don't know how to pick yourself up, brush yourself off. You've never had to consciously decide to move on with your life. You've just always *been* moving. And now you've stopped."

So it was about inertia. Well, maybe I liked being still for once.

Week after week I told Harry that it made no sense for me to be writing three thousand dollar checks every month to some guy who'd just tell me bullshit I either already knew or advice that was wackier than I supposedly was.

"Just relax, will you? The guy's a miracle worker. He turned Sean Bickerson around; he'll fix you."

I told him I didn't know who this Sean guy was and didn't care. Then I reminded him that I wasn't broken.

"Golf pro," Harry said, ignoring the second part. "Poor guy got the yips after losing Augusta in sudden death to Floyd Vandersen. One-point-four million bucks—*poof!*—lost after he drove himself into the stands."

It always came down to money with Harry. Plus, it kind of pissed me off knowing someone could make that kind of coin on a sunny weekend by hitting a tiny white ball around with a stick.

"So what the hell does this Bickersly guy have to do with me?"

"Bickerson. Not Bickersly." Harry tapped his head with his finger and said, "It's all up here, my friend: success, failure, winning, losing. Winning is mental. So is failure."

"Thanks for that bit of trivia, Confucius."

"We need to fix your head."

"Yeah, well, it's not my head that was shattered, it was my knee."

"Your knee is fine."

Easy for him to say. He didn't have an eighteen-inch-long scar that itched like a sonofabitch sometimes. But I humored him and dutifully saw Frank once a week.

A couple months in, Frank suggested that we consider something a bit more radical.

"How much more radical?" I asked, thinking he was talking electroshock or drug cocktails or some other shock therapy. Waterboarding, maybe. Yeah right. The guy thought watching people was therapeutic. Radical probably meant playing word association. Or hypnosis.

It was hypnosis.

"Are you whacked?" I said. The guy was a regular freaking groundbreaker. "That's so—what's the word I'm looking for? Nineteenth century."

"It works."

"Look," I told him, "I'm not trying to quit smoking. I'm trying to get over my fear of

(flying)
racing."

"But you're not getting over it, Gary. Maybe because you don't really want to."

"Bite me, Frank. Bite me on my ass and see if you like it! And it's Stack, for the hundredth time!"

He tapped the pad on his lap with the chewed-off eraser of his pencil, as was his habit, and watched me for several minutes; I knew his games by then and so kept quiet.

"Gary—"

"Stack, for chrissake. Stack Miller, supermoto champion"

"—why do you think you're here?"

"You tell me. You're the shrink."

He smiled and nodded thoughtfully in a way that felt supremely condescending. "You're in denial."

What the—?

"You're blocking your real emotions, Gary, and they're manifesting themselves as this irrational fear of death. It's paralyzed you."

"I don't think it's irrational to be afraid of dying."

Frank shook his head. "It's not just that you're afraid, it's *how* you think it's going to happen. You're preoccupied with death… And the dearly departed."

So, okay, maybe I'd taken to watching a lot of *Dawn of the Dead* flicks lately.

I said, "Yeah, well, Frank, the next time your bike falls apart when you're going a hundred seventy—"

"I don't ride motorcycles."

"—then you can talk to me about being afraid to die."

"Stop making excuses. You see yourself dying a million different ways, which is why you refuse to do anything. Ride a motorcycle. Fly in a plane. Date. Walk down the street. Hell, you see danger even in the act of clipping your nails or—"

"Fuck you, Frank. Just…fuck…you. Okay?"

After a while, he moved the sessions into his tenth floor office in West Hollywood. Harry drove me there himself. They said I was too easily distracted at my home, but it was obvious Frank was trying to draw me out of my comfort zone. Fine, I'd play along. I didn't like the ride over, but if I closed my eyes and pretended I was in bed, it wasn't so bad.

He kept pushing the idea of trying hypnotic suggestion. "Just consider it, Gary."

"No."

Tap. Tap. Tap.

"Would you knock that off?"

"Why?"

"It's annoying."

"Good. Talk about how you feel."

"Are we done? 'Cause I feel like we're done."

He sighed deeply and shrugged.

"Look, Frank. This isn't working. I've decided that I'm not coming back. I'm done."

"You're not—"

"I'm done."

He told me to go out into the waiting area and wait for Harry, like I always did, but then he and Harry must have talked privately on the phone on the way over, because by the time he picked me up, Harry pretty much had the whole trip arranged. I guess he figured he already owned fifteen percent of my ass, that he could just go ahead and do shit like that without asking for my permission first.

I refused to go.

Yet, somehow, here I was. And now I was going back home again and none of this had helped. I was alone and some fat jerk was asleep in the seat next to the one I was supposed to be sitting in, except I couldn't get to it. The aisle was even more packed now with passengers and there was no way I was going to get anywhere close to my seat until they stopped boarding and everyone else had already sat down.

I slid the lavatory door closed behind me and did one of those toy soldier about-faces; I thought since I was here I might as well take a leak, but I probably stood there for a good five minutes before I realized I didn't need to go. I tucked everything back in where it belonged and hopped back around and sat down on the toilet lid instead. The bathroom had that canned eau-de-shit smell to it, but I didn't really care by then. I took a deep breath and tried to relax. It seemed to work as long as I didn't think about how this was actually a small space inside a much larger one that would soon be zooming six miles over the open ocean at a brisk five hundred miles an hour.

Over the Triangle of Death.

(Science fiction. There's no such thing as the Bermuda Triangle.)

After a while, I started feeling a little better, although the face staring back at me in the mirror sure looked like crap. I didn't like how pale it was, sickly white, despite having spent the past week and a half in a place where you had to be dead not to get a tan. My eyes were sunken in from too much drinking and too much sleep and not enough exercise. I'd wasted nearly the entire ten days crashed out on the couch inside my bungalow flipping channels, looking for horror flicks and instead watching a butt load of Sponge Bob Square Pants and Myth Busters. The only day I'd gone out was the day it had rained.

And yesterday.

I hadn't planned on drinking as much as I had last night, and I guess I'd blacked most of it out. When I woke this morning, I had a bitch of a hangover, a galaxy of bruises spreading down my right side, a cut on my scalp—now hidden by my baseball cap—that had since clotted into a tangle with my hair, and one big, fat, ugly question mark dangling inside my head and demanding an explanation. The Question Mark of Damocles. Except I couldn't remember a damn thing I'd done. Well, besides drink.

The blood from my scalp wound had soaked into the pillow and the bed sheets, but I couldn't be bothered to worry about that. What bothered me was the way the other pillow on the bed looked like it had recently been used, by someone whose scalp hadn't been bleeding. I didn't remember picking up a girl, and when I checked after getting up to take a piss, my parts didn't look like they had been used in any sort of entertainment capacity.

By the time I got the taxi to the airport, my headache was gone, but the rest of me felt like I'd done an encore presentation of the Phillip Island crash.

The sound of the jet's engines took on a new timber and the vent above my head started blowing air over me. The stink of burnt jet fuel and tarmac made me nauseous. As I reached up to dial the vent off, the door accordioned in, whacking me on my left knee, the one with the whopping scar and the titanium pin in it. I batted the door with my hand to keep it from hitting my head and croaked a rough, "Occupied." In return, I got a muffled apology. Or maybe it was a curse. I don't know. I didn't care. I gritted my teeth and lowered my shoulders, wondering if there would come a time when my leg didn't feel as brittle as a glass Christmas tree ornament.

After a while, I became aware of movement, of the whole bathroom jiggling and swaying. The jet was doing this lazy, rolling, side-to-side thing. It felt like I was on a boat on a gentle swell, except there was this weird ticking noise, like a cheap plastic clock ticking. I'd never liked the way airplanes seemed to creak and crick before, but now it jarred me, like it was falling apart at the seams. I could feel the terror I'd been trying to suppress rising up inside me. We were bouncing slightly. Taxiing. I knew I should get up and return to my seat, but I couldn't move.

I sat through the safety speech, barely registering it, catching only random words here and there: belt buckle…oxygen masks…smoking …federal offense…blah, blah, blah. I kept my head down, measuring my breathing, exhaling into the stiff fabric of my jeans and wishing I'd put on a pair of loose shorts instead. I worried that maybe I was suffering from dehydration because I thought I should be sweating more than I was and why the hell was I worrying about dehydration when we were about to explode on the runway?

"Flight attendants, please take your seats."

The jet engines began to whine. We were in position to take off and it was too late to do anything about where I was except sit tight and hope I didn't get into too much trouble when they found me here—assuming we were all still in one piece.

I felt the tug of gravity shift to my right and we started to shake.

As the front of the plane lifted from the tarmac, I reached up and shoved the latch to the "Occupied" position. I tried to picture the inside of my home. My bed.

(Christie.)

God, I hadn't realized how much I hated her for leaving me.

We'd been in the air for some time when someone knocked on the bathroom door.

(Now you're screwed.)

Honestly, though. What could they do to me now, throw me off the plane?

"Someone in there?"

"Be out in a sec," I mumbled, rubbing some feeling back into my face. I wasn't looking forward to going back out there, not with that guy sitting there. I could picture him spilling over my armrest, taking up half of my seat.

I got up and washed my hands in the cramped metal sink, pulled a paper towel from the dispenser, dried them. I checked my face in the mirror. It was looking pretty bad under these lights. I lifted my baseball cap to fix my hair and was once again reminded of how much more of my forehead had made my acquaintance over the past few months. The cut on my scalp had leaked a bit, a clear, tacky liquid that had crystallized, embedding some of the hair around it. I wetted another paper towel and dabbed the spot, then tried to tweeze out the clot, but it wouldn't come.

The next thing I knew, the floor had dropped out from underneath me and the walls of the bathroom were tilting. My face smashed into the mirror, knocking me backward. A jolt of electricity shot up into my shoulder as I rammed my elbow into the wall; my arm went numb, right down to my fingertips. I tried bracing myself, but the plane overcorrected and I tumbled to the floor in front of the toilet, banging my ear in the process.

(Fly, you idiot!)

The engines roared. But there was another sound, animal-like, high and keening. The wind! We were in some sort of dive.

(God damn it, fly!)

We continued to lurch and shudder as the whine of the engines increased. People were screaming.

The dive ended just as abruptly as it had started. I tasted blood and realized I'd bitten my tongue, so I got unsteadily to my feet and spat into the sink. Then I sat back down on the toilet. It creaked beneath me.

The plane gave another thump, and the shouts in the cabin intensified for a moment. But then we settled into what felt like level flight. The intercom chimed. "This is Captain Calder." The voice was a bit excited but commanding. "My apologies for the turbulence this evening, folks."

(Turbulence my ass! That felt like engine failure!)

"There's a bit of a disturbance in the area, as many of you may have guessed. It's extending a little higher than we thought. We're going to gain some altitude, see if we can't clear it. In the mean time—"

The plane gave a slight jounce, then plummeted briefly, then leveled. I heard several frightened yelps from the passenger compartment. Then, relative silence.

"In the mean time, folks," Calder continued, still sounding in control, "I've turned the fasten-seatbelt sign on again, so if you would all please remain seated until we've cleared this rough patch of weather, I'd be most grateful. Sit back, relax, enjoy some of TropicAir's fine selection of entertainment options. Remember, with TropicAir, flying's a breeze."

More like a thrill ride.

The intercom clicked off, leaving a momentary hiss of static before that, too, was gone. The plane continued on its way, still spasming a little. I couldn't move. I knew if I tried, I'd either vomit or scream. Hell, I was screaming inside my head like it was going out of style!

The ride eventually smoothed out again, but I'd decided by then that I was going to stay put until someone dragged me out. At least in here I could suffer in private, avoid the embarrassment of public displays of terror. But the screaming inside me just kept right on going—or so it seemed, before I realized it wasn't me but coming from somewhere out in the cabin. I heard someone run by the bathroom, first from the back of the plane, then returning. Someone shouted a few words, but I couldn't make them out.

What the hell is going on out there?

I pressed my ear to the door and listened. Now I could hear snatches of words, phrases: "...your seat...calm down...*help!*...CALM DOWN!" Despite the worry I was feeling about the plane, I found not having a clue what was going on was much worse.

(Get out there and find out.)

Frank wouldn't want that. He'd tell me to sit tight.

(Frank's not your shrink anymore. Go on, see what's the matter. Take control.)

There was a buzz of voices coming from what sounded like the galley across the aisle, but there were too many to understand any one of them. I didn't move. I didn't breathe.

After a while, everything grew quiet again—almost too quiet—and it remained so for a long time. It was as if everyone had disappeared, like some *Twilight Zone* episode. Stupid, I know, but that's why I nearly screamed when someone knocked at the door.

There was a murmur, then I thought I heard my name.

"Hello?"

"Mister Miller?"

"Yeah," I said, my voice coming out rough and shaky.

The person on the other side of the door moved away to speak to someone else. "No, Michael, it's Miller. We're still missing Calvin and…"

"Mister Miller?" Different voice this time, male, right outside the door. "I'm Michael, one of the flight attendants. Are you all right in there?"

"I'm fine."

"We need you to take your seat please. Now."

The voice was pleasant enough, but I could tell his request was anything but a suggestion.

The plane lurched and the door buckled slightly as something hit it. I heard the attendant utter a muffled curse.

"You okay?" I asked.

"Fine. Please, Mister Miller. We need you to go back to your seat."

I got to my feet. My legs were wobbly but after a moment I was sure they'd support me. My arms, on the other hand, felt as stiff as steel rods and just as heavy. I fumbled with the door latch for a couple seconds, unable to push the damn door open before remembering that it folded in. I stumbled out into the aisle and was glad to hear the engines take on a more normal timbre. We finally seemed to have found a stable patch of air.

"Mister Miller? Are you okay?"

I turned toward the voice. It was the same attendant I'd spoken to earlier, the woman—Ashia, according to the gold tag on her chest. Her hair was in disarray and her scarf had come undone.

"I'm…fine. I'm okay. That was pretty damn rough."

She nodded distractedly. "What's your seat number?"

Michael referred to a paper printout, then said, "Twenty-one F, Ash."

"Twenty-one? Isn't that—" But she stopped short. There was a frown on Michael's face.

"What?" I asked. "What's the matter?"

There was a small cut above Michael's left eyebrow and a tiny line of blood was running down the side of his face. He saw me looking at it and he turned slightly away. I wondered if he'd sustained the injury on the bathroom door just a moment ago.

"What was all the yelling about out here?"

"Nothing," Michael said, a bit more tersely than I thought was necessary. But then again, that had been a pretty bad set of turbulence. I couldn't blame him for being off. "Just, please get back to your seat while the seatbelt sign is still lit."

"Can you make it?" Ashia asked, taking hold of my elbow. I felt like an invalid, but I let her lead me up the aisle.

A number of the overhead bins had popped open, and their contents had spilled out into the aisles. Another female attendant was busily picking things up, repacking the bins, reclosing them. Several passengers stared after us as we made our way up the aisle; most just had these dazed looks on their faces, but there were still quite a few weeping softly as their neighbors tried to calm them.

(And you thought you had problems flying.)

I didn't see a single person asleep. How could anyone sleep after that?

"Twenty-one F," Ashia said, turning around at the row ahead of mine. "Do you need anything before I leave you?"

I shook my head.

"There are bags in the seat pocket," she informed me. "For when you feel sick." I was tempted to reply with a bit of sarcasm, but before I could think of anything to say, she'd gone back the way she'd come.

I scooted into my row without looking at anyone and settled into my seat. By the time I realized I was alone, Ashia was already too far away for me to ask her about the fat guy. Not that I wanted him back or anything.

Must've slipped into first class when no one was looking.

Well, good riddance.

†

"Mister Miller?"

I opened my eyes, turning my head toward the sound of that voice, but my neck was stiff and the throbbing between my temples was almost unbearable. It looked like the hangover headache had returned.

Ashia was leaning over the still-empty seat next to me. Her hand was on my arm, gently shaking it. Her face seemed pale in the darkness.

"Yes?"

It was then that I realized just how dark the cabin was and how much quieter than it had been when I'd sat down just a moment ago. A quick glance at my watch confirmed that I'd been asleep for almost two hours. I must've crashed almost immediately.

I noticed that all of the window shades had been pulled down, and that made me feel a little better. There's nothing worse than being blasted by the sun coming up through the clouds on a crystal clear morning at thirty-five thousand feet. But it wasn't the sun I was worried about, it was those damn blinking lights floating around out there in that bottomless sea of blackness. Just imagining it made me shudder.

Feeling suddenly resentful of being woken up, I mumbled that I'd take a rum and coke.

Ashia tapped the seat back impatiently, then tilted her head toward the aisle. "Would you mind coming with me, please?"

"On second thought, better make it a double." I was having trouble focusing my eyes. They felt like sandpaper.

"Please, Mister Miller."

"What's this about?"

She didn't answer.

The fog of a week and a half of inactivity, plus heavy drinking and the day's exhaustion, refused to clear out of my head.

"Can't you just tell—"

"Please don't make a scene."

Scene? I remembered my little indiscretion during takeoff and groaned.

"Look," I said, pinching the bridge of my nose. My throat was dry and scratchy; I really needed that drink. "If this is about earlier, I—I'm sorry. It won't happen again. I get in these moods sometimes, you know. It's the only way I've found to keep from going crazy."

Ashia's frown deepened and she straightened up. She turned her face toward the front of the plane and gestured quickly, then turned back to me. A man in jeans and a denim shirt appeared by her side, asking if there was a problem. I considered telling him that there was going to be one if people didn't stop bothering me, but Ashia spoke first, murmuring from the side of her mouth though still looking at me: "This is Mister Miller. He's not..." she cleared her throat. "He's not cooperating."

The man raised his eyebrows questioningly at me.

"Mister Miller," he said, keeping his voice low, presumably so he wouldn't disturb the other passengers, "my name is Stan Felder. I'm a federal air marshal with the Transportation Security Administration. Would you come with me, sir? I'd like a word with you in private."

(Tell him to go screw himself.)

I unbuckled my seatbelt and got clumsily out of my seat and followed him. We passed the curtained-off galley and kept going toward the front of the plane. Aisha trailed along behind.

Physically, I was feeling pretty crappy, a combination of lethargy and jumpiness. Mentally, I was even worse off. I was angry and confused about what was going on. And, maybe, a little concerned that I really was in some deep shit for stowing away in the bathroom during takeoff. But a federal air marshal wasn't someone to mess with.

(You can take him.)

Most of the passengers were asleep. The few who weren't raised their eyes tiredly and watched us go by, some showing curiosity, most just resigned to knowing they were going to be a mess for the next couple days. Redeyes have a tendency to do that to people.

Stan pulled back the curtain for first class and we slipped through. Now I was leading; I just kept going until he told me to stop. I found myself looking around as we went, checking out the people in the seats, and I realized that I was looking for the fat guy who was supposed to be sitting next to me. But I didn't see him anywhere.

We approached the foremost galley, just aft of the cockpit. Stan passed me once the aisle widened, then he stood to one side and gestured for me to enter. The male attendant I'd spoken with earlier, Michael, was already there, standing at the back. He'd cleaned up the cut above his eye, but a few drops of dried blood spotted his white shirt. I felt a twinge of guilt, but quickly dismissed it. I hadn't been the one to cause the turbulence that made the plane tilt that threw him into the bathroom door. Hell, I was lucky I wasn't sporting a matching gash on my own face. Though now that I was thinking about it, my cheek did feel bruised.

The other female attendant—Stacy, according to her name badge—was standing next to Michael. None of them appeared to be in a pleasant mood. It didn't look like they were going to ask me for my autograph. I didn't waste any time getting to the point.

"Would you mind telling me what's going on?"

"Just a few questions, Mister Miller," Stan Felder answered.

I didn't like the sound of that. I also didn't like the way it was four to one. But I shrugged and tried to be agreeable.

Nobody seemed willing to be the first to speak, which only set me more on edge. Plus, it seemed that the Benadryl was finally taking effect, because every noise sounded like it was bouncing around inside my head. I cleared my throat. "Well?"

Michael crossed his arms and said: "What were you doing in the bathroom earlier?"

"Bathroom?" Stan asked, a look of surprise on his face.

Michael nodded. "Yeah. He was in one of the bathrooms earlier, during that rough patch we flew through. Spent quite a while in there, too. Stacy and I were busy with the overhead bins and calming passengers down. He wasn't in his seat."

"When was this?"

"When Ash was doing the recount."

I raised my hands then, hoping I might speed things along. "Okay, you got me," I said. "I confess: it was me."

All four of them stopped, a combination of puzzlement and surprise on their faces.

"It's not like I planned to do it," I explained. "Write me a ticket, or whatever it is you have to do, but just let me go back to sleep. I'm really not feeling all that great." And I wasn't. The smell of breakfast heating up was suddenly very cloying. Not sure what they were feeding first class, but it smelled like vomit.

"Ticket?" Michael asked. "Sleep? You think this is funny?"

Stan waved Michael away. "The gentleman in twenty-one E. The seat next to yours. How did you know him?"

"The big guy?" I shrugged. I was confused enough about being pulled me up here, and now they were asking me about him? It wasn't my job to keep track of passengers. Besides, I was glad the guy had moved somewhere else, even if it was first class. As long as I didn't have to sit with him.

"Yes, him. His name's—" Stan Felder glanced at the paper in his hand. "Kiernan...Charlie Kiernan." He tilted the manifest toward Aisha, who nodded. Stan gave me an expectant look. "Were you two traveling together?"

Charlie Kiernan? Now it was my turn to frown. The name sounded familiar. But then again, when you meet as many people as I do—or did—then everyone's name starts to sound similar after a while, just like everyone's face sort of blends in with the next one.

"No," I said, "we weren't traveling together. I didn't even know the guy. What makes you think I did?"

"Did you two speak to each other? Either before or after boarding? Get into an argument or anything?"

"Argument? No. He was already asleep when I boarded, and—"

"Is this your boarding pass?" Michael interrupted. He reached over and snatched something off Felder's clipboard and thrust it in my face. I could see my name and seat number on it, so, yeah, it had to be mine. I reached for it instinctively, but he pulled it away.

"We found it in Mister Kiernan's possession."

I shook my head, shrugged. "So. Not sure why he'd have it, unless I dropped it. Maybe when I was trying to wake him up?"

"When was that?"

"When we were boarding."

"And did he wake?"

"No..."

Aisha gave Michael another meaningful glance, but what it meant, I had no clue.

"Anyway," I said, "it's not like it's a big deal, right? The boarding pass, I mean. Once we're on the plane, it's no good anymore, right?"

"It's a legal document. Mister Miller."

"Right," I said. "And nobody ever just tosses into their seat pocket two minutes after they've sat down."

"But why did Kiernan have it?"

I exhaled in frustration. "Why aren't you asking him? He'll probably tell you he picked it up off the floor or something."

"Stop playing games with us, Mister Miller. You know as well as anyone else here that we can't do that."

"What games? I have no goddamn idea what you're talking about."

Again, nobody spoke for a moment. There was only the drone of the engines and a soft ticking coming from somewhere, regular and persistent, like a timer or something. Maybe it was a timer for the food heater or something. Whatever it was, the smell and that freaking ticking were driving me nuts.

"He's dead, Mister Miller," Michael finally said.

"What? Who's dead, the fat guy?"

"Are you telling us you didn't know that?"

"How the hell would I know that? I haven't seen—"

"He was poisoned."

"Enough," Stan interjected. "That's enough, Michael. Just let me handle the questioning, okay?"

I opened my mouth, but nothing came out. It was one thing to discover that there was a corpse on the plane, quite another to be

(a suspect in the murder)

questioned about it.

"Can I see him?"

"Why the hell would you want to do that?"

"Michael!" Stan snapped. He rubbed his temple. "Actually, I'd like to know the answer to that, too."

"I—I don't know," I stammered. I honestly didn't know why I'd said that. Was it morbid curiosity? Was it because I'd become so preoccupied with death that I wanted to look it in the face? Was it like Frank said, that I was obsessed with the recently departed?

"Is there anything you'd like to tell us, Mister Miller?"

I shook my head. "Are you sure he didn't just die of natural causes? I mean, the guy was a walking, talking time-bomb. Poster child for a coronary bypass. What makes you think he was poisoned?"

"I thought you didn't know him."

"I didn't. But it doesn't take a genius to see he was one cheeseburger shy of a massive heart attack."

"He didn't have a heart attack."

"Okay…" I said. I gestured at Michael. "But it's like he said: I was in the bathroom when it happened. I didn't even know the guy had died. I just thought he'd snuck up to one of the empty first class seats."

For some reason, this made Ashia start to giggle. I gave her half a smile, but she turned away, embarrassed.

"Do you have any carry-on luggage, Mister Miller?"

"Huh? No. I didn't bring any bags."

Stan frowned, and I realized my mistake. A man without luggage looks mighty suspicious. He said, "Would you mind emptying out your pockets?"

"Why?"

"Because I asked you to, Mister Miller."

"Not until you—"

"Mister Miller," Stan snapped. "Don't make me ask twice."

I glared at him for a moment, then reached into my pockets, withdrew my cell phone and wallet and laid them on the counter. Michael immediately picked the phone up and began inspecting it. He was like a goddamn kid. I wanted to slap it out of his hands, but resisted the urge. I reached down again and pulled the linings of my pockets inside out. "See? Nothing. Not even a comb."

"Take off your hat."

"Excuse me?"

He repeated the command, then instructed me to place my hands on the countertop and spread my fingers. Placing one hand on my shoulder and the other on my back, he used the toe of his shoe to spread my feet apart. Then he told the flight attendants to check all the bathrooms and the seat pockets around where I was sitting.

Michael tossed my phone back on the counter and sneered at me. "*Supposed* to be turned off during flight," he said. He stuck his face right up to mine, daring me to respond. When I didn't, he huffed and left.

I closed my eyes and waited for Felder to finish frisking me. Believe me, I wanted to resist. I wanted to turn around take a swing at the guy. The little voice inside my head was screaming for me to do it. But it would've only made things worse. Up here, Felder was the law; I wasn't so out of it that I didn't know that much. So I bit my tongue and kept quiet instead, even though I felt violated and bullied and ashamed. I didn't move a muscle, just focused even more on that quiet tapping noise, feeling myself falling into its rhythm.

"We need to be sure, Mister Miller," Felder said.

"Of what?"

He didn't answer.

"There's a hundred-plus people on this plane," I said. "Why are you harassing me?"

"One hundred and thirty-six people, to be exact. One of them is dead, one hundred and thirty-four are innocent. Do the math. I don't need any more trouble."

(Well, you got it!)

"I wasn't making any trouble. I was asleep when you came and got me."

I stared at my hands. That goddamn ticking was still there. What the hell was it?

"Would you at least tell me what makes you think I had something to do with it?"

In answer, he flipped my boarding pass onto the counter. It slid to a stop next to my hand.

"Turn it over," he said.

On the back, written in a jagged, spidery hand and smudged by a fat thumbprint were the words: "Push Miller. He knows, even if he says he doesn't."

I felt the blood run from my face, my skin grow numb. What the fuck did it mean?

Nothing. It meant nothing. How could it? The guy had a heart attack, nothing more. And now I was being blamed for it.

(Fight them! Turn around and lay a good one on that fat schnoz of his.)

"Is that you're handwriting?"

(Yes.)

"No."

"Would you tell me if it was?"

"I didn't write it. And I didn't poison anyone."

He sighed. "Maybe you didn't, but this just seems a bit too…coincidental, don't you think?"

"I don't know what it means."

Felder shrugged. "Maybe you do. Maybe you don't." He began thumbing through my wallet. "You reside in Malibu?"

I nodded.

"How long in Bermuda?"

"Ten days."

He pulled something else out, a business card from the looks of it. I couldn't tell if it was Frank's or some other card someone had shoved into my hands. It happened all the time. I usually just threw them away, but one or two would occasionally show up inside my wallet from time to time. He waggled it. "Ever fly a jet?"

(Yes.)

"No. What the hell gave you that idea?"

He stopped and looked at me for a long moment. Ashia, Stacy and Michael returned as we were standing there like that. I could see them shaking their heads and shrugging, which apparently indicated they hadn't found anything, nothing that might implicate me further in this supposed conspiracy of theirs. Felder handed my hat and phone back. He kept my wallet.

"Can I go now?"

"Not yet. What were you doing in Bermuda?"

"The same thing everyone else comes here for." I could hear Harry's laughter right then, his voice as he told me he'd booked this trip: *A little tropical pussy is all the R&R you need.* All the R&R he needed was more like it. I wondered if his wife suspected.

"Not business?

"No. I'm a motorbike racer. And Bermuda's not exactly a motorcycle mecca, if you know what I mean. Look, am I under arrest?"

"So it was personal?" He asked, and I frowned. He tried again: "Were you following Charles Kiernan?"

Now I remembered where I'd heard the name before. Charles Kiernan—*Charlie* Kiernan—had been the name of the guy who'd written that piece about me and Christie breaking up. The guy from

(The LA Times)

The Juice. I remember going off to Harry about it, about how the article had made certain... allegations, potentially damaging allegations—not that there was much left of my career to damage at that point. But I'd wanted to sue.

Harry eventually talked me down, saying it'd just make matters worse. "Suing draws the wrong kind of attention. The *threat* of a lawsuit, however..." he'd added, smiling deviously. "We can probably work this to our advantage, maybe get a settlement out of court." So I forgot about it, and the whole thing eventually just faded away.

Talk about coincidence. Here he was. In Bermuda. On the plane. With me. And he was dead and my boarding pass had some cryptic message on it suggesting I knew something.

(The truth.)

It didn't make any sense.

"Am I under arrest?"

"If you don't cooperate—"

"I didn't do anything."

"Mister Mi—"

"I'm done," I said. I'd reached the end of my patience. "This is ridiculous. I don't know what you think this is all about, but I didn't do anything. I certainly didn't *kill* anyone. You've got over a hundred other people on this plane—a hundred and thirty four...or six, whatever—and yet I don't see you talking to any of them."

I brushed past Stan and the flight attendants, barely managing to hide my surprise when they just let me go. I was shaking from anger by then, outraged at the accusation and furious at myself for

(being such a wuss)

letting them get as far as they had with it. The old Stack Miller wouldn't have put up with any of that crap. He would've put that goddamn air marshal—and that smug prick of an attendant Michael—in their places. Stack wouldn't have allowed himself to be humiliated like that.

(Wouldn't have blamed himself for what happened to Christie, either.)

I failed her.

(It's not your fault.)

"Shut the hell up," I growled.

This time, nobody stared at me as I returned to my seat. Everyone, it seemed, was asleep.

Passing the galley mid-ship, I hesitated. Now I knew why the curtain was drawn here. If there was a dead body on board, they'd have to stash it somewhere. Here was as good a spot as any, I supposed.

I couldn't help it: I really was curious. I still didn't understand why, but I wanted to see the body—*needed* to see it. I needed to prove that he really was dead and that this wasn't some kind of sick joke being played on me. I could almost imagine Harry putting the crew up to it, though I couldn't imagine a reason why he would. He was twisted, that's for sure, but he never did anything unless it was somehow related to money, to making *him* money. I just didn't see his fingerprints on this.

I checked the aisle behind me, but Stan and the flight attendants had apparently already forgotten about me. Either they knew they had nothing on me, or they weren't afraid I'd try anything else.

(Idiots.)

What the hell was I thinking? I didn't do anything in the first place.

I slipped past the curtain and into the galley, and there, just as I'd suspected, was a pile of blankets on the floor, and underneath them was the completely unmistakable shape of a very large person.

Cold fear settled over me, displacing my anger. Fear and disgust. And maybe a little pity. Whatever dislike I'd held for the jerk before, whatever new animosity I'd felt after realizing who he was, he was still a human being. Dying on a plane just seemed so...undignified. And lonely. Die on a plane and you're totally at the mercy of your traveling companions. "Is there a doctor on board?" I muttered to myself.

I reached over to lift a corner of the blanket.

"You sure you want to do that?"

I straightened up with a gasp, my heart leaping into my throat. The blanket fell back over Kiernan's face. All I'd seen was a shock of greasy hair, enough to confirm that it was him.

"Where'd you come from?"

She shrugged.

"What did you mean, if I was sure?"

She gestured. "It's not pretty."

The purse strings mouth was gone. Her cheeks were flushed and there was this playful pout to her lips, a sparkle in her eyes. She clicked her throat.

"The face of Death never is."

I couldn't speak.

She pushed herself away from the wall. "Once you see it, I've heard it's hard to find your way back." She shrugged. "You do want to come back, don't you?"

What the hell was she talking about?

"What do you want?" I managed to say. "Why are you here?"

"Didn't you ask for a doctor?"

"You're a doctor?"

She shrugged.

I struggled to find something else to say. "I was told he died of poisoning."

"Poison?" She shook her head. "Is that what you think?"

"I don't know."

"No, not poison. Something much…worse. If I were you," she said, turning to leave, "I wouldn't touch him. You know, just in case." And then she was gone and I was alone with the corpse.

Don't touch him? Just in case of what? What the hell was that all about?

I didn't know.

I almost turned around right then and left, but then, as if drawn against my will, I reached down again. I grabbed a corner of the blanket and drew it away from Kiernan's face. And the woman was right: what I saw made me recoil in horror. Even her warning hadn't prepared me for this.

I knew that Kiernan hadn't been dead more than a few hours, and yet he looked like he'd been dead and floating in a tub of water for several days. His face bore the palest of death masks—rendered ever paler by the harshness of the galley lights—and his eyes bulged from their sockets as if everything that had been held within his colossal frame had liquefied just as I'd imagined it earlier, and it was all now being forced through the funnel of his neck and into his skull. The eyelids were stretched tight, pulled away from each other, and the whites of those unseeing, bloodshot eyes had turned to lead, losing their sheen in the dry, recycled air. Heavy folds of cheek flesh avalanched to either side of his face, flaring his already ample nostrils even wider. They were fumaroles, through which I expected his brains to ooze out of at any moment like magma.

But the worst of it was his tongue, already blackened and swollen. The corpulent thing protruded from those cyanotic lips like the appendage of an oil-slicked mollusk. My half-digested dinner rose in my throat; bile burned the base of my skull. I swallowed it back down, but knew it would take a lot more to keep it there.

The plane jerked slightly from some minor turbulence, and the movement rippled through Kiernan's face before rolling down his neck. I'd dropped the blanket in my fright and so reached down to cover him back up again. My mind was screaming to get the hell out of there. It was telling me I was a fool for looking and why hadn't I just gone back to my seat?

The plane gave a sudden lurch, throwing me off balance. I tumbled face first onto Kiernan's corpse.

I shrieked, then inhaled to continue screaming, but my mouth filled with Kiernan's fetid odor and I gagged. I tried to push myself away from that horror, but there was no solid surface to push against. It was all swampy flesh. I clambered desperately for any sort of handhold, and finally managed to wedge my palms underneath his chin.

Not poison, something worse. Don't touch.

The weight of my body dislodged a death moan from that cavernous chest. It escaped through his swollen lips. More rancid air caressed my face, stinking of old cheese and cured meat. I had to bury my nose into the hollow of my shoulder.

The plane gave another shudder, but by then I'd gained some traction. I heaved myself up on my elbows, then got to my knees. The body jumped and quivered with each jolt of the plane, almost as if it was being shocked by a live wire. But that wasn't the end of my torment. My mind took the image and ran with it. Now I almost believed he'd come alive, that the collision of our bodies had somehow revived him. In a moment, Charlie Kiernan would sit up, and with that sudden certainty, I groaned in despair.

Somehow I managed to get back to my feet. I was shaking horribly by then. I wanted desperately to run from there, but my body wouldn't allow it. Terror flooded through me, riveting me to the spot. I could only watch, mesmerized, as each roll and tilt of the airplane further solidified the illusion of Kiernan's revival. He nodded his head at me, seemed to be looking with those dull gray eyes. Senseless as they were, they were full of a terrifying

(truth)

knowledge.

The floor slanted. My feet betrayed me—or perhaps it was my bad knee. I had no strength anymore. I was slipping toward Kiernan again. A sound escaped my lips. I felt his cold, dead hand flop against my ankle. His fingers slid around it and began to tighten.

(Face the truth, Gary!)

I shrieked with panic then and stumbled from the galley. I only made it to the aisle before collapsing against the far wall. I was whimpering and didn't care if anyone saw me. But then the plane gave another shake and I heard a sound coming from behind the curtain. I scrambled to my feet, managing to get out of my own way long enough to throw myself into the bathroom. This time, I made sure to lock the door.

The plane continued to creak and rattle, but I heard nothing else outside the bathroom, no footsteps or moans. And it struck me as odd that there were no cries of panic from the passengers, either. But then again, hadn't everyone been sound asleep?

All that separated me from Kiernan was a flimsy sheet of plastic and cheap aluminum. I fell against the door and sat there, powerless to defend myself against whatever might want to come through.

I wondered how Frank Gorme would try and explain this one.

At some point, after several minutes passed without a sound coming from outside the door, rationality returned. It was insanity to believe Kiernan had come back from the dead.

But he grabbed my leg!

(You don't really believe that, do you?)

So why did the skin around my foot feel so strange? Why did my foot feel like it had been

(infected)

grabbed?

"It didn't," I told myself. I sat rocking on the toilet, repeating those words over and over again. Meanwhile, the plane flew on, back in its slumberous journey over smoother air. I wondered if we were past the infamous Triangle.

"The mind is a muscle," Frank once told me. "Its grip on reality can be tenuous, especially when it wants to substitute something wholly irrational so it won't have to face a more unpleasant truth. But you have to fight the urge to accept what isn't true. It'll take all your strength, all of your force of will, to wrest yourself away from your fears, and to find what is real and separate it from what isn't."

I'd laughed at him, accusing him of thinking he was some kind of philosophical or psychological genius, but he'd dismissed my insults out of hand and continued undeterred.

"Sometimes it helps to have a little guidance. That's what the hypnosis can help you with."

"The truth," I murmured to the pale face staring back at me in the bathroom mirror, "is that I'm a supermoto champion. I had an accident and it screwed with my head. I'm on a plane and, no, there aren't such things as zombies."

(Well, at least you're half right.)

I ignored the voice inside my head and concentrated instead on what I knew to be real.

But what about that business last night with the bartender? He had said zombie, hadn't he? Maybe I'd heard him wrong. I'd been drunk. Maybe I'd heard Kiernan wrong, too, back in the terminal. It was the Benadryl speaking. Yes, that had to be it. Besides, it made no sense that Kiernan would be working on a zombie story. His specialty was chasing after sports celebrities like me.

I realized there was a new sound, adding to the drone of the engines, a tapping outside the door.

I ignored it and instead lifted my foot up to my lap, crossed it over my knee. For once there was no pain in the reconstructed joint, no stiffness; those things now seemed to belong to the ankle that

(Kiernan had grabbed)

I'd imagined Kiernan had grabbed. I had to prove to myself once and for all that there had been no grabbing. I'd twisted it falling out of the galley, that's all. Or maybe when the plane tilted and I fell. I just hadn't realized it at the time. I hadn't felt anything, certainly not his hand.

The tapping sound sped up.

No, it was stupid, entertaining such thoughts. Corpses don't grab.

(So check. Prove to yourself you're not crazy.)

I pulled the cuff of my jeans up, past my calf, over my knee. The scar glistened, a shiny white thing that made me think of snail trails for some reason.

I sat like that for several minutes, not moving, just staring at my sock. Finally, I peeled it away from my ankle.

It took every fiber of my will to lower my eyes. My vision blurred for a moment. My breath came out of me in a gush.

There was nothing. Not a mark anywhere on my skin. No bruise or redness. No evidence that I had been grabbed. Nothing.

I laughed then and I knew. The truth was Kiernan's corpse hadn't come back to life. It had just been my imagination.

The tapping had stopped.

Still laughing, I let my foot drop back to the floor, and I leaned back on the toilet with my eyes closed.

Suddenly, I wasn't afraid anymore. I was on a jet. So what?

There was a dead body across the aisle. Big deal.

I was alive and he wasn't and that was that.

I stood up and flicked the latch from OCCUPIED to VACANT and opened the bathroom door.

The curtain across the aisle hung crookedly. It was still slightly open and I could see a corner of the TropicAir blanket through the opening. The guy was dead, all right. It was unfortunate, yes, but I'd had nothing to do with it. More importantly, he wasn't alive. Or undead. Or whatever.

I reached over and tugged the curtain closed, then I headed back to my seat. I was ready for this flight to end. I smiled for the first time in a long time.

I was ready to get back to my old life.

†

I was screaming before I even knew I was screaming.

How long I'd stood there in abject terror, I had no idea, but I eventually became aware of what was going on around me when the first hands grabbed my shoulders and arms. Other hands thrust themselves at my face. They were pushing. Pulling. Tearing.

There were other people shouting, too, not just me. The hands were pushing me into a seat, to the floor, pulling me down. I screamed and screamed and my body could do nothing else. It was like something inside me had cracked and all the horror inside of me was pouring out as sound.

The hands slapped over my mouth, smothered my nose. And there were faces that came with those hands, faces and voices and bodies, but I could only see one face, the one in front of me: Charles Kiernan.

"Mister Miller!"

I felt myself violently shaken. I felt pain. Someone slugged me and the screaming stopped. That's how I knew it was me. The hands gripped my shoulders and twisted me around, but I couldn't tear my eyes away from the seat next to mine.

"Miller! Goddamn it, what the hell's going on here?"

Stan Felder's voice this time. He was running toward me, shoving his way past passengers who were now crowding into the aisle. Hearing him seemed to bring me back into the moment. He thrust his face at me and it was red and angry. Michael grabbed me and shouted, forced me to look at him. "Mister Miller!" he screamed. "Sit! Your! Ass! Down!"

More people were waking up; some were asking what was going on. I could see their faces, their bleary eyes, anger over having been so violently wrenched from their dreams. Not all of them were waking, though, which struck me as odd. Maybe half. Slightly less.

"What's going on?" Stan demanded.

I pointed at the corpse in twenty-one E.

Michael turned and stared for a moment. Nothing in his body language suggested surprise or dismay, and for that second or two, I thought the whole thing had been a dream. Kiernan wasn't dead. He was right where he was supposed to be.

(And the woman? Is she right where she's supposed to be?)

I looked around me. The woman who'd talked to me in the galley, the doctor—her seat was empty. Had I imagined her, too?

"No…" I moaned. I felt myself sinking.

Michael turned around, his face a mask of disgust.

"What the hell is this, Miller? Is this some kind of sick joke? Because if it is—"

There was a gasp behind me and I turned. Ashia was there, her hands over her mouth and her eyes glued to Kiernan. She backed away, her eyes, flicking between me and him and suddenly I knew I hadn't imagined

(Kiernan grabbing me)

any of it at all.

"You're a sick bastard!" Michael shouted. He grabbed my collar and shook. "Why would you do—"

"Me? Are you a fucking nuts?" I shouted. "You think I did this? Why the hell would I move a dead person?"

"Calm down," Stan shouted. "I said calm the hell down, Mister Miller! Michael, you too!"

But I couldn't calm down. I was shaking all over and my knees were giving out and my head was pounding.

But then Ashia screamed and we all turned, except she wasn't screaming at all because her mouth wasn't even open. And yet the screaming didn't just continue, it was getting louder. And then I realized it was coming from behind her, from first class. Stan spun around and began to push his way toward the front of the plane. "Sit down, people," he was shouting.

I could hear a low humming sound underneath all the shouts, low and dissonant in the way whale songs are low and dissonant, and my skin crawled as I realized what it was: moaning. A second scream rose from behind the curtain, then a third. Now there was a whole chorus of them, a whole freaking tabernacle choir of them joining their voices in unholy worship!

Michael cursed and told me not to move. He tried to shove me aside, but then he stopped when a woman stumbled through the curtains holding her head. She jerked straight up, as if she'd been yanked from behind by her hair, and I could see blood pouring from a wound on her scalp.

"What the f—!"

And now there was new screaming, this time coming from the back of the plane.

Even then I wanted to believe that none of this was happening, that it was just some strange form of mass hysteria.

But then I saw that the rest of the passengers were rising, the ones who hadn't woken before, and I could see by the way they stumbled clumsily from their seats, not screaming at all but moaning, their eyes expressionless. This was no hallucination.

Michael still had a hold of my shirt and his own sudden scream hit me like a slap, like a splash of icy water. I felt a calmness settled over me—not the calm of tranquility, but of a system shutting down, refusing to accept what was happening, going into complete denial.

I became aware of movement behind us, but I couldn't take my eyes off the bleeding woman as she took yet another step toward us before being yanked into a seat. Arms were on her, wrapped about her, tearing at her face. The moaning and screaming grew louder and now there were shouts of anger and pain and terror from all around the cabin. The curtain tore from its hangers with a machinegun rattle. And the dead came, a roiling writhing tidal mass: first class, economy, young and old. They converged to where we were standing. And they were hungry.

I knew this without registering that they were eating. I knew it with a sudden irrefutable conviction, as if I had always known. The dead were hungry. And they would turn the rest of the living into them as they fed.

They struggled out of their seats—some, not all. Some weren't able to escape their seatbelts. But enough rose that it became clear that more than half of the passengers had died in their sleep and all I could think was the woman in the galley telling me it wasn't poison, but something worse. Was it a virus? Were we all infected?

They came, lurching across the seats, blankets slipping from their shoulders, glasses askew and falling away unneeded, their grotesque mouths in a pantomime of hunger. They tripped over their own feet, fell, rose again with horrifying determination. Shirts and dresses snagged on armrests, tore free. These things were temporary obstacles; once they managed to reach the aisles, the speed of their onslaught was terrifying.

They came down both aisles, their faces bloated and waxy, bruised and pale, just as Kiernan's had been. They stumbled against each other, knocking and falling and rising, reaching, moaning, their swollen, purplish-black tongues protruding obscenely. The smell was sickening. They would stop only when they came across a living passenger. I saw that the living were quickly falling. We numbered fewer and fewer.

Michael's hands jerked on my shirt, pulling me off balance. I turned to catch myself and saw the corpse of Charles Kiernan standing inches away. He had risen from where he had settled, as if he had simply stopped there to rest. He had Michael's head in his grip. Michael was gawping at him in bafflement. Then he started screaming. Kiernan opened his mouth and his tongue fell out and onto Michael's face. Michael tried to whip his head from side to side, but Kiernan's grip was too tight. The corpse ignored the thrashing and kicking; its dead eyes betrayed no emotion.

With a sudden *slup*, one of Kiernan's fingers slipped into Michael's left eye socket. The eyeball bulged, then collapsed, and a glistening jelly oozed out and ran down his cheek. Michael's screams abruptly stopped. Charlie bent down and bit off his nose.

(Bastard deserved it.)

Blood spurted from the hole in Michael's face, and he began to gurgle. His hands slapped at the air, batting at Kiernan's head and face. The monster bent down again undeterred, and when he lifted up again, half of Michael's face tore away with him. It dangled from Kiernan's mouth for a moment, like a giant shitake mushroom. Blood dripped from it, splattering what was left of Michael's face, then the flap of skin fell. It hit the floor with a *slap*, sounding like a wet rag.

And still Michael fought. He had no leverage, bent over backward as he was, his feet barely on the floor anymore. Only Kiernan's grip on his head kept him from falling over onto his back.

I saw his fleshless jaw open and close like a fish in the air. His teeth and bones glistened bright pink, pulsing deep rivers of blood that flowed down his neck. He looked like some kind of gory prop in the window of a fly-by-night Halloween shop. With each shallower exhale, blood bubbled forth in a crimson foam; with each raspy inhale it collapsed back into that living skull. Michael was drowning in his own blood, and yet he fought on.

You have to admire the guy—

Kiernan bent down and bit him a third time, this time thrusting his mouth wide over Michael's neck and ripping out his throat. The body slumped, twitched, then rotated on its tenuous connection with the head. His arms fell limp to the floor.

Kiernan still had a hold of Michael's head. Then, quiet suddenly, the skull imploded in his hands, collapsing with a sickening crunch. Blood and tissue sprayed forth, staining the seats, the floor, me. Everything within a five foot radius. Michael's brain leaked between Kiernan's fingers. The monster lowered his face and began to feed.

I had been unable to move a muscle, unable to conjure any sort of control over myself, but when Kiernan raised his head and his unseeing eyes locked onto mine, when I saw the hungry look he gave me, when he dropped what remained of Michael and stepped toward me, only then was I finally able to force myself to move.

I stumbled backward but couldn't go any further than a single step. I was blocked by the seats across the aisle and I shrieked with fright.

Something heavy hit me square on the back, jolting me forward and nearly into Charlie's grasp. I twisted away, fending off the woman who had fallen against me. She dropped to the floor and was dead before she hit. Her neck and scalp and arms were covered with bite marks and torn flesh, like bloody tattoos. Almost before her hair settled about her face, she began to stir again. She opened her eyes and they were black as night and just as quiet. She rose stiffly to her knees and moaned.

Kiernan reached out to me. His fat fingers closed on my shoulder. I spun away, yelping with surprise and pain. His hand closed on the scalp of a man who was trying to crawl between the seats. The man rose, screaming, dangling from Charlie's outstretched arm as if he was pulled on a string. He punched blindly and kicked the air. One of his elbows caught me on the cheek. I grunted and fell. I heard a ripping noise and the man fell to the floor. Charlie stood a moment longer before dropping the bloody scalp.

Passengers and zombies were coursing down the aisles, crashing into each other, crying and yelling and whimpering, moaning. Those who were still alive tried to climb over the seatbacks, crushing each other in their panic. The general movement was toward the rear of the plane, but once there, there was no place else to go. To my horror, we were becoming quickly overwhelmed. Our numbers were dwindling: two dozen, one. Now, most of the faces I looked into had that same lifeless affect, their faces and hands covered in blood, their eyes blank.

I felt my shirt being grabbed from behind and suddenly my terror was so acute that I yanked myself away so hard that I banged my head on an armrest. I heard my shirt tear, but now I was being pulled back again by my pants. I twisted around and kicked at the dead-eyed teenager behind me. I felt my repaired knee buckle as my foot connected with his face. Pain flared into my thigh, coursed up my back in red-hot ribbons of fire. And still the boy-thing didn't let go of me. I kicked again, ignoring the pain, and finally his fingers tore free. It fell, face-first, to the floor, then rose again.

There was no hope of escape. The aisles were a mass of bodies, some eating, some being eaten, many already dead, most beginning to rise again. Yet, I fought through them, scrambling over seats, kicking and punching the living and the dead alike. I became aware that I was uttering incoherently, despairingly. Tears poured from my eyes, blinding me. I was certain I'd pissed myself.

I saw Ashia go down. I saw her rise up again. Her brown skin was ashy pale and her jaundiced eyes glowed with the dull fire of death. She ripped the top of Stan Felder's head off, then reached into his shattered skull to feed. The young boy from the terminal snapped at his mother's crying face as she batted his arms, pleading with him to recognize her. The boy's father lurched back and forth in his seat, unable to free himself from the seatbelt.

There was a squeal of twisting metal, then a snap, and the father suddenly lurched forward. The shredded ends of his belt dangled from his waist, then fell away. He joined his son in feeding on the woman who had been both mother and bride. But before they could finish, she rose. Now the three of them stood and stumbled into the aisles.

Still others were tearing free from their seatbelts.

I sensed that the focus of the monsters had shifted. They were now heading toward the front of the plane, perhaps drawn there by the smell of the food in the galley. Several were already there, and I realized what they were doing. They were trying to get into the cockpit. I saw the door open and I screamed and the door slammed shut. But then it was yanked open again and I saw the captain pulled through.

"No!" I shouted.

The copilot tried to come to his companion's aid and he, too, was quickly overwhelmed. I saw them go down. A moment later, they rose back up again, their white shirts now tie-dyed in shades of ochre and crimson.

The door to the cockpit flapped, as if in a wind, and through it I could see the empty pilot seats. And yet we flew smoothly on, and I had to conclude that we were on autopilot.

I found myself at the back of the plane, me and a few others, and there was truly nowhere else to go. To one side of me was the exit hatch, to the other, the rear galley. A drinks cart had rolled against the back wall and it was this that I now tried to hide behind. The monsters had nearly completed their massacre of the main cabin. Now it seemed that they were turning on each other. The screams had fallen away. Taking their place was a strange and melancholy chorus of breathless moans. The stink of blood and rot was everywhere.

I was shaking so hard that the drink cart was rattling, the glass liquor bottles inside tinkling against each other. I peered around the side. Almost as if by some silent command, the horde turned as one. They started moving toward me.

I was alone.

There was only the bathroom behind me now, only the bathroom with its flimsy door. And it was occupied.

I pounded on the door. "Let me in! Oh, god, they're coming. Please!"

They were drawn by the sound of my cries. The ones in front fell and the ones behind scrambled over them, only to fall beneath the feet of those that followed. That was how they came, like a roiling tide of death. The moaning grew louder; the stench grew.

I heard a click and saw that the latch had been drawn to the side. I tugged, but the door wouldn't open.

You don't even know what's inside, Stack, m'man.

(But you need to find out.)

I jerked away, suddenly afraid of what I'd find. But the monsters were closing in on me now, rising and falling, rolling ever closer. Twenty feet, fifteen, ten.

The door collapsed in and a bloodied arm reached out at me. I shrieked and pulled away.

"Fine, stay out there then!"

I threw myself into the bathroom just as the first dead fingers brushed the back of my neck.

"Close it!" a voice shrieked above me. "Close the goddamn door!"

I couldn't get any leverage! I could barely turn. Hands were on my neck and my shoulders, yanking my hair! I leaned my shoulder into the door and shoved, but those dead arms felt no pain and wouldn't pull away. They had my shirt and were pulling me through the opening. I'd be torn apart by the door before they got me through it.

I could hear the woman panting. I felt her hands drop to my shoulder and she began pulling me *away* from door. I jerked myself out of her grip. I couldn't hold the door closed with her pulling on me like that! But the zombies had my shirt and it was cutting off the circulation in my arm. I could feel their cold, lifeless hands on me, frigid cold, pulling and scratching. The door was beginning to open wider. More arms pushed through. They were on my legs now. I felt myself being pulled through!

With a cry of desperation, I yanked it fully open again and reached out and gave the zombies in front a massive shove. I kicked with one foot and pulled my arm back. The monsters' grips fell away, but then another grabbed me from the side. I stepped halfway out through the opening, elbowed the thing in the face, turned and did the same to yet another. But there were too many hands and snapping jaws!

The first zombie was still trying to rise beneath the feet and bodies of others who were trying to get to us. A hand grabbed my collar and pulled me down with such force that I was choking. I couldn't get any air in my lungs and blackness was descending over me. But then I gave one more heave and rose up. I felt myself yanked back into the bathroom. The door slammed shut. A heavy thud hit the outside, shaking it. A hand reached out and slid the latch over.

Occupied! my mind screamed, as the last shred of sanity threatened to leave me.

We were safe, at least for the moment, but for how long? The door would almost certainly fail. How long before the zombies broke in?

"That's not what we need to be worried about," the voice said behind me. I turned and for the third time found myself looking at the mysterious woman from the galley.

"What...do you...mean?" I panted.

"Listen."

I did. "It sounds like they're leaving."

"They are."

"Where are they going?"

"Nowhere. They're waiting."

"What do you think will happen to us?"

She didn't answer. She didn't have to. We would die. The plane would crash. We would eventually run out of fuel or get shot down. All my fears were coming true. I just never imagined that it would be at the hands and teeth of the already-dead.

"Maybe it's for the best," I said. "We can't risk them surviving and getting loose in LA."

I glanced up at her standing on the toilet, her eyes above mine.

The sounds of hands on the door grew softer. A few were still there.

"Are you willing to die?" she asked.

"What other choice is there?"

"There's always a choice."

"What?"

"Fight them. Kill them."

"Then what?"

"Fly the plane. Land it. You can fly, can't you, Gary?"

Cold white fear washed over me. I'd never told her my name. "Who the hell are you?"

She didn't answer at first, just stood there looking at me, her face familiar and yet totally unplaceable. Finally, she said, "I'm nobody, Gary. At least, I'm nobody that matters. But them?" She tilted her head toward the cabin. "It's them you need to name."

I shook my head.

"They are your fears, Gary." And this time when she smiled, her teeth were bloody and her eyes were dead. That's when I saw the bite marks on her arms and neck.

I screamed, but she just shrugged.

"*Nooo*," I wailed, trying to escape, but the latch wouldn't budge. "This can't be happening!"

"Gary." She said, and she stepped down and grabbed my face in her hands, and she was so strong! She pulled herself close, then slipped her tongue into my mouth and I could taste the death growing inside her. The tongue swelled, reached down toward the back on my throat and I started to choke.

"No!" I screamed, shoving her away.

But she just smiled sadly. She handed me a card of paper and I saw that it was my boarding pass, and suddenly meaning of the cryptic words written on it became clear. She was Christie—not exactly her likeness, but close enough.

"You've always known the truth, Gary," she said. "You just refused to face it."

"No, I— What the hell are you talking about?"

"Are you ready to face what really happened, Gary?"

"It's Stack," I growled.

I threw my fists at her, but none of my punches landed. She stepped around me and her body pressed against mine once again. I could smell her sweet scent, the light perfume—roses and cinnamon—mixed in with the stink of decay.

She touched the door and it somehow opened, and she was through it before I could pull her back.

"Christie!"

"Take care of your monsters first, Gary. You need to defeat them, or else you'll die. Your choice. Then you can have me back."

"But I don't know how to fly a plane!"

"Check your wallet."

Instinctively, my hand went to my back pocket, even before I knew it wouldn't be there. Stan had taken it. But there it was. Inside was a single item.

It was a pilot's license.

Apparently I did know how to fly.

I must have forgotten.

†

I didn't know what was real anymore. Everything was falling apart.

I looked at my knee and the skin there wasn't scarred and I wondered what it meant. But I knew. It meant there hadn't been a motorcycle accident.

(But there was an accident.)

Had I made that up, too? Why?

I cracked the door open and found the aisle outside empty. But they were out there. I could hear their moans. Cautiously, I extended my head out of the bathroom, turned it to the front of the plane. Now I could see them, lined up all the way up the aisle to the front of the pane. Even Charlie was there, right at the front. And she was with them now, Christie. My Christie. She was a monster like all the rest.

They turned their dead eyes to me and, one by one, they cleared a path, and I knew what I had to do, but I didn't know if I could.

That first step was the hardest. My foot made a dull thud as it landed on the thin carpet. My joints felt stiff. I took a step, wrenched my hand away from the door, took another.

The moaning grew louder, but the monsters didn't try to stop me. I was crying then, shaking with terror.

An eternity later, I sat into the pilot's chair. I placed the headphones over my ears and thumbed the transmitter switch.

"LA Control," I said, wondering how I knew which words to say. "This is TropicAir Two-Seventeen requesting clearance to land."

Learning to fly had been the easy part. I'd taken it up as a hobby. But I certainly didn't know how to fly a jet. That was Frank's doing.

Oh, and I was a supermoto champion. At least I hadn't dreamed that part up.

"But zombies?" Frank said, shaking his head. "Never would have thought your fears would manifest themselves that way. But...whatever works, right?"

"I still think you're a quack," I said. And Frank laughed.

We continued the sessions, but never the hypnosis, and the zombies never showed up again after that first try.

Finally, one day in August, about nine months after the accident, Frank suggested we give it another go.

I was standing at the window of his office, watching the passersby down on the street ten stories below us. I'd gone back to racing about six weeks ago and had just come off a successful tour that culminated with me winning the Tokyo 300. The purse was just over a million, so Harry was back to being his usual ecstatic self. Team Kawasaki was ecstatic, too. And I'd just gotten a new sponsorship with Red Bull, so I was rolling in the dough. Life was good. Sure, I still had doubts and fears that haunted me, but why rock the boat, right?

"I'm not so sure that's a good idea."

Frank evaded my resistance by changing the subject. "Have you been to see Christie lately?"

He came over to stand beside me, and I could smell the soap on his skin. For some reason, I'd grown acutely aware of such things. Smells, sounds. Even the light seemed brighter. Sometimes it was even too bright.

I looked over and noticed him tapping the chewed end of his pencil against his notebook. I cringed for a moment before calming myself. I told myself to ignore him. I knew his tricks by now. The tapping didn't work that way on me anymore.

"Still no improvement," I managed to choke out. "She's dying."

"You're not responsible, you know."

I nodded. But if we hadn't been seeing each other, she wouldn't have been with me down in Melbourne. She wouldn't have been on that plane that day I decided to go for a little sightseeing flight out over the coast.

I closed my eyes and the image of her lying in her hospital bed came to me. It was always there, branded onto the surface of my consciousness. She'd lost her leg below the knee, her left one, and she was still in a coma. They didn't think she'd ever come out of it. She was dead to the world. And yet she wouldn't die. The gray liquid they fed to her through a tube in her stomach looked like pureed brains.

I hadn't told Frank I wasn't sleeping very well. I had nightmares about the wires and tubes connecting her body and the machines that ticked away, day in, day out. More and more I found myself avoiding beeping noises.

And I also didn't mention the voice I was still hearing.

(What voices?)

"You're still not fully better," he told me, as if reading my mind.

I could hear him moving over to his desk. "I'll pencil you in for next Thursday. I've got the whole afternoon free. I'll block it off." He clapped a hand over my shoulder and I jumped. "Until then...get lots of rest and eat right."

I nodded. He opened the door, then hesitated.

"What?"

He shrugged. "I probably shouldn't mention this..."

"What is it, Frank?"

"Well, you'll probably hear about it on your own. Actually, Harry'll probably spill it first."

I waited. Frank rubbed the back of his neck and winced, like maybe he was having second thoughts about telling. I had an idea what it was, but I wanted him to tell me.

"Well? Are you going to tell me or just torture me with it?"

"That article the *Times* wrote about the plane crash? Christie's? The one that talked about your affair?"

"There was no affair," I snapped. He waited for me to calm down again before continuing.

"The writer died."

"So? Good riddance," I said, perhaps a bit too hastily.

Frank's eyes flicked over my face. He sighed, shrugged. "He was murdered."

I felt a shiver pass through me.

(Miller knows the truth) the damn voice whispered inside my head.

"Charlie Kiernan was a tyrant," I said, waving my hand dismissively. "His staff and editors hated him. He was a slob and a prick."

"They said his head had been smashed open." I could see Frank shuddering.

"Okay..."

"Just a weird coincidence, huh? Happening like that."

"Like what?"

He studied me for a moment.

"They say the murderer took the man's brain."

I chuffed. "There's no such things as zombies, Frank." But then I could hear the voice of the bartender inside my head telling me there was. "Remember?"

Frank chuckled nervously, patting me on the back. "If you say so." He sighed. "Don't mean to push you out the door, Stack, but I'm meeting someone for lunch."

"Let me guess: Harry?"

Frank laughed. "No, a…former client of ours, though."

I lifted my baseball cap to straighten it, and my fingers found the old scar just at the hairline, the one that looked a little like a bite, like someone had decided to take a little nip at me. A little taste test. It still itched sometimes.

"Well," I said, "I'm sure you'll be able to cure him."

I found myself whistling *Don't Worry, Be Happy*. Frank's face got a faraway look on it. He was such a sucker for that tune.

I let myself out.

From the Associated Press News Wire:

[Los Angeles]   PGA golfer Sean Bickerson was found brutally murdered in his car yesterday afternoon. Investigators are still gathering evidence at the scene of the crime just outside the posh restaurant Giordano's on Fifth, a popular watering hole for sports figures. Given the viciousness of the crime, police believe a hatchet was used as the murder weapon. "We have a suspect in custody," LA Police Chief Rodney Fastoff announced late last night. The identity of the suspect has not been released, but sources close to the investigation speaking on condition of anonymity told reporters that the man police arrested is a well-known sports psychiatrist. In a bizarre twist, those same sources also claimed that the murderer may have eaten part of the victim's brain. The murder shares similarities with the gruesome killing of *Times* sports writer Charlie Kiernan, who was discovered in his home…

‡ ‡

Author's note

The idea for Occupied *was borne out of a question I posed to my Twitter followers: "What is the scariest setting for a horror story?" The answers ranged from the expected (cemetery, morgue, forest, haunted house) to the surprising (the office, a deserted island, the internet), from the ironic (high school senior ball, Disneyland's Small World, Chuck E. Cheese, a wedding) to the amusing (Charlie Sheen's bedroom; Ashton Kutcher's marriage). What it means, I suppose, is that given the right story, any setting can become a place of horror. Even the mind of a supermoto champion.*

I was rather surprised, however, that no one mentioned the cabin of a passenger jet. It's a very commonplace setting and one which practically anyone can relate to. It's a setting that, for me, presents perhaps the most untenable of situations for a character enduring an attack (whether external or internal): limited space and mobility, no possibility of escape (unless you brought your own parachute and can survive the 500-mph blast), dependency on others (unless you possess a commercial jet license), lack of communication with the ground, a high likelihood of a gruesome death, and horrible feng shui. And do I even need to mention the food?

Very few books and even fewer films exploit the constrictions of the passenger jet cabin as a crucible for the horror protagonist. Admittedly, even Stack, the narrator in Occupied, *ultimately escapes through a seemingly artificial means by waking from his hypnotic state. But if you think the flight he was on never occurred—at least for him—then you're as deluded as he is.*

And a friendly word of advice: the next time you're in LA, keep an eye out for the woman with the purse-strings mouth.

‡ ‡ ‡

Mr. November

There are all manner of hauntings: of places, of things, of people. There are hauntings of the mind, just as there are hauntings of the body and of the soul. But the worst sort of haunting is the kind which infects the spirit, entwines with it, subsumes it. The kind that cannot be easily exorcised.

Not, at least, without first killing the host.

STANDING there on the sidewalk, enveloped in the hot July sunlight, I can't help but be struck by how little the place has changed over the past twenty years. The newspapers had called it Malvern Manor, so named after its last owner back in the nineteen-eighties, but as kids we'd always just called it The Place On Dunbury Hill. Even now, as I look at it through an adult's eyes, it still feels as possessed of evil as it had back then.

Despite the brightness of the day, a pall of oppression hangs over the lot, a hazy sense of perpetual decay and yet, at the same time, a self-indulgent refusal to concede the passage of time. As if a structure made of wood and stone can feel resentment, much less express it. Maybe it can. Maybe the place resents its abandonment so long ago; or maybe it's offended by the rumors that persist about it, stories of pain and suffering that have survived despite the waxing and waning of so many generations

There are people who say the rumors are just malicious stories, conceived by parents wishing to keep their children safe. But they are mostly transplants to this place; they don't know this town of Edgemont as I know it. They don't know what it can do to a person.

The house had already stood empty for some twenty years by the time I was old enough to begin making my own memories of it. And so it has continued to stand for another twenty, alone and empty, brooding on its overgrown lot on the side of Dunbury Hill, overlooking the Southside and the dark, tattered remnants of what was once a dense forest: Alden Wood.

I have tried desperately to run away from here, but for the last twenty years the house has called me back. It presses itself upon me, no matter how far I go. It has left its mark on the skin of my soul just as Derrick's memory leaves its own impression there. But while my brother is a pile of whisper-soft bones in an old box in a cold grave—while I am a rattling pile of bones in a living coffin made of weathered skin and neglected flesh—the Malvern house remains just exactly the same as it ever was: hard and tall and unyielding, looming over the world, haunted and haunting. It is in that last part that the house has become something of the brother it took from me.

Nothing stands between us now, neither distance nor time. The faded front door holds slightly ajar, inviting me in, daring me, teasing. I've been staring at it for twenty years, in my mind's eye, and yet this is the closest I've come to going back inside.

The house hadn't killed Derrick right away, but whatever it stole from him—his soul or spirit or whatever life-giving essence that fills us all—it took from him in that one single night. I'm sure of that, as sure as I can be of anything.

The thought makes me uncomfortable, even after so long getting used to it. I shift my feet on the old sidewalk, toe a crack filled with grass and pebbles. Why have I returned? To reclaim what was lost to me? To Derrick? Why am I here?

We'd numbered four that Halloween night that it happened: me and Derrick, plus the two next door neighbors, Lenny and Marcus. They were my brother's friends, boys roughly Derrick's age. They lived in the houses to either side of us. I was the youngest of the bunch, and the only reason I was even included was because our mother had made Derrick promise to take me. It was the only way she would let me go trick-or-treating without parental supervision. Unfortunately, there were no boys my age living in the neighborhood, no one for me to accompany. I was stuck with Derrick.

Or, rather, he was stuck with me.

"And don't scare Bobby, Derrick," my father warned as we finished preparing ourselves for the grand adventure

My parents had tried to hide their own eagerness in letting us go unattended by pretending to be stern and disapproving, but we all knew it was an act. That night was the fourth game of what would turn out to be an unforgettable World Series. Arizona was leading two games to one, and they wanted to stay in and watch it on the TV. But they couldn't do that and take us door-to-door, so they compromised. It was the perfect opportunity for us kids to enjoy the night the way we were meant to enjoy it: without parental constrictions.

I knew that Derrick had some reservations about the arrangement, not solely because I was his little brother, a scaredy-pants little kid who practically wet himself watching cartoons and was therefore a supreme embarrassment to him in front of his friends, but also because Derrick was so heavily into baseball at the time. He was torn between going out for candy and watching the game with Mom and Dad.

By the age of nine, Derrick had already learned all the teams' names, knew their day-to-day standings, their primary playmakers, could recite a ton of stats. By thirteen, he was a starting pitcher on Edgemont's Little League team, the Bullets, and the high school was already drooling over the prospects of having him play on a team that looked, for the first time in the town's history, that it might have a shot at taking Regionals and possibly even State someday. He was a good pitcher, accurate and fast—no, not just good; he was *talented*.

He was also a budding New York Yankees fan. This often irked my father to the point of sudden anger. And while Dad wasn't exactly a Diamondbacks supporter during the regular season—the Cubs were his team—he became a D-backs fan when it was them against "those damn Yankees," as he liked to call them. One got the sense that the team had once betrayed him. Badly.

The game was early in the fourth, score tied at one-all, and the D-backs were looking to extend their series lead. It was killing Derrick not to stay home and watch it. But the lure of trick-or-treating with his friends and no parents proved to be too strong, even for him. As a freshly minted teenager on the cusp of becoming a young man, he must've realized that there would be other World

Series to enjoy, but there wouldn't be too many more Halloweens. Plus, there was Marcus, his best friend, to consider, as well as the mask that he'd made so much fuss over.

For me, the benefits were more of the practical sort: No parents to tell us not to eat too much candy or cut across people's lawns or flowerbeds. No "Stop climbing fences." No one to tell us not to run across the road without looking both ways first. No one claiming "That's enough; you're bag's full; time to go home."

I'm sure Derrick would've preferred to have me stay home or my parents take me, rather than tag along with him and his pals, but he couldn't very well refuse my mother's conditions, either. By agreeing to take me he'd extracted my promise not to tattle on him to our folks about the mask, the one he'd gotten at the Scare Store at the mall. Mom had told him in no uncertain terms that it was too horrid of a thing for anyone to wear, much less a boy of thirteen, and certainly not around me. I was nine and sure to have nightmares about it, a claim I vehemently refuted, though to no avail. She told Derrick to throw the mask away, that she didn't want to see it again, and how could he even think it was okay to bring something like *that* home?

But, like I said, he was on the lip of adolescence and, besides baseball, he was getting into things that I was still too young to understand at the time: horror movies and horror paraphernalia, as well as girls (which, to my young mind, were one and the same). It didn't help that Marcus's dad let the boys watch slasher films at their place. Splatterpunk is what they used to call it I believe. I can still remember the way they treasured the cover of the *Chainsaw* DVD, much the same way I would come to treasure the Vani Desmont centerfold eight years later. Derrick had hidden the disk under his mattress and whenever he wanted me out of his room he'd flash it at me. And I just knew by the look on his face whenever they were planning to watch it at Marcus's house late into the night when my parents thought they were just hanging out and playing Lego Battles. Marcus was a year older than Derrick, which made him cool. There was no way in hell Marcus played Legos.

Then there was Lenny, who was thirteen, like my brother. He claimed he liked gore, too, but honestly, I think he was just along for the ride.

As for me, I never went through a horror phase. I just could never understand the appeal.

After a last minute check of our costumes—including Derrick's pockets and his empty pillow case—Mom guided us to the back door. It was obvious she hadn't forgotten about the mask and didn't trust Derrick to be honest about throwing it away. If she'd just thought to ask me about it, I'm sure I would've spilled the beans. But she didn't. "Be back by eight," she told us.

"That's too early, Mom," Derrick complained. He was wearing a skeleton tee shirt with glow-in-the-dark ribs and had painted his face white and black. "Can't we at least stay out till nine?"

Mom sighed and looked at Dad, who shrugged in his typically unhelpful way. She frowned. "Okay, but first you have to bring your brother home by eight. After that, you and your friends can go back out for another hour. No later. It's a school night. And if you come to a house without any lights on, then—"

"We know, we know," Derrick said. "Don't go to it."

Now it was my turn to complain. Why did Derrick get to stay out till nine when I had to be in by eight? But there was nothing I could say to convince her to budge on my curfew. She practically pushed us out the door and down the steps. The last thing I remember as we left was hearing the staticky sound of the crowd coming from our television. I had to drag Derrick off the steps to get him moving.

We skirted the back of the house and went next door to the Cordova's. Marcus's dad was the kind of father a kid wouldn't get embarrassed about having around. He liked to play tricks on us, like he'd never grown up himself, so neither of us was surprised when he jumped out of the shadows on the front porch shouting, "Booga booga! Did I scare ya?"

We both nodded obligingly.

Mister Cordova gave my fake parrot a friendly jab with the top of his beer. His words sounded slightly slurred to me. A half dozen crushed MGB cans wobbled on the picnic table when he bumped into it. "And who might you be, matey? Blackbeard?"

"Cap'n Hook," I said, laughing and brandished my K-Mart plastic hook at him.

"Arrr! I was talkin' to the bird. Blackbeard, the Parrot!"

He was wearing an old pair of dark green mechanics coveralls splattered with something dark, and although my mind automatically registered it as blood at first, I quickly realized it was really just red paint. There was, however, a very real-looking hatchet with real-looking blood on it leaning against the front door, all part of his props.

"Open up!" he said, swinging the candy bowl over our empty sacks like a metal detector. We did as he said, and he shook a generous helping of chocolate into each of them, the whole time smiling around the butt end of his cigarette. "Can't let you boys go out there empty now, can I? That oughta get you started."

"Thanks, Mister Cordova," we chorused.

Derrick asked him if he was going to watch the game.

"Not watch, son, listen. That's why I gots me this," he answered, pulling an old transistor radio and earbuds out of his breast pocket. "Won't be missing any of the action sitting out here on the porch."

He followed us into the house to find Marcus and Lenny.

"Check it out, dude," Marcus said, his face lighting up when he saw us. He pulled something out of a paper bag that looked like road kill. I stood in rapt horror as he pulled it over his head before realizing it was a werewolf mask and not a dead possum or raccoon. Mister Cordova gave an exaggerated shudder and held his hands up and pled for mercy. We all laughed, although my own laughter was as forced as it sounded. Even knowing the mask was a fake, I didn't like seeing it on Marcus. It transformed him into something that looked, not just dangerous, but wicked.

"Cool," Derrick said. "You got mine?" The Marcus/Wolf Man-thing nodded and went over to a cabinet. With one hand on the top of his head to keep the eyeholes aligned, he reached in and withdrew the mask that Derrick had bought with his recycling money a couple weeks before. I was disappointed that he hadn't changed his mind about wearing it.

There had been a terrible argument that night he'd brought it home. Mom got angry with Dad for not agreeing strongly enough with her, but when he did, Derrick started shouting that Dad always took her side. "That's not true, Derr," he'd said, and Mom had snatched the mask off the table and threw it out the back door and into the yard. She told Derrick if he wanted it so badly then he could sleep with it *outside*, but under no circumstances would it be coming back into the house again.

That was the end of the discussion, but dinners for the next few nights had been especially quiet, at least until Derrick finally agreed that he'd dress up as something other than the rotting zombie he'd originally planned to go as. After that, things settled back into their usual pattern, and the whole thing was forgotten.

It was only through some unintentional eavesdropping that I'd learned Derrick hadn't thrown the mask away, but had given it to Marcus to hold onto. He still intended to wear it come Halloween night. I told him I knew about his plans and would tell on him, although, truthfully, I doubt I would have. I think Derrick knew that, too. He knew the last thing I wanted was for Mom and Dad to have yet another reason to fight. I would've agreed to sleep with the mask myself if it meant keeping them happy.

But now, seeing it again up close, I was no longer so sure of that. Even as a lifeless, limp rubbery thing in Derrick's hand, it seemed to possess some kind of innate malice, its empty eyes filled with a cruel intent that I imagined would insinuate Derrick when he put it on. I must have shown my feelings on my face, because Marcus suddenly grabbed it out of Derrick's hand and swung it over at me, waggling it in front of my nose and saying, "You're not scared of this, are you, Bobby? It's just rubber. Or maybe it's not. Maybe it's real human *flesh*!"

"I'm not scared," I told him, taking a half-hearted swipe at the thing. I didn't want to touch it. And I was scared. But I wasn't scared for just me; a part of my fright had to do with what I believed would happen to Derrick when he put the thing on. I knew it was ridiculous to think that. I knew the mask was just a cheap, mass-produced piece of garbage. I probably should've been more worried about the lead content in it, except, of course, I was just nine years old and when you're that age, such mundane considerations don't even register on the radar, not like the fantastic and improbable.

"That's nothing," Lenny exclaimed. "Check this out!" The three older boys were very competitive with each other, so I expected Lenny's mask to be even more grotesque than the other two, but I quickly saw that it was just a clown's face, rubbery white and red with curly red and green and yellow hair. It looked as harmless as a balloon animal. And yet, both Marcus and Derrick were inexplicably impressed by it. They acted like it was some kind of masterpiece of terror. I wasn't sure that they weren't putting me on.

"Awesome! That's gonna scare the crap out people!" Derrick shouted.

"It's a clown," I said, laughing. "That's not scary!"

"Wait till we're done with the makeup," Marcus said, nodding smugly. And he dug around inside the bag before producing a tube of fake blood.

Suddenly my pirate's costume, complete with a plastic gray sword and press-on beard and fake leather hat, felt woefully fake and all too childish.

"Well, you boys are too scary for me," Mister Cordova exclaimed. "Besides, I gots me a game to listen to and hordes of little beasts and beastettes to be scarin'." He made his way out of the kitchen, swinging his hatchet and whistling, *Take Me Out to the Ballgame*. As he passed me, he gave me an exaggerated cringe. I laughed and pretended to stick him with my hook. He skipped off down the front hall, grabbing his ass and yelping like a hurt puppy.

I chose to wait in the darkened hallway while the boys busied themselves with their makeup, dribbling the thick, red slime over their arms and spreading it over their shirts. I heard the first kids arrive out front and chuckled when I saw Mister Cordova stand up and brandish his axe and gleefully shout, "Booga-booga!" The kids shrieked with delight.

On the radio, the announcer said the score going into the seventh inning stretch was tied at one-all. An organ played and the crowd yelled, "Charge!"

"They're tied," I yelled.

There was no answer, just a lot of laughing and fooling around. Someone was doing armpit farts—Lenny, if I had to guess—when someone let off a ripper, eliciting a whole new rounds of groans.

"Hurry up!" I shouted in at them. It was a quarter to seven by then and all I'd collected so far was the candy from Mister Cordova, which didn't really count. Plus, I'd already eaten half of it. "All the good candy's going to be gone!"

"Aw, quit your whining," one of them said. I think it was Marcus. The three boys laughed. There was a crash, a curse, some more laughter. It sounded like they were making a real mess in the kitchen.

"I'm not whining. You're wasting time."

"Keep your britches on, Captain Goobers!" Even more laughter.

"You promised, Derrick."

They tumbled out of the kitchen, their tattered rags for costumes flapping behind them, their arms painted to match their masks. I refused to look at Marcus and Derrick faces, but when I saw Lenny, I had to suppress a shudder. They had given his clown face a grimace and darkened the area around his eyes; a trickle of blood spilled from the corner of the mask's mouth and out of one nostril. He was still a clown, but they had made him look positively gory. Suddenly I was cursing the baseball game on the television and regretting agreeing to go with Derrick.

Marcus knocked the parrot from my shoulder and laughed.

"Leave him alone, man," Derrick told him. "Not cool."

It was nothing, just a quick roll of the eyes and a little shove to push Marcus away from me, but it was enough to change my mood. In that moment, I would have followed my brother anywhere, no matter how scary the mask he might be wearing.

Marcus did leave me alone—for a while—and we made pretty quick work of the Southside. In those days, our street, Alden Lane, was in one of the newest and outermost neighborhoods of Edgemont, just across the river from the main part of town. You had to head north, otherwise you'd be into farmland pretty soon; beyond the fields was what was left of Alden Wood. And beyond that was the power plant.

So we headed north, back towards town, zigzagging along familiar streets. We crossed the river at the old train trestle—against our parents' orders—before winding our way up Fifth Street. Our bags were getting heavy, but we weren't even close to heading back.

It wasn't until we came to Dunbury Park that Derrick remembered my curfew. It had been weighing on my mind, but I'd kept quiet about it.

"Anyone know what time it is?" he asked, but the others shook their heads. Nobody had worn a watch.

The woman who answered the door at the next house told us it was ten minutes before eight. We heard a TV on in the background. Derrick asked if she knew the score.

"Three-one D-backs," a man shouted from his chair farther off in the room. "Bottom of the eighth. Arizona just scored a pair off Stanton, so New York replaced him. But Mendoza's throwing crap."

Derrick groaned.

"You boys wanna come on in and watch?" said the man. "We got soda and chips."

We all looked at each other. Thoughts of my parents telling me never to talk to strangers or go anywhere with them or take candy from them suddenly came to mind. I could see it in the others' eyes that they were thinking the same thing. Yet everything about Halloween seemed to negate all that. Our parents had practically shoved us out the door with their blessings to go up to people's houses, people we didn't even know, to knock on *their* doors, to beg for candy.

"Want to?" Derrick said. He had lifted his mask to the top of his head, and his face was glistening with sweat. We were all hot. It was a warm evening, and we'd been running from door to door almost nonstop for over an hour. "Just for a few minutes. I need a break."

I remember thinking what a lame excuse that was. Out of all of us, Derrick was the strongest and most athletic. It was obvious he just wanted to watch the game.

Lenny backed up a step, shaking his head. I couldn't see his face, since he still had that stupid clown mask on, but from his body language I knew he didn't think it was such a good idea.

The man got up and started walking toward the door.

"Let the boys alone, sugar," the woman told him, her voice low and tired-sounding, but he kept coming, the smile on his face suddenly looking much too wide and way too eager.

"Come on, Derrick," I said under my breath.

The man stopped at the door and his body, as thin as it was, seemed to block nearly all of the light coming out. "Hey, it ain't no big deal, boys. It's just a *baseball* game. Just the World Series." He held out the candy bowl, even though the woman had already given us something. None of us reached over.

"Our Mom gets really mad when we're late," I said. "She might even call the police."

The man chuckled and nodded at my brother. "So, you like the Yankees, eh?"

Derrick nodded. I was pulling on his sleeve, backing off down the sidewalk. I lost my grip and stumbled. Lenny caught me. I didn't try to grab my brother again. The man was too close for my comfort. He could grab me if I wasn't careful.

"Come on, Derr," Lenny whispered.

"Aw, half an inning won't hurt," the man told Derrick, winking. "Our boys are up at bat. The Yanks, right? We're gonna crush those losers, you wait and see. Arizona's got Schilling up on the mound, but he's no finisher, right? Just a pussycat. What do they call him?"

"The Schill," Derrick croaked.

"Right, the Schill. And what do they call you? The Kill?" He laughed and my brother laughed weakly with him. "You know, because you're dead."

"Derrick?" I said, pleading now. I was shivering by then.

The man was out of his house, standing over Derrick, guiding him inside with a hand on his shoulder. It was a skinny, boney hand, and the man's legs were long and skinny, too. His jeans were faded and loose, the fronts beginning to fray. The baseball cap on his greasy head was stained and ratty-looking. I realized with a growing sense of alarm that it wasn't a NY cap and I remembered what he'd said: *Our boys are up at bat. The Yanks, right?* Except the cap was the wrong color. It was Arizona's colors. And the woman had vanished.

"Derrick!" Lenny shouted. "Come on!"

But it was another group of trick-or-treaters that broke Derrick's trance. He snapped his head up as the kids crowded around him to get to the candy bowl. He turned and looked at us, then back at the man. "Sorry, Mister," he mumbled, then hurried over to where we had gathered near the road. We all pulled him into our circle, as if we could protect him.

Looking back, I saw the man finish handing out candy. He closed the door and went back inside. We could see him through the picture window settling back into his chair, reaching for a handful of chips. The walls of the room flickered blue and white. A car commercial was on the screen, a beautiful woman in a white dress driving through a city that was much cleaner and newer looking than ours. She was laughing, and the top was down.

Suddenly we'd had enough trick-or-treating for the night. Our pillow cases, not yet full, were full enough. Our feet were tired. Our excitement had flagged.

"Come on," Derrick muttered, and we followed him across the street and in the direction of the Southside. For the first time I noticed how empty the streets looked—no trick-or-treaters in sight—as if by crossing the road we'd somehow stepped into another place and into another time, a night that wasn't Halloween. Streets that weren't occupied by kids in costumes, but instead with creatures that were decidedly more sinister. Even the air felt different, colder. The wind had picked up and was blowing off the river. I could smell the faint, greasy smell of the train yard on it.

A church bell rang off in the distance. I counted the tolls. There were eight. We were now officially late.

"Is that true about your mom?" Lenny asked Derrick. "Do you think she'll call the cops?"

Derrick brushed past him, but didn't answer.

"Because I wouldn't mind seeing a cop car right about now," Lenny finished. He gave a nervous laugh.

Marcus shook his head in disgust. "You're such a chickenshit sometimes, Lenny."

But it was me he was looking at, smirking. It was me who was the chickenshit. That's what he was saying, just not saying it out loud directly to me because of Derrick. I lowered my eyes and kept walking. Nobody said a word as we topped Dunbury Peak and started back down the other side past the memorial park. The lights of the Southside spread out before us, thinning toward the edges, looking like an unfinished Lite-Brite creation.

Somewhere out there, close to the edge of the darkness, was my home. But it suddenly seemed like a long way away.

Fifth Street dead-ended at the railroad tracks, so we took a right onto Edgemont Terrace, which we followed around the edge of Dunbury Park. We encountered a few other groups of trick-or-treaters, older kids mostly by then and fewer parents. We were all huffing and slightly out of breath.

Lenny suggested we cut through the rest of Dunbury rather than going all the way around. The park was long, stretching nearly three miles, and we still had a third of it yet to go. But it was fairly narrow. We could see the lights from the streets on the other side twinkling through the trees. The park itself was shrouded in darkness, deep and mysterious. There were a lot of potential hiding places between us and the other side.

"Derrick," I said, slowing to a stop. All three of the boys had taken off their masks by then, for which I was grateful, and had stuffed them into their candy sacks. Somewhere along the way, my parrot had slipped off my shoulder and was lying across my back, pecking at me as we went. I took the opportunity to pull it off of me. It joined the candy in my sack. "I think we should keep going."

"Baby," Marcus taunted.

Derrick glared at him.

"What? If we hadn't brought Bobby along, we'd have twice as much loot by now," Marcus complained. "And we wouldn't have to be heading back yet, either."

"I've got enough candy," Lenny mumbled.

Marcus frowned at him. "Aw, man. This sucks! I don't even have to be home till ten."

"Never mind that," Derrick said. He grabbed my wrist and pulled me in the direction of those twinkling lights. I resisted at first, but he started jogging, and, before I knew it, we were all sprinting through the dark.

Our feet whispered over the soft dewy grass and our breaths came in staggered gasps. For much too long the bobbing lights didn't seem to be drawing any closer, and I started to feel a bit panicky by then, imagining things coming out of the shadows after us. I don't know if the other boys felt the same way, but it did seem like we were all running faster than we might have under different circumstances. Even Marcus was looking like this was no time for standing around discussing things. No one said a word until our feet started slapping pavement again.

"See?" Derrick said, looking at Marcus. "No one's a baby. Now let's go." He still had a hold of my hand and ended up almost jerking me off my feet. He twisted around and gave me a glare, but I wasn't looking at him. I was looking at the house looming out of the darkness behind him. Malvern Manor. The House on Dunbury Hill.

It rose above us, stark and silent, the last house on that dead-end road. Everyone knew the Malvern place back then, or at least knew *of* it. It was a massive structure, an old Victorian, one of the first houses built on the hill back in the eighteen-hundreds. The original owner was a successful furniture maker named Octavius Dunbury. He had owned the entire hill and hundreds of acres of the surrounding forestland. Remnants of the forest are still scattered about, a few copses on the hill, broad swaths of it south of the river, including Alden Wood. He had been rich and famous and powerful, and his name still adorns several street signs, buildings and businesses in the area. But it wasn't until the descendants of Octavius Dunbury relocated to the Eastside and sold the place to a man named Frederick Malvern that the house he'd built earned itself its name.

Malvern had been a town selectman in the nineteen-sixties. He'd made his money as an oral surgeon years before he entered into local politics. After he retired from public life, he returned to the trade, reestablishing his practice in the mansion's spacious lower level. At the time, the locals joked good-naturedly about the place, calling it Maleficence Manor (or Manner), in first part because of the house's gothic appearance, but also because the good doctor was known for having a rather gruff bedside manner. But if Malvern wasn't exactly warm and cuddly, he was an excellent physician, and people didn't go to him to be chummy; they went to him because they needed their teeth fixed.

Malvern's practice thrived for the next twenty-some odd years, until Frederick suddenly keeled over of a massive brain aneurism at the age of eighty-seven. He was right in the middle of doing an extraction on the chief-of-police, who happened to be enjoying a generous helping of laughing gas at the time. When he came to, his rotten tooth was in Malvern's dead hand, and the good doctor himself was lying on the floor staring straight up at the ceiling.

Over time, the nickname Maleficence Manor became simply Malvern Manor, although the former name's dreadful connotation stuck. After a while, people started saying that the place was haunted. Whether it was or not, the house stood empty after the death. It has never been offered up for sale, never rented out, never used by anyone or anything save possibly a few stray animals and adventurous (and amorous) teenagers—enough of the latter, anyway, to sustain a steady stream of ridiculous tales sufficient to pique the curiosity of the town's kids and the stern warnings of their parents, while being too outlandish to be taken too seriously.

"Place gives me the creeps," Lenny said, shivering.

The weeds had grown tall in the front yard, but they were now dead, dried and brown and whispery. The leaves of the thick ivy growing up on its walls had already fallen away, giving the house the appearance of a skinless creature whose exposed blood vessels had shriveled dry.

"What does condemned mean?" I asked, pointing to the sign that had been wired to the front fence.

"It means it's haunted," Marcus answered, barking out a harsh laugh.

"Really?"

"No," Derrick said, whistling through his teeth. "Now come on. We're already late."

"No, wait!" It was Marcus, and I didn't like the look he was giving me. His eyes were especially dark, hard to read, but his teeth seemed to glow as he grinned. He held up his candy bag and jiggled it. I could hear the wrappers inside crinkling. "Want some more candy? You can have some of mine. I'll let you grab a handful, as much as you can hold with one hand." He jerked his thumb at the house. "But you gotta go and knock on the door."

"Marcus—"

"Oh, come on, man. Easy peasy. It'll only take a second." He turned to me again and said, "I'd do it, you know, for a handful from your bag, but it doesn't look like you have as much to spare." He shook his sack again, and it did look heavier than mine. I don't know how it could be, since we'd been to all the same houses, gotten the same candy. And yet my bag did look quite a bit smaller.

"Nobody's going to do anything, Marcus," Derrick said, losing his patience. "Least of all Bobby."

"Yeah, he's a chicken," Lenny chimed in. He actually looked relieved, probably because I was the butt of Marcus's attention and not him.

"I am not a chicken," I snapped. "And I'm not a baby."

Derrick pulled at me again, but then he let go when I refused to budge. I was torn between taking Marcus's dare and knowing he was right about me. But then Derrick started walking away, and by doing so it was like he was telling me he knew I wouldn't do it—

that I *couldn't* do it. Knowing this made me even more determined to prove myself to him that I wasn't a chicken.

"Come on! It'll be quick," Marcus shouted after him. "All he's got to do is run up the steps and knock... And turn the door knob."

"You didn't say I had to do that," I complained.

Derrick's voice sounded flat as he yelled back at me. It was almost as if the air around us was dead. He was already fifty feet away and quickly fading into the darkness. "I don't care what you do, Bobby. Mom's gonna be mad at you for being late, not me."

Marcus reached into his bag and pulled out a handful of candy, then let it sprinkle back in.

"A handful from *each* of you," I stammered, hoping they'd back down.

Marcus seemed to consider this, then nodded. "Okay, but then we'll need to up the stakes, won't we?"

"No way," Lenny cried, clutching his bag to his body. "I didn't agree—"

"Shut up, Lenny."

"What do you mean? What stakes?" I said.

"If, after you try the doorknob, you find that it's unlocked, then you have to go inside."

"It won't be unlocked," Lenny said, managing to look both upset and hopeful at the same time.

"Then there's nothing to worry about, right?" Marcus said, still looking at me.

"Is that all?"

"Uh...no. If you go inside, then you have to close the door and stay inside for a full ten alligators."

I was sorry I asked.

"Make it twenty alligators," Lenny said.

I looked back up at the old house and shivered. It hadn't seen a coat of paint in so long that it was impossible to say what color it might have been to begin with. It seemed to lack any color at all, just an indefinable pale hue that seemed to bleed through from within. The windows stared out at us, looking like the black, soulless eyes of the alligator I'd seen last summer at the animal park upstate, and the darkness below the front porch overhang made me think of it with its mouth frozen open in mid-gulp.

"Promise?" I said. It wasn't the candy I was after now, it was for Marcus and Lenny to stop thinking of me as a little baby, as a chicken. But was it worth it if I actually had to touch the house? And what if the doorknob did turn and the door opened? What then? Could I stand inside in the darkness, cut off from Derrick, shut off from the world? Would I even be able to count to ten—no, *twenty* alligators?

Then again, I could just pretend to try the doorknob. They'd be none the wiser. I didn't think Marcus would check. I'd just pretend it was locked. Besides, why would it be unlocked? It didn't make sense that it would be.

"I'll hold your candy bag for you," Marcus said, his smile growing wider.

"I'll keep it," I snapped, yanking it back out of his reach.

I pushed on the front gate and it squealed on rusty hinges. The bottom corner dragged over the concrete. I lifted it so it wouldn't grate, but the hinges still squealed. I snatched one last look over my shoulder. Derrick was out of sight by then, but I knew if I hurried and did what Marcus asked, that I'd be able to catch up with him.

I stepped quickly through and made my way toward the front door. The night seemed to hold its breath, but I was shaking like a leaf on a windy day. I held the bag in front of me with both hands, ready to swing at anything that moved. Other than the wavering shadows thrown off by the clouds drifting past high above, everything was still.

My toe hit the first step with a dull *thump*. I stopped.

Lenny and Marcus chuckled behind me, then whispered something that was half encouragement, half mockery. I lifted my foot, set it on the riser, shifted my weight. The step creaked once, softly. I lifted my other foot, placed it upon the next one up, shifted my weight. Three more steps to go before the landing.

From somewhere in the distance, I could hear the faint cry of some night bird, the sound of a car. The church bell rang the quarter hour. Two more steps beneath me and I stood at the boundary of the shadow the overhanging porch roof cast down. I squinted into the darkness. It seemed so much deeper now than it had from out on the sidewalk. I didn't turn around to look at the other boys then, mostly out of fear that if I took my eyes off the shadows, something would come out of them and grab me.

I swallowed a breath and stepped into the darkness.

The CONDEMNED sign is long gone. So, too, the old wrought iron gate. Its hinges have rusted away and broken off; the rust has bubbled up beneath the black paint, distorting the metal into grotesque shapes. Where is the gate now? Probably sitting in someone's garden somewhere, supporting a row of pole beans. Or maybe in a heap of trash at the bottom of a gully or storm drain. I can picture the sign hanging in some kid's dorm room. Twenty years is a long time for something to happen. Who knows what has become of such things?

But the rest is the same. The sidewalk to the front porch is unchanged: cracked and tilted by seasons of frost and drought, stained by rotting leaves and the desiccated corpses of earthworms resurrected during the most recent rainstorm. The July sun beats heavily down on me, bright and searing, and yet the darkness under the porch remains as cold and lifeless as if it were late October, on a night when the Diamondbacks were beating the Yankees three-one, and the Yankees were about to tie it up.

I light another cigarette and shove the lighter back deep into my pocket and stand there puffing on the filthy thing. I stand and gaze at the house that stole the life from my brother. The memories come rushing back, not with the patient, erosive ebb and flow that they have over the years, but in a sudden tidal rush that leaves me drowning in misery and wondering whether my coming back to this place was such a good idea after all. I don't belong here. I never did, neither two decades ago, and definitely not now.

But I'm here. I'm not turning around now. Not when it has cost me all of these years and a wasted career, a wife who left me because I wouldn't stop beating her and a girlfriend who left me because I couldn't stop beating myself.

I would rather die than turn away now.

A dry chuckle crawls up my throat. It's not the first suicidal thought I've ever had. And it certainly won't be the last.

†

†

"Bobbeeeee..."

Derrick's voice came drifting out of the darkness, sounding distant and hollow.

I paused, listening. Marcus and Lenny stood on the sidewalk below me without saying anything, just watching.

"Bobby, come on," Derrick yelled. "Mom and Dad're going to kill us." From the sound of his voice, the way it was fading, I could tell he was still heading downhill, away from me.

I turned back to the porch, my head ratcheting on my neck like it needed oil. I'd come this far without anything bad happening. I could feel my confidence building, even as I felt an unspeakable terror rising from someplace deep inside me. I could feel it close to the surface. It was a race to see which of them would win.

I took a breath, then stepped out of the moonlight and into the swamp of darkness beneath the porch. There was no turning back now.

In all of my years on this earth—the nine that preceded that moment and the twenty since—I never felt more alive than right then. Not alive as in glad to be living, but alive as in suddenly aware of my mortality, of the delicate and vulnerable nature of the thing we call life. My nerves were reporting every sensation in high-definition stereo. My brain was having trouble processing the information. Every sound was multiplied a hundred-fold. I felt everything, tasted everything, smelled everything. My eyes pierced the inky blackness and discerned every crack in every board, every stained nail head, every mote of dust. The air tasted acrid and smelled of mold and negligence and forgotten memories. I was hyperaware. Anything that might have existed before that one moment was suddenly immaterial; and anything that might come after was irrelevant. Only the present mattered.

It took an uncountable number of steps, an inestimable amount of time, to reach the door, but I finally did manage it, and once I had it seemed as if it had not been so long or so far as I thought. A few feet, mere seconds. The rotting floorboards beneath my feet had held. They hadn't opened up, hadn't devoured me. Nothing pounced out of the darkness to get me. No monsters or snakes or bats. There were no suspicious sounds, no malignant moans of hunger or want;

there had been no evil red eyes blinking terrifyingly at me. Just my own imagination.

And that was enough.

I waited about as long as I could, but I knew by then that I could wait forever for something to happen and that nothing would; the next move was mine.

The door appeared to be locked.

I can't really explain what I mean by that. What does a locked door look like? How does it distinguish itself from an unlocked door or announce itself as such? I can't say, but as I stood there, my face just inches from it and my hands strangling the life out of my pillow case, all I could think was that the door looked like it didn't want anyone to pass through it. Or maybe it was just wishful thinking on my part; my mind was screaming for it to be locked. I was hoping and praying the thing would be secured, and not just by a series of deadbolts, but by a dozen boards nailed across it from the inside.

I raised my hand, brought it up to the doorknob. My fingers had barely brushed the cold metal when it seemed to jump at the touch of my skin. It acted as if it had been wakened, and it turned of its own volition, twisting inside my hand. I stood in abject horror, watching as the tarnished brass of the knob, with its ornate carvings that looked like the skin of a reptile, rotated. The latch clicked and released. There was not a single sound as the door opened, not the creak of hinges or the whisper of air. The door opened and the darkness presented itself to me. Only then did my terror breach the surface. And yet I stood there frozen, unable to move.

I could see nothing inside. Still, I knew that what filled the darkness which my eyes couldn't penetrate was *not* nothing, but a definite something. I knew that the house had been waiting for me, or at least a boy of similar build, with my height and weight and appearance. I would do just fine, thank you.

I heard the boys behind me. I heard their whispers. I hadn't heard them throughout those terrifying moments leading up to the door opening, and yet I somehow remembered afterward that they had been talking the whole time. They suddenly stopped as they realized what had happened. I'm sure they were as surprised as I was that the house would be so amenable to our—to *my*—trespass.

It was probably fortunate that my heart was in my throat, since it kept the scream rising up within my chest from escaping through my mouth. I couldn't move. I couldn't even turn to run. My heart was in my throat, as dead as a cork, and the darkness before my eyes turned to whiteness in my mind as I struggled to breathe.

"Well?" Marcus said. His voice sounded shaky, but I thought I heard a quiver of amusement in it, too. I heard the crackle of his candy bag as he shook it. What would he say if I were turn and renege? What would he do?

I knew what he would do. He would redouble his teasing, and there wouldn't be a thing that Derrick could say about it, because how can you defend someone like that? Marcus would keep on teasing me, and so would Lenny. In fact, that's why Lenny was pushing me, too. In that strange calculus of adolescence, my success or failure would determine his own stature in Marcus's eyes.

"That's one handful you've earned," Marcus shouted. His voice sounded weak and muted, as if he too was losing substance. "But only *if* you finish the second part. Go inside, close the door and count to twenty."

"Twenty *alligators*," Lenny said.

It didn't make me happy to hear the fear in both their voices. They were a good fifty feet away, safe on the sidewalk beneath the protective dome of a streetlamp. They were somehow outside of the house's reach. And yet they were as scared as I was. But they were also grateful they weren't standing in my place.

"Stop," the voice hissed in my ear.

I nearly wet myself when Derrick suddenly appeared beside me and grabbed my arm. I didn't, but I did jump and give a yelp of surprise. I'm sure he saw and heard me do that, but he didn't show that he did. He began to pull me off the porch, and now I could hear Marcus and Lenny below me complaining, calling me names and threatening that I wouldn't get any of their candy. Not that the threat meant much to me anymore.

I pulled out of Derrick's grip. "No," I told him, and he swung angrily around at me and reached for my arm again. "No, Derrick! Leave me alone!"

"We're late, Bobby!"

"I don't care."

He sighed. "Look, I'll give you a handful of my own candy. Two, even. Who cares? It's not worth whatever punishment we're going to get when we get home."

"Punishment?" I said to him. He was worried about punishment? I was worried about the rest of my childhood.

"It's just forty seconds," Marcus called up after us.

"You said twenty," Derrick countered over his shoulder.

"I doubled it, you know, since there's two of you now."

I could see Derrick wavering.

"Fine. Come on, Bobby. I'll go in with you."

"Just Bobby," Lenny said.

"It's me and Bobby together and he gets a handful of candy from each of you. No, *two* handfuls."

"No freaking way!"

Derrick turned and faced them fully this time. "Yes. Way."

They didn't argue.

He turned back to me and asked, "Are you ready?"

I tried to push him away. I didn't want his pity. This was something I needed to do on my own. I needed to prove that I wasn't a baby. But he deflected my hands and stepped past me toward the darkness, leaving me feeling more alone and more dependent than ever.

"Look," he said, stopping at the door, "I'm not going in by myself. I need you with me."

"You do?"

"Yeah, Bobby." And suddenly I wanted him with me.

"Forty alligators," we heard Lenny shout, as we stepped over the threshold into the silence of the old Malvern house. "And you can't start counting until—"

Derrick reached past my shoulder and swung the door closed.

It didn't matter how long we needed to be in here. Twenty alligators or forty. I was with Derrick. He wanted me with him.

In that moment, I could've stayed in there with him forever.

Twenty years. That's how long I avoided coming back. For ten of those, I couldn't escape Edgemont. I was held captive by this town, by my parents and their inability to leave. But even when I did escape, as soon as I was old enough and could secure my own way, as soon as I had enough savings to guarantee I would never have to return, even following all that, Malvern Manor continued to pull at me. It wouldn't let me go. It called to me in my dreams, sneaking into my thoughts at the oddest of moments, when I least expected it, whispering for me to come back. It haunted me.

I did return, but never all the way. Each year, in July, I would come back to Edgemont. But I would stay away from this house. I would not come to this exact place. Each year I'd drive into town and I'd pretend not to care; I'd drive down the highway with my eyes never leaving the road. But just as I'd come over the tracks on the north side of town, I'd always look over, and the house would be there, off in the distance. And my heart would skip. A part of me would always wish that they'd torn the damn place down; another part knew that the house would never allow it, not while there was unfinished business.

For twenty years it continued to stand.

So here I am and so the house rises before me and it dares me just as those long forgotten boys once dared me. Come in, it whispers. I have something of yours. And I know that this is my moment of truth. The house stands before me, a looming, foreboding presence, smoldering with age and resentment, and it's no wonder that it still stands, for it has been waiting, patiently even, if a house can be patient. It can. I know that it would wait another twenty years if it had to.

But I cannot.

I lift the cigarette to my lips and take a drag, and my hand lingers for a moment in front of my face before I let it fall again to my side. I purse my lips, exhale, and the smoke swirls past my face, speeds away behind me, dry and powdery.

I drop the butt—it's nearly spent anyway—and sparks skitter away as it hits the sidewalk. I lift the toe of my shoe and give it a twist, making sure it's fully extinguished. In this heat, a fire could consume acres before it would be extinguished.

When there are no more tendrils of smoke, I step past the iron fence, now tangled with lush weeds and wildflowers. I make my way up to the house.

The door closed behind us with a soft click, not the loud echoey boom that I'd been expecting, almost as if the house knew not to wake its hidden inhabitants. Not yet, anyway. The door had closed and latched on its own. Looking at it from the inside, I was once more overwhelmed with the sense that the door was locked. In fact, I was sure of it this time.

I heard my brother take in a breath beside me, but that's all the sound there was. Nothing came from the darkness before us, no cricks or creaks of drying, rotten boards, nor the wind in barren eaves. Nothing maleficent or otherwise, and nothing in between. The silence seem to be trying to reassure us that Malvern Manor was just a house, a decaying framework of wood on a plot of hillside in small rural town, just a box. But it wasn't just a box, was it? The house had once held living, breathing souls. It had a memory of those people forever trapped in its rooms, etched within its stairs, written upon its walls. Memories of laughter and pain; memories of heartache and joy. Memories that seeped out of the wood.

And now it had a memory of us.

"Forty," I whispered, completing the count. Then, when Derrick didn't move, I said, "Come on!"

"Bobby, quiet!"

My eyes had adjusted to the gloom by then, and now I could see Derrick staring off into space, staring hard into the rooms that opened up away from us. His face was directed toward the rear of the house. I felt his breath on my cheek, slow and patient, quiet. I pulled on his sleeve.

"You hear it?" he said. His voice was a whisper, though harsh with urgency. Even in the darkness, I could see the sharpness of his features, the hardness in his eyes.

I shook my head then realized he wasn't looking at me. "No, I don't hear anything." But I was listening, as hard as I could. And yet I heard nothing.

"I just want to check on something."

"It's time to go, Derrick. Mom and Dad—"

But he dropped his candy bag by the door and stepped away from me, his face pointed upward, as if he were sniffing the air.

"Derrick!"

He turned slowly toward me, holding his finger to his lips, shushing me. I stopped again, wondering what he could be hearing that I couldn't. But there was still nothing to hear. Nothing at all. I hesitated. He took another step and the scrunch of his sneaker sounded loud in the darkness.

Somewhere, as if through the scrim of time and distance rather than a plank of wood, I heard Lenny calling for us: "Okay guys, you can come out now. Derrick? Bobby?" I thought I could hear panic. I heard Marcus call, too. The same note of fear had crept into his voice, too.

Now Derrick was in the center of the room. I had my hand on the doorknob, but I didn't turn it. I held onto it like it was an anchor, even as I glanced back. Derrick's ghostly shape was drifting away from me. I could tell that the room was bare, save for a chunk of shadow to one side that, with concentration on my part, finally resolved itself into a broken couch with its cushions missing. Now I could see the torn fabric, the exposed springs, the rabid spume of stuffing foaming through.

The floor beneath us was worn to bare wood; ancient paper peeled in long strips from the walls, curling in their slow-motion race to reach the ground first. High above us, the ceiling was stained and streaked; dust sifted down through eruptions in the paint. A single uncurtained window to the right allowed some light to filter in from the street. A second window upstairs cast a dull, gray glow upon the wall on the landing. In one corner, I made out the shape of a door; on the opposite side of the room, the staircase.

"Derrick!"

"Shh!"

And that's when I heard it, or thought I heard it: a whisper, a dull staticky noise, faint, the sound of musical notes, a *crack*, as if someone had snapped a small twig. The sounds faded from my ears and my head as quickly as they had come, immediately calling their existence into doubt. Even now, twenty years later, I'm still not sure I heard anything. Was it real or just in my head? Or had those sounds been planted there in the days and weeks and years since?

But whether or not I heard them didn't matter; what mattered was that Derrick heard…something. He was following those sounds. He turned toward the back of the room. I heard his sneakers grind the dirt and the old flaked paint. I didn't want him to open that door. I knew if he did, then out of it would come all the horrors of the world.

"Please," I whimpered. "It's time to go."

But he was beyond hearing me by then. I'm not even sure if I did speak. The memories twist, reform with other thoughts, wishes I've since made about what happened, with wants that will never be realized. I stood frozen watching him, straining my ears, willing my heart to beat more softly, holding my breath to still the rush of the ocean inside my head and the creature that stirred within.

But whatever Derrick was hearing, whatever sound I might've heard—had thought I'd heard—it did not repeat itself to me. And whatever I may have said or didn't say, Derrick was deaf to it. He drifted onward, forward, toward that door, away from me.

It was the soft scrape of another shoe against wood that roused me, set me into motion. With a yelp, I twisted the knob that was still in my hand. I spun round, whipping the front door open—exulting that it wasn't locked after all—and launching myself onto the porch with every intention of leaping off of it. But I had been mistaken. The sound hadn't been inside the house, it had been outside the door!

I would have screamed then if my breath hadn't been stolen from me. I would have flown down the steps, if I hadn't tumbled to the floor of the porch with Lenny falling beneath me and the squeak of his surprise suddenly sobering me up.

"Hey," he shouted.

I jumped up and tumbled down the steps, my body still reacting to my fear, not yet having fully processed what my brain had already figured out. I could hear Lenny flat on my heels. It was only when I reached the sidewalk and curled myself around Marcus that I stopped. I would have kept running, except an image of Derrick rose in my mind. I couldn't abandon my brother inside the house. I couldn't just leave him in there alone.

Marcus was laughing, holding his belly and pointing at Lenny, who skidded to a stop as soon as he reached the sidewalk. "I thought you were going to wet yourself," he said, but Lenny only grumbled unhappily and shook his head. His face was pale in the lamplight, and his eyes were wide and frightened. He was trembling. But so was Marcus.

Suddenly I realized something about him I hadn't known before: I knew without asking that he had put Lenny up to coming up to the house to fetch us.

He turned to me. "How about you? Did you pee your pants, Chicken Little?"

I didn't answer. At that point I doubted I could still remember the fundamentals of speech.

"Where's Derrick," he asked. "Where's your brother? Hey, Derr! Come on!"

I was still panting, hands on my knees, shaking. But Marcus was really laughing now and Lenny was beginning to laugh as well, a nervous hiccupping, hitching laugh, tentative at first, then loosening up. He'd realized there was nothing to be afraid of, just a half-crazed nine-year-old boy who'd thought a monster was after him. But nothing had come after us. Nothing had chased us from the house save my own irrational fears.

"Inside," I panted, raising an arm, one hand still on my knee. I tried to look braver than I felt. "He thought he heard something. He wanted to check it out."

The boys stopped laughing.

I looked up at the house, at the still-open front door that had swung partially shut in my haste to leave, and somehow the place seemed smaller, though no-less ominous, like it was settling back in for a rest. It looked...satisfied.

"Derrick!" Lenny called, startling me.

Marcus shushed him. "You want the neighbors to call the cops? Stupid!"

"But you yelled."

"Just...shut up."

Lenny was shifting from side to side, looking like he had to take a leak. I stepped away from Marcus. I just wanted to leave. I wanted Derrick to come out of the house and down the steps so we could go. I stared at the front door and willed it to open and spit my brother back out. But the front door didn't move, and not a sound came to us from inside.

Another minute passed. The clock bell rang the half hour. Marcus shifted impatiently. He opened his mouth to speak, thought better of it, shrugged. I was just about to go back inside when there came sharp report from inside the house, followed by a series of splintering sounds, of wood breaking. There was a half second of silence, then came a loud crash, and this time we all jumped for real.

"What the—"

But the rest of the sentence was cut off by Derrick's screams.

Marcus was the first to run, and in his terror to flee he knocked me on my ass. He dropped his bag in the process, but then thought better of it, spun, retrieved it. He took off down the sidewalk looking like the devil himself was chasing after him. For all we knew, the devil might soon be, but first he had to finish with Derrick.

From Derrick's cries, it sounded like it might take a while.

The screams grew louder over a space of maybe a dozen seconds, though it felt an eternity, then they suddenly started to fracture. Derrick was crying then and his sobs rose and fell before they too grew ragged. The sound of it tore into me. I felt shattered by it. I was crying, too.

Lenny gave me a look of desperate hopelessness, then he, too, ran off down the street and into the darkness. Marcus was already out of sight, though I could still hear the raindrop patter of his shoes on the concrete.

"Come back," I shouted after them. "Lenny! Marcus... Derrick!"

"Oh, god!" I heard my brother wail. "Ahh, god, no! Help me. Bobby, help me! Bahh haa haa beeee... No!"

But I couldn't go in there. I couldn't even stand. My legs were rubber. I sat on my ass and sobbed out on the sidewalk in the middle of a colorful sea of candy. I put my hands in my face and bawled until someone heard me and picked me up and took me to my parents. I don't even know how they figured out where I lived. And my parents where there trying to calm me down, but even then I couldn't stop crying. I heard them talking to the people who had found me, and I also heard the announcer on the TV saying that the game was all tied up and that it would be going into extra innings and I knew that Derrick would be upset when he found out what he was missing, though he'd be happy to know that the Yankees were mounting a comeback. But then I was being picked up and belted into the back seat of the car and the car engine was starting and we were going somewhere behind a vehicle with flashing lights.

I remember the brightness of the hospital, the hard plastic seats. I remember my breath hitching as I finally ran out of tears and woke up to find my parents standing off to one side talking to a man in a white coat and then, finally, what seemed like hours later, Derrick walking out of the bright peach-colored room with the light green curtain and his arm was in a cherry red cast that I knew as soon as I saw it that it wasn't blood but still I imagined it was. His already shredded shirt was torn even more. His face was streaked with dust and the ghosts of his tears. Bright red spots of fake blood were intermixed with the darkened real stuff, and his hair was an absolute mess.

But what scared me the most were his eyes: how empty and red they were. I knew right then that Derrick was gone: here was his body, but something had been stolen from him, from *inside* of him, and it was still in that house on Dunbury Hill.

But Mom and Dad didn't seem to notice the difference. They were yelling at him, yelling all the way home from the hospital. "We trusted you, Derrick!!" They promised a grounding that was sure to last "until you're eighteen."

But Derrick never did last that long. His body managed to hang on for his fourteenth birthday, but no more. The house had stolen away all his remaining years.

They didn't realize how sick he was for several more months, when it was pretty obvious something was seriously wrong with him. It was as if the fall from the second story landing had shattered more than just the bones in his forearm, it had broken his will to live. Believe what you want, but that's how I saw it, anyway. He forgot how to live.

He was sick a lot, and he grew paler by the day; he lost his appetite, lost weight. At first the doctors thought it was a series of nasty colds, the flu, stress, hormones. He was anemic. They finally discovered the cancer when they x-rayed the arm again, since the bones didn't seem to be knitting properly. A tiny spot near his shoulder. More x-rays. The rest of his body was riddled with malignancy.

The next several months passed with all of us suspended in a state of perpetual terror. Derrick was in and out of the hospital a dozen times. Each time he went in he was pretty bad; each time he came out he was worse.

"It's not your fault," he'd tell me, not that I'd ever indicated as much to him. I refused to accept these little reassurances. I knew he was wrong. I knew if I hadn't been such a chickenshit, if I had just thrown Marcus's dare back at him instead of allowing myself to be suckered into a situation where Derrick felt like he had to take the dare with me, then this wouldn't have happened to him.

We took him to the hospital for the final time the following May. His bone marrow transplants had failed; the chemo was killing him faster than it was taking out the cancer. As much as I wanted to help him, to trade places with him, I could do nothing for my brother. My own bone marrow turned out not to be a match for his. In fact, it didn't seem like there were any matches anywhere.

None of this surprised me. The house had planted the seed inside Derrick. It had wanted him and wouldn't give him back. What it had done was supernatural, not organic; there was no science that could neutralize it.

I am such a fucking hypocrite.

I say I wanted to help, but the one thing I could've done, I didn't. I never returned to the house. Not once. I often dreamed of it in those days. I dreamed of going back and doing something once and for all. I fantasized about setting it on fire, of burning it to the ground. But I knew it wouldn't let me. That's what I told myself. The truth was, I was too chicken.

Derrick held on for two more months. Two months of living hell tethered to a hospital bed by wires and tubes and beeping machines. Finally he died. His body may have forgotten how to love, but it knew how to die.

My parents buried him in a cemetery plot at the top of Dunbury Park, in a casket made of white spruce and lined with dark blue velvet—the Bullets' colors, Yankee colors—and it had polished brass rails that shone like gold in the brilliant sunlight. The box seemed so small, and yet it had ample room inside to spare. Two of my brother could've fit inside by the time it was needed.

Half the town showed up for the service, even Marcus and Lenny, though I didn't speak with them. I couldn't even meet their eyes to draw their attention.

I remember standing there at the burial, watching the casket float away from the hearse, over to the side of his grave. It was as if the pall bearers were ghosts and I could see right through them. All that mattered was the casket. I watched it as the preacher gave his eulogy and I remember thinking how empty it was. I knew my brother wasn't inside of it; he had been left somewhere inside that house, the house whose rooftop I could see even then, poking up over the greenery that hid the rest of its walls, peeking at me with its evil eyes. I watched as the casket was lowered into the ground, and I watched as the first shovelful of dirt sprayed over that polished white lid, hitting it with a dull *thuh* and followed by the harsh whisper of the dirt avalanching over the sides. I wondered if Derrick might even now be watching us bury his body. I could certainly feel eyes on us, watching from somewhere inside Malvern Manor.

Lastly, through the veil of my own tears, I watched my parents cry. I made myself a promise that I would leave this place the first chance I got. I would leave and take the memory of that night away with me. I would never return.

Except, here I am.

I started playing ball in the sixth grade. The Edgemont Arrows. After that, the Bullets. Same team as my brother. I played short stop and was actually pretty good at it. Filled a whole record book with double plays and even a few dozen triples; made a fair number of homeruns, too. I could easily have been better. It wasn't for lack of trying. Bad things always seemed to happen to me.

By the time I graduated, I had dropped sports altogether, been arrested for B&E, spent a week in juvie before getting probation. I got a girl pregnant. This was much later. She wasn't the nicest girl— had a cocaine abortion—so maybe not everything that happened was exactly bad. No, I can't mean that, but it was probably the best thing that could've happened to me, as well as the mother, all things considered. As for the baby, I try not to think about it. I've had enough on my mind as it is.

Carla Zuñiga was her name—the girl, not the baby. The baby never got one. I don't even know what it was.

Carla's dad told me he if he ever saw my face again, he'd shoot me as soon as turn away. I told him that wouldn't be a problem. So I have no idea where Carla is now, if she's married and has kids, if she's even still alive. She could be lying in some gutter somewhere or in a shallow, unmarked grave. I think about how that could've been me; I think about what a blessing it would be, to be able to forget everything.

The ex-wife and ex-girlfriend came several years later. I believe there might've been some overlap between them. I don't remember exactly. It wouldn't surprise me.

I suppose it was a miracle I even graduated from high school, but I did. I got a job in the warehouse district, over on the Eastside, north of the river and the train yards. When I had enough money to buy a car and leave town, I did. I was eighteen, and I knew if I stayed in Edgemont even one more year, I'd probably end up in the river, the jail, or the morgue.

I remember a time—I was probably six, Derrick ten, so this was shortly before Marcus and Lenny came into my life—we were in Derrick's room. He was lying on his bed and the morning light was shining in through the window. Or maybe it was afternoon, I don't remember exactly, I just know that the light shining on his face gave me this warm feeling and he was lying on his back and tossing a ball against the wall and catching it. It must've been late afternoon, because Mom and Dad weren't home; they usually worked late. It was just us two alone in the house. Maybe I was a little older, like eight and he was twelve. Anyway, the folks weren't home, because if they were, they'd never have allowed all that banging on the wall.

So there we were, and Derrick was telling me how he wanted to play in the majors. I was too young then to really understand what he was talking about, but I could tell by the look in his eyes that it was something really important to him. I don't know how long I sat there on his floor, playing with a toy that I can't seem to picture anymore—it's not important—just watching him toss that ball and thinking how much my brother loved baseball. And how much I loved him.

He'd turned to me and said, "And when I play, Bobby, you can come and watch. I'll have a whole section in the stands reserved for you and Mom and Dad."

"The Cubs?" I'd asked, because they had been his and Dad's favorite team when Derrick was younger.

He shrugged. *Thump...slap*, went the ball off the wall and into his glove. "No, maybe those damn Yankees," he said. He looked over at me with a sly grin. It was the first time I remember him ever choosing to disagree with my dad just because he knew how much it would irk him.

I imagine Derrick's death was equally as hard for my father as it was for me—well, both my parents, of course, but my father, especially. He and Derrick had always been so close when we were little, but as Derrick got older they started drifting apart. It's one thing to lose someone when you're holding them tight up against you. It's quite another when they're already at arm's length and slipping through your fingers. Or when you're pushing them away.

The old wooden steps creak and groan beneath my weight. I'm a lot heavier now than I was back then. The boards sag a little, but they hold. One step...two...three. And the porch spreads out before me as my eyes rise above the level of the floor and I can see old leaves rotting in the corners, deposited by breezes that have long since passed on to other places. I see the dried-up remains of an old rag. I see chucked stones that failed to reach their intended target of the windows. Even the kids who threw them are now just memories.

Now I am fully up on the porch, standing erect, eight, nine feet away from the door, and the faint scent of decay and neglect, of urine and charred wood, reach my nose. My shoes make soft *kuh-lunk* sounds on the boards, and the wood protests, but it, too, holds. The house must really want me to finish what I have come to do, though what that is I have absolutely no idea.

Twenty alligators, my mind whispers. As if it could be that simple.

I pause at the door, listen, but if there are whispers, I can't hear them. There are only the whispers inside my head, the ones that drove me from this place in the first place, drove me halfway across the country, drove me back.

I step inside and close the door.

There is no counting this time. Twenty alligators or twenty years. It doesn't matter. I will know when I am finished. The house will tell me.

This time, rather than waiting by the door, I make my way to the back of that front room, back toward the heart of the house. There's a door there, the one that Derrick had tried, after I'd run away that night two decades ago. It stands partially open, as if inviting me, and I take hold of the knob and slowly draw it open enough to see in.

I can make out the top few steps of a flight of stairs leading down into pitch darkness. A damp, warm smell rises up at me, a whisper of air rising, the musk of earth and decay. And now I wish I'd brought a flashlight, so that I could see down into the cellar. But then I know that it doesn't matter, because whatever is down there is not for me. Maybe it was for some other child haunted by other memories, but it's not for me. Just as it wasn't for Derrick. What claimed him wasn't down there, so I leave it be.

I shut the door; it doesn't stay shut. It swings open on dry hinges, squeaking quietly, sounding like a murmur of somebody stirring in their sleep.

The police had said he'd fallen over a rotten banister; they'd found him lying on the floor in the foyer. The railing would be above me, if it was still there. But the broken wood has disappeared in the intervening years, and whatever remained has been torn out, probably for improvised campfires. Only the ragged stumps of the balusters remain, like the bottom jaw of a sleeping giant with a bad case of tooth decay. The thought reminds me of the old, ridiculous Malvern stories. Kids have the craziest imaginations.

The landing gawps above me. I will go up there, but not just yet. I'm not quite ready.

I wander through the rest of the ground floor level, making my way through the empty rooms, reassuring myself that I must go up. Some of the rooms are still guarded by doors, warped in their frames, refusing to shut properly. Some rooms are open. They are all empty, stripped of decoration, save a few scorch marks and graffiti. All of the furniture has been scavenged. A mouse-eaten pillow sits in the corner of one room, bleeding stuffing, but that's it. Even the ratty old couch in the front hallway is gone. The place feels completely devoid of anything. It feels sterile, obscenely so, bare to the point of pornographic. Suddenly I fear that the soul of the place has fled, too, cheating me just when I found the courage to face it.

I am uneasy. All the while, I am listening for that whisper, but all I hear are the soft clops of my shoes, the rustle of my clothes, the dull throb of my heart. My throat aches for another cigarette, but I only have one left. I've decided it will be my last.

With a sigh, I head for the stairs.

There was a period of time—I must've been in my mid teens, since I was still playing for the Bullets then—when I considered coming back to the Malvern place. It wasn't like I lacked opportunity. Our house on Alden Lane was no farther than a quarter mile away. Just a quick shortcut along the railroad tracks, over the river, up the hill.

But I couldn't. Not even after our little league started taking practices up in Dunbury Park and I would walk home from there, Saturday afternoons and Wednesday and Sunday evenings, my bat slung over my left shoulder and the waxy sun melting into the distance off to my right. I'd always find an excuse to take the Third Street Bridge down into the old neighborhood, even though it meant losing the sun sooner, rather than taking the trestle. I stayed away from the end of the park where the Malvern place stood, so much like a sentinel watching over the Southside neighborhoods. If there was one good thing about where we lived, the house wasn't visible from our street. I don't think I'd have been able to last as long as I did if it had been.

When I was sixteen, the Cordovas moved away. I'd known that Marcus had gone into the Marines; he was a few grades ahead of me and each time someone would go into the service, there'd be an announcement over the loudspeaker at school; each time one of them came back, there'd be another. Sometimes the announcement would be joyful; sometimes it wasn't.

I was in juvie when the news about Marcus's return reached me. He'd been injured in some remote place just north of the Sudan-Libya border, had been granted a medical discharge. He came back with a head wound, was never the same afterward. They put him into a convalescent center up in Stepford and so that's where his mom went to live, to be by his side. By then, Mister Cordova was living in a trailer park up near the train yard. I don't know if he visits his son. I don't know if he still celebrates Halloween like he used to. I hear he's rarely sober these days.

Lenny, I'd been told by someone I can't remember, went to college up in New England. Not sure what he studied. His parents still live in the house next to my parents, but I don't talk to the Baileys when I'm home. I don't really talk to anyone. I'm sure he must be doing well because each July when I come back, there's always a nice, fairly new car in the driveway next door, a BMW or a Lexus or something like that, and it looks like they have a gardener come and take care of the lawn once or twice a week. Though, why they never moved to a better part of town and into a nicer house or even a smaller condo, I could never understand. People get stuck in one place, and they can never leave. Or, if they do leave, they always end up coming back.

Each year, on the anniversary of Derrick's passing, my parents take a drive up to the cemetery. I'm not sure why I go, since I never believed Derrick was in that white box—his body, yes, but not him. What the EMTs had brought out of Malvern Manor was an empty shell, a golem, and that's why he had faded so quickly afterwards. Without his soul to sustain him, there was nothing to keep it well. And so my brother's spirit has remained up there for the past twenty years, lost somewhere inside that wretched house, not in the grave that bears his name.

Each year I go back with my parents and stand over the plot of land that swallowed his white and blue casket. I go through the motions. I bow my head to the marker with the words DERRICK MICHAEL NASH written in block letters on it. With the words HE WAS A BELOVED SON AND BROTHER. And each year I'd feel nothing but a restless stirring inside me, rather than closure.

I set my foot upon the first riser and shift my weight, listening for the telltale crack of the wood splitting, failing. My hand reaches automatically for the railing and, failing to find it there, I nearly tumble over the side. In fact, I do lose my footing, but it's a short step down. Arms flailing, I hop back to the landing. I curse my distraction.

I find if I step on the stairs near the wall, they feel much more solid, and it's just as well for me, since I am terrified of the edge. I've imagined Derrick falling over it a million times in my nightmares, a million and a half it's me in his place.

Once I reach the second story landing, I glance over my shoulder at the floor beneath me, at the front door still standing wide open and the glassless window to one side. Above me still, and down another hall, is a second window, out of view from below. The glass has also been stripped from this one over the years. The sun is still high enough in the sky that most of the room is still in shadow, but there's enough scattered light to tell me there is nothing hidden there waiting for me.

So now I stand, listening and waiting. There's nothing to hear, nothing welcoming me or warning me, nothing telling me what I need to do. I experience a moment of vertigo, when I feel as if the ground is shifting beneath me and my hands reach out and over that precipice, out over the space through which my brother had once fallen. I imagine the curve of his arc, the air displacing before him. What must he have thought in that moment? Had he been afraid? Sad? Exultant?

I open my eyes and look down over the edge. Maybe it's a trick of the light. Or maybe what I see just then, the shape of a body down below, twisted and broken, the soul seeping away like a shadow, or blood, or being sucked away from him. A trick of my imagination. It seems real, though, this ghost of a memory that isn't a memory at all. His screams come back to me then, echoing inside my head, and the figure below me shifts, looks up at me with a face that is mine, accusing. And then I really am falling.

I spin my arms, kick out, and somehow the motion throws me back. I fall against the wall, slide down to the floor of the second story landing. And as I sit there, pressure behind my eyes, I want so badly to cry for my own cowardice. Twenty years of tears and anger and guilt finally come pouring out of me then and I can't stop it. Only when I am exhausted, when I'm drained, do the tears stop. Now there is room inside of me to take the next step.

With shaking hands, I light my last cigarette. The flame of my lighter dances in front of my exhale, then stands still as I hold my breath and stare into its depths. The lighter grows hot in my hand. I relax my thumb and the flame goes out. I take a long drag, hold the poisoned air inside me, let it out.

When I next open my eyes, the cigarette is ash, extinguished, the butt cold. Sunlight streams in against the far wall at an angle that tells me it's late afternoon. I get to my feet and go down the steps. The restlessness is still there, but it feels smaller, more distant.

I make my way out through the front door and across the porch. Bright July sunlight spills over me as I head down the steps, envelops me, washes past. I make my way through the overgrown weeds crowding the walkway, choking the fence. Now I'm on the sidewalk. Even then I don't stop.

By the time I hear the whisper, I am already halfway down the street and I know it has followed me out of the house: *The count is full, two outs, bottom of the tenth inning. Score is tied at three-all.*

Only now do I stop. There's a young boy playing in the yard of the house I'm standing in front of. He looks up at me, then goes back to tinkering with his plastic truck. Slowly I turn, as that old memory comes.

Kim gets set, checks the bases...throws, and...Jeter nails it! He nailed it! It's going...he's...Derek Jeter has just hit the first November homerun in World Series history! He's just won game four for the Yankees!

The cheering goes on and on, and I know it'll never fade away. Not now. Not ever. But the house now fades, imploding upon itself in my mind. In its place stands an empty overgrown lot. The old house is finally gone.

I know I should feel relief, but as I read the new sign out in front, I know I never will, just an unending sense of loss.

COMING SOON: MALVERN MANOR APTS.

‡   ‡

Author's note

I've always wanted to write a classic haunted house tale, which is what Mr. November *originally started out to be. In fact, I originally called it* The House on Dunbury Hill, *and I was going to fill it with the most loathsome of spirits imaginable. But Malvern Manor refused to give up its ghosts, and I soon realized that it wasn't the house that was haunted (or, at least, not just the house, for I suspect the place will one day prove to be possessed) but the story's narrator, Bobby.*

I also wanted to write the story as a Halloween trick-or-tale, for what more perfect night could there possibly be to visit a haunted place? And that got me remembering Halloween trick-or-treating with the kids the year the San Francisco Giants won the pennant. I remember asking at each door for scoring updates. This became as much a part of my memory of that night as all the rest.

In researching this story, I learned that the first World Series game to be played on a Halloween night took place in 2001. The Yankees won that game on a tenth-inning walk-off homer by Derek Jeter in the opening minutes of November 1ˢᵗ, earning him the nickname Mr. November, and tying the series at two games all. The D-backs would end up winning the pennant in seven, I'm sure much to Derrick's disappointment.

And what of the man who'd invited the boys in? Was he just a fan of the game?

The coincidence of my character's name, Derrick, with that of Derek Jeter is just that: coincidence. I'd chosen the name before I realized the link; before, even, the story incorporated the World Series aspect. In fact, I prefer to think of Bobby Nash as this story's Mr. November, for it's he whose effort brings Derek home. And besides, I thought the title lent an air of mystery and nostalgia to the story. It just fit so well.

This story is a tribute to the strength of those Halloween memories, to fans of haunted houses, and to the boys of October (or November). May they all haunt us evermore.

‡ ‡ ‡

The Headhunter

Promise me, darling. Promise you won't rest until you take my killer's head.

WHEN THE LAST SHARD of the day's sunlight fell from his ceiling and twilight painted the walls crimson in a sweet seduction of darkness, Bill Hawkins unfolded his legs and levered himself off of the ancient couch he used for his bed. His joints ached, though neither from the chill of the approaching winter nor the stiffness of age, nor even from the hardness of the cushions, but from the tension that had parasitized his body since the Uprising, since the time the killings began. The world had died a living death, and now it was the curse of those who remained to relive it each and every night that followed.

Stay in.

She haunts him: his beloved wife. She haunts his every thought.

Stay in, or at least go back to the old place where we were once so happy.

He raised his arms, stretching, rotating his head until it no longer creaked like an old pine bending with the wind. The twilight lingered, as if the day were reluctant to go. It would pass soon enough. Night would fall and it was best if he were dressed and gone before the hordes of undead began their nightly crawl out of their holes to search the city for hapless victims.

He'd promised Reggie a week ago that he'd hunt with him tonight.

You promised me, too, darling. Remember? Reggie won't mind.

"I owe him. And, yes, he will mind," he uttered into the darkness, hoping she would leave him be. Knowing she wouldn't. "Just one night, my dear. I promise."

She didn't answer.

It felt like a betrayal. Just like it felt each and every morning he returned without the head of the murderer, the she-beast that had taken his Karen from him forever.

He reached for his pants, so carelessly flung onto the armchair fourteen hours earlier. They were spattered and stiff, smelling strongly of copper and brine and something vaguely sickly-sweet. But it was old blood, dark and coagulated, almost a week old. A week since he'd made his last kill.

He'd planned to wash the clothes, had promised himself this morning he'd do it, but after a meager breakfast of tasteless jerky, he'd practically collapsed onto the sofa in exhaustion. He hadn't even remembered undressing.

Sleep eluded him. As desperately tired as he was, he could not find peace in sleep. His wakefulness had tormented him for days beyond counting. Even the memory of sleep seemed like nothing more than a dream he'd once had.

As the sun rose and pushed back the shadows, he'd lain, restless and hungry, his joints congealing like old fat and his head thickening as if from some indefinable ague. An eyelid twitch pestered him, on and off, for hours, like a fly buzzing around inside his head. His body was wracked, his soul ruined.

Focus, darling.

His anger roiled, rose to the surface of his consciousness, threatened to erupt from him. But then it would sink away again with little more than a pathetic psychic burp as his mind teetered on the razor's edge of unconsciousness. Teetered, yet never dropped.

There were moments when he'd wanted to scream out, in anger and frustration, in pain, in the substitute that had taken its place. But then fear would take hold of him, fear of being discovered for what he had become. He was ashamed. Ashamed that he had let them take his Karen. Ashamed that he was still here when she was gone. Ashamed of what he'd been reduced to. He was a lonely Headhunter who hunted for revenge. There was nothing more shameful than that.

His guilt clutched at his throat, strangled all but the loneliness from him. *That*, he held too deep for anything to touch, like a treasured secret, the heart of his very existence. Shame and loneliness. They were why he hunted. Selfish reasons.

There were moments of recklessness when his mouth would open and an anguished groan or shout of desperation threatened to spill out. But then he would clasp his hand over his lips. The consequences, if he let himself cry out, were…. Well, he tried not to think about them.

Not until I am avenged, darling.

A noisy clatter rose from the people on the sunburned sidewalk below him, from the machines they operated, their feckless routines. Like anything they did made any difference now. The noise drifted up to him in beckoning waves. A scream would certainly be noticed, would draw the wrong sorts to his door. Angry men who killed recklessly and for no other reason than fear of what they did not understand.

When it was nearly noon, he'd gotten up to tug the curtains closed. He was careful not to be seen through the cracked glass. Heat radiated in, clawing at his already parched skin, which felt like so much softened plastic. After so many nights, the light was like acid to his eyes. The flimsy curtains muted the images below him, turned them into phantoms flitting around. For an hour or so he'd stood there, motionless, mesmerized, stoic, watching the shapes of the people who dared venture out while the sun was still up.

Did they really believe they were safe down there?

He considered the question while his stomach rebelled from his miserable breakfast. A memory brushed up against his mind like a tide seducing the shore. He and Karen, at one of the local cafés downtown, laughing, enjoying a ham and cheese panini. A memory from before the Uprising. When life had been…normal. He knew what the memory meant. It meant that as it passed from him, the monster would soon follow in its wake, the monster and memories of its brutal attack and how it had taken his Karen away from him.

He tried to think of other things, but images came unbidden, uninvited. And yet he welcomed them: Karen's happy smile; the sound of her voice; the smell of her skin; the soft, delicious moans of their lovemaking…

Another life. A lifetime ago.

And then, just as he'd expected—and yet could never prepare for—there was the face of her attacker, rising up out of the ground like a spectral mist, taking his Karen from him for the thousandth time. He could almost hear her pleading with him as she lay dying. Her voice growing dimmer. The sound of his own footsteps as he'd run off like a coward.

He winced from the memory, the pain of the memory. He groaned, low and to himself, doubling over in anguish, letting it run its course through him like some malarial fever. He knew that when it finally passed, he would pine deliriously for its return. Excruciating as it was, the pain somehow made him feel more alive than he had in a long time.

I will find you, he'd promised. And he had, hadn't he? He'd found her once.

But then she'd been taken away from him again.

So, standing there at the window, he'd renewed his vow to kill the monster—to kill *all* of them—no matter how long it took. He'd kill them as mercilessly as it had taken the life of his beloved wife.

And then, maybe he'd finally be able to sleep.

With his resolve renewed, he'd torn himself from the window and fallen back onto the couch; the twitch in his face resumed its tiresome harassment.

With a deep sigh, almost a moan, he slipped each leg into his pants, zipped the zipper, secured the belt. His clumsy fingers, stiffened by the heat and the dryness of the day, stumbled over the clasp until, finally, the thing was done.

The darkness had deepened considerably by then. He found his shirt and draped it over his shoulders. The front was stiff as cardboard, as were the collar and one sleeve. He felt his skin drawing away from it in revulsion. Some hunters got used to the gore; he never did.

Tomorrow, the voice persisted.

Tomorrow, he agreed. He'd wash everything tomorrow. The stains wouldn't come completely out, nor would the stench their blood left behind, but at least he wouldn't have to feel it against his skin.

He settled once more onto the couch, sinking deeply into it, for the springs were old and cheap and had been sorely abused in another lifetime by other souls. His hunting boots were similarly stained and just as putrid as the rest of his clothes, though that mattered little to him. They were boots, after all, meant for such abuse. There are many things much worse than blood and vomit to defile them, he thought, as he laced them up.

Finally, he put on his glasses.

Now the night was fully upon the city. The streets below were as silent as the inside of a crypt and just as desolate. Pausing at the door, he reached down and quietly withdrew the machete from the old umbrella stand. He flipped it in his hand and watched, mesmerized for a moment, as the spinning steel glinted in the faint green glow of his apartment's security system's digital readout. Reflexively, his hand snatched the handle in mid-air. A soft ringing sound filled the air as the handle struck a knuckle.

He blinked, frowning, momentarily distracted by the absence of his wedding ring. Where had it gotten to? And then he remembered: he'd lost it one night, several weeks ago. It had slipped off as he finished bagging a head. An especially gruesome kill. The beast had struggled, refused to die. So much gore. The ring had slid off his finger and gotten lost. The ring that had always been too tight before.

It was just another reminder that he wasn't taking care of himself, wasn't eating enough. His body was wasting away. In the six months since Karen had been gone from him, he'd lost nearly a third of his weight. His clothes fit him poorly. Only his promise for revenge kept him strong, even as thoughts of death plagued him more and more frequently, like a siren's song.

Drowning. He'd heard it was the best way to go. He wondered how it might feel.

Darling, don't think such thoughts.

He straightened up then, shivering, and looked through the peephole in his door. The hallway sloped away in both directions, as if the darkness that grew from either end was too heavy for the world to bear. He watched, but nothing moved in those shadows.

Finally, convinced he was alone, he thumbed in the security code, waited for the timer to set, then slipped out into the waiting night.

†

†

A warm October mist had begun to fall by the time Bill reached the old trestle at the edge of the river. The opposite side was where Reggie preferred to hunt. It was far from Bill's own haunts in the city, the former warehouse district downtown that had, for a while before the Uprising, become *the* place to shop and eat and be seen. Now it was a wasteland of vacated buildings and empty avenues. Second Street was where Karen had been taken from him, one evening at dusk. So it was there that Bill focused his hunting efforts, always searching for the hideous figure of the she-beast that had attacked them. Always secretly fearing that some other hunter had already gotten to it first.

It wasn't unlikely. In the six months that had passed since then, the numbers of hunters in the city had swollen considerably. Heads were harder to come by, and he'd heard nothing of that one particular monster for quite some time. Yet he persisted.

Besides, there was something about the river that he disliked. It always made him feel restless.

A week had passed since he'd been out this way, since the last time he and Reggie had teamed up. But even in that short amount of time, the fall rains and unusually warm days had triggered an explosion of new growth along the trails, making them difficult to find in the dim light.

She's still out there. Just keep hunting.

He pushed her back. "Tonight isn't about you, Karen," he whispered.

Then what is it about?

"It's about…"

What? Doing a job?

He wanted to laugh with the bitterness of it.

"Doing God's work," he muttered spitefully.

That was how Reggie always put it. Reggie, the exiled preacher-turned-Headhunter. After all that had happened, how could he still believe there was a God?

The first time they met, just days after the attack on the Eastside, Bill had been sure he'd come to despise Reginald C. Le Grange. Or if not despise, at least resent. Reggie was a study in contradictions, a devoted father and husband, yet an extremely efficient hunter. "Ice flows through his veins," the other hunters said, laughing maniacally.

Reggie's thick black skin had turned nearly as pale and translucent as Bill's own was now—evidence of the countless nights he'd already spent hunting by the time they found each other. Hunting! Such a strange habit for a former man of the cloth. And he was an imposing presence too, nothing like the emasculated priests Bill had known in his own childhood growing up, when he'd attended catholic school at St. Christopher's. Reggie had the heart and compassion of a saint, the warmth of a man untouched by such horror—if any such man still existed. But he also had a killer's hands and a killer's instincts.

While showing Bill the proper method for separating a head from its diseased body, he'd pray: "In the name of the Lord."

Reggie believed the Uprising was God's Rapture, and that they were left behind to deliver the Damned into Heaven.

It was such a ridiculous claim that Bill often wondered why Reggie continued to believe it, especially after the way his own church had treated him. After the Uprising, Reggie had begged his congregation so show mercy on the Undead. Was it any surprise when they turned on him and his family, when they mercilessly hounded them until they'd been forced to flee town?

"Where in the Bible does it say anything about...well, about zombies?" Bill once asked.

"For starters," Reggie had answered, "Matthew, chapter twenty-seven, verses fifty-one through fifty-three."

"Right."

"*And, behold,*" Reggie said, quoting, "*the veil of the temple was rent in twain from the top to the bottom; and the earth did quake, and the rocks rent; and the graves were opened; and many bodies of the saints which slept arose, and came out of the graves after his resurrection, and went into the holy city, and appeared unto many.*"

"Bodies of the saints? Seriously? That's whacked, Reg. You know that? That's just... Anyway, what you're describing sounds nothing like what's happening now."

"You want zombies? How about this one from Zechariah: *This will be the plague with which the LORD will strike all the peoples who have gone to war; their flesh will rot while they stand on their feet, and their eyes will rot in their sockets, and their tongues will rot in their mouth.*"

Bill hadn't answered, though he had found himself shivering involuntarily. Even now, such words elicited a visceral reaction. He didn't think he'd ever get used to them.

That first night, as Reggie took Bill under his wing, his eyes had seemed to glow in the darkness, as if some inner fire had been lit. He'd recited verse after verse of scripture, trying to convince Bill that what they were doing had been foretold in the Bible and therefore was sanctioned. "Enough!" Bill had protested. A part of him had wanted to burst out laughing, another part crying.

"Just teach me how to hunt."

So Reggie took him into the darkened house where one of the Damned awaited. That night, Bill had taken his first head. He owed everything he knew about headhunting to Reggie. Without him, he wouldn't have survived as long as he had. But he still didn't share his beliefs.

Deep down he suspected it was Reggie's way of rationalizing everything that had come to pass. Of justifying the very practical matter of survival. Headhunting, as grisly an occupation it was, put food on the table, and with three mouths to feed in such hard times as he had at home, one did what one needed to do.

Even so, it must've been impossibly difficult for someone like Reggie to defend what he had become.

It made Bill's own guilt pale in comparison.

There was no moon yet, but so far from the city, the landscape glowed with its own natural light. A luminescent fog rose from the fields, reminding him of steam rising from a fresh cup of cappuccino. He realized with a start that the last time he'd enjoyed such a treat was exactly a year ago, the morning he and Karen had wandered down to the Starbucks in the lobby of their building, only to hear the first breaking news of the Outbreak on the loudspeakers. The sirens had sounded. They'd thought it was a tornado, a terrorist attack. Nobody could have guessed the truth. Nobody could have prepared for it if they had.

A full twelve months to the day. An illegitimate anniversary: the birth of the first Undead. He doubted anyone was celebrating tonight.

The trestle's metalwork rose high above him, a dark spider web against the coffee sky. They intended to cross over the river tonight, a task that Bill had always abhorred. It would be so easy to become trapped on the structure. But, as Reggie reminded him, hunting was better on the opposite shore. The area was dotted with a few small neighborhoods where the rich and spoiled had once lived but which now served as wayside stops for travelers, shelters for hapless squatters. Beyond the rundown mansions, downriver, a cozy little town still existed, still peopled by a few brave souls. He'd call them brainless, but it would just be too ironic, considering what was at stake.

Upriver, only farmland and scattered ranch houses existed. Most people lived in the cities now, huddled in clusters of apartments like his own; most zombies, too. For the most part, each kept to their own side of twilight if they could, but encounters were inevitable. The city was the front line in the war that seemed to have no boundaries.

An overgrown path led away from the walkway and tumbled down past the crumbling cement piling and into the blackness underneath. Bill descended, cursing the darkness and his forgetfulness. He could picture the flashlight on the hook next to the door of his apartment and his hand itched to reach out to snatch it from that vision. He thought about going back for it, but the apartment was too far away to return to now. He'd have to make do without it for the night.

He stopped to listen. The only sound coming to his ears was the whine of the crickets that lined the river's banks. In such quiet, it was easy to believe he was truly alone in this world. It was equally hard to forget how close to the truth that was.

The grass was wet from mist and the worn soles of his old boots constantly threatened to betray him. He moved slowly, deliberately, concentrating more than he wanted to on staying upright and less on his surroundings. But then his legs did fly out from underneath him and his arms were pin-wheeling for balance, but to no avail. He landed heavily, his shoulder impacting the hard ground with a soft, sickening *crunch*. Pain immediately radiated outward, coursing over his neck and down his back, before quickly collapsing back in on itself, a cold white ember that he knew would burn indefinitely. He heard his machete *ping* off an exposed rock next to him.

From the darkness under the bridge, there came a soft click. Then everything exploded in light, a silent, brilliant, blinding glare. He threw a forearm up to protect himself.

"Bill? You scared the crap out of me."

Bill let out an exhale of relief, dropping his arm and turning his head away from the light. "Wanna turn that off, Reg?"

"Sorry, brother."

He could hear Reggie shuffling around in the darkness, gathering up his backpack and tools. Bill stumbled to his feet, found his machete, stepped back onto the trail. His shoulder throbbed, but the pain was already fading. No permanent damage.

"Sorry I'm late."

There was a soft scraping sound—Reggie's boot against cement—then the ex-preacher was standing beside him, his white eyes and teeth glowing in the darkness. The unmistakable coldness of polished steel brushed against Bill hand.

"What's this?"

"Gary's," Reggie said.

"When?"

"Two nights ago."

Bill grunted. He remembered the hunter, short and brutally ugly, breath that stunk halfway to Tuesday. Gary walked with a permanent stoop, the result of a close encounter in the chaos that had infected the city in the days immediately following that first attack. His left arm had been nearly torn from his shoulder; afterwards, it remained paralyzed. It was easier for him to just strap it to his side, which partially accounted for the stoop. The sling made it easier to hunt, easier to fight. Easier to run.

Except this time he hadn't run fast enough.

"Where did it happen?"

"The old mall," Reggie answered. Bill noticed something new in the other hunter's voice, something tight and fragile that he'd never heard before. The ex-preacher sounded almost defeated. "He was one of mine, too. One of my flock."

"Sorry."

"They ambushed us, a whole gang of them, at least a dozen. It was... It was like they had coordinated the attack. Like they knew we were coming. I barely escaped."

"But you did. That's what counts."

"I was the only one."

"How many did we lose?"

"Including Gary? Four. Jed Macon—"

"I knew Jed. Back in the day. Never really liked him much, though. One of yours?"

"No."

"He was more of a closer, would let someone else do the hard work before he swooped in for the kill. Hated that. Still, a shame he's gone."

"A loss," Reggie agreed. "The other two were brothers, Charlie and Sev Cartwright."

Bill frowned into the darkness. He hadn't known the other two, but it didn't lessen the ache that grew inside of him.

"They're getting smarter," he said. He felt his chest tighten. Anger, maybe, or bitterness, although he wasn't sure who it would be directed at. "Either that or we're getting dumber."

"Neither," Reggie countered, "but they are getting more desperate. I heard they raided some of the camps over down near the train yards. It was a bloodbath."

"Fucking monsters."

A click came from Reggie's throat. Usually he tolerated Bill's foul language, but tonight it seemed he had less patience for it. Maybe the attack at the mall had set him on edge.

"What were you guys doing all the way down there? And why such a large group?"

"Planning," Reggie answered, though he didn't elaborate.

"I take it you prayed for them?"

"I pray for them all, Bill."

He nudged the handle of Gary's knife into Bill's palm.

"No, you keep it."

"I already have two, one for each hand. Can't use it, don't want it. You take it. Use it…for Karen. And the others."

Bill sighed. The knife had good balance, a wide blade, though much too short for his liking. He preferred longer weapons, like the machete. He didn't like getting so close to his prey.

"For Karen," he murmured. "And the others."

He slipped the knife into his belt behind him and pulled his shirt over it.

†

"This is the part that scares the shit out of me," Bill muttered, as they hurried over the trestle.

He tried to make out the shapes in the shadows beneath him along the shore, imagining they held hidden armies ready to attack them—the hunter become the hunted. He grew more and more certain that something dreadful was waiting for them on the other side.

He sniffed the air, but detected nothing other than the reek of the river.

What would they do if they were trapped up here? They'd have to jump into the river. That, or stand and fight. He thought he'd take his chances fighting, if it came to that. The river current was much too slow to carry them away quickly enough, which meant they'd have to swim. But their attackers would simply follow along on the shore and wait until they either sank in exhaustion or came ashore.

And what would happen when the sun rose?

The idea of drowning once more suffused his thoughts.

Focus, Karen whispered.

So he did.

They made it safely across. Then, without a word, Reggie headed upriver, away from the abandoned mall and the small town, toward the spread-out farms, much to Bill's relief.

They followed a winding road whose surface glistened from the mist, keeping their ears pricked for sounds that didn't belong to the night. They checked a number of darkened houses, their doors smashed in, their windows broken, taking turns directing the beam of Reggie's flashlight. But they found nothing: no evidence of recent habitation, whether by the Living or Undead.

At an intersection, where the signal lights blinked red in all directions, they found a car, its headlights soaking into the darkness ahead. The hood was still warm, though the engine was silent. The doors were open and the keys were still in the ignition; the driver was gone.

"Bad place to run out of gas," Reggie remarked. Bill snorted nervously.

A baby seat in the back was empty. In the flattened weeds alongside the road, they found a long smear of blood and the bodies of the family. Steam still rose from them in the humid night. Their skulls were cracked open and the tops of their heads were gone. The brains were missing.

"Fucking monsters," Bill said, turning away in disgust.

He went over to turn off the car's headlights. A strange twilight descended upon them, a red washed glow alternating with the coldness of gunmetal gray.

"We're all God's children," Reggie commented. He quietly adjusted his backpack, then kneeled over each of the bodies and said a quick prayer while Bill stood on, impatiently scanning the shadows. Except for Reggie's quiet murmur and the click of the traffic light, the night was silent.

"Just make it quick. This place makes me jumpy."

They walked on for some time, but saw nothing. The newly risen moon gave off a meager, pasty glow from its perch low on the horizon. They eventually came to a farm.

Once again, no lights showed in the windows. There were no cars parked out front and no animal sounds came from inside the barn. A single white shirt hung on the line, flapping like a ghost trying to warn them away.

"Check the house?"

Bill nodded, though the barn would've been his first choice.

Reggie led the way across the patch of barnyard and around the corner to the back porch. He held the unlit flashlight like a club in one hand, a knife in the other. He'd walk a few steps, stop, sniff the air, then take a couple more steps. As far as Bill could tell, there was nothing that indicated they were anything but alone.

But he couldn't be sure.

The first porch step creaked quietly under Reggie's boot. They paused, but only the wind answered. Two more steps, two more creaks, and then they were fully in the shadows beneath the porch roof. The torn screen door stood open, but the inner door was shut tight. The glass embedded in it was, miraculously, still intact.

"What if it's locked?" Bill hissed.

Reggie fumbled with his flashlight, switching it to the hand that held the knife, but the fog had greased his grip and the light slipped out of his hands. It hit the wooden floor with a loud *bang!* The light snapped on and the beam jabbed the darkness around them as it tumbled down the steps.

"Fucking Christ," Bill whispered.

The back door crashed open. Instinctively, Bill stepped back. The figure hurtling out at them narrowly missed him. It howled incoherently and crashed into Reggie, who lost his knife. The blade flew into the yard. The two figures, zombie and human, tumbled down the steps in full embrace, hands grasping, teeth clacking.

"Bill!" Reggie screamed as he fell.

Bill snapped out of his stupor and leaped off the porch. His ankle twisted painfully beneath him as he landed and his glasses flew off his face, but he ignored the pain and threw himself at the grappling pair. Hooking his elbow around the attacker's neck, he pulled it off his partner, but the monster was too strong and twisted out of his grip. Now it turned to face him. Bill swung his foot up and kicked it in the stomach. It backed clumsily away before tripping over Reggie's knife.

"Need some help here!" Bill cried. He chanced a quick glance behind him, but Reggie seemed to be having trouble getting to his feet. He was stumbling around like a drunken sailor, apparently still dazed by the fall.

Bill turned. The attacker was stupidly reaching down for the knife. Taking advantage of the distraction, Bill raced across the yard, willing his injured ankle not to collapse under him. Lunging at the hideous thing, he swung the machete with every last ounce of energy in him.

For a moment it seemed that he'd missed. The beast continued to bend down, then, slowly, as if it were reconsidering, it paused. Without a sound, it pirouetted on its toes then tumbled onto its back on the dirt. Its head rolled to a rest at Bill's feet.

He kicked it away, then fell to his knees. He suddenly felt drained. Hunts were not supposed to go this way. *He* was supposed to be the hunter.

He dropped the bloodied machete and crawled over to the porch railing where he tried desperately to vomit, but his stomach was empty and all that came out was a dry cough. He dry-spat, then wiped his mouth.

After a few moments, he turned. Reggie had recovered and had already bagged the head. He was standing over the body, finishing his prayer. When he was done, he bought the sack over to Bill.

"You take it," Bill panted. "You have a family to take care of and—"

"No," Reggie said firmly. "Your kill, your trophy. That's the code." He pulled it out of the sack by its hair and nodded appreciatively, trying to make light of the situation. "You bagged a good one," he joked. "A few more like this and you might even be able to retire to the Bahamas."

"Put it away," Bill growled, though he managed a weak smile. He took the sack from Reggie's hands, tied a knot in the drawstring and slipped the loop through his belt.

"You okay, Bill?"

"Think so."

"Good. Now get with the program. There's likely to be more."

They made a quick sweep of the downstairs of the house. The staircase leading to the upper floors had long since been torn down, leaving a gaping hole in the ceiling. But all they found was a soiled mattress in the back room, darkly stained and stiff. The barn was similarly deserted. A few stray shafts of hay dangled from the cobwebs, the rest long since carried away by rats or the autumn winds. Stalls stood open and empty, their gates hanging loosely on rusted hinges. In the center of the barn stood a large wooden chopping block, the top softened by blood and scarred by hatchet marks. The hatchet was long gone.

They headed away from the road then, striking out across an open field that looked as if it hadn't been sown in several seasons. The weeds stood tall and dry, their seed pods rattling in the night breeze. Bill had never been out this way, and the unfamiliar terrain was playing havoc with his knees. His ankle felt hot and stiff and swollen inside his boot, but like the shoulder injury, it was more of an aggravation than anything serious.

He couldn't help feeling like he was being watched. He knew Reggie felt it too. Several times he caught him glancing nervously in the direction of the dark trees that crowded them on either side. He disliked the openness of the field and the light of the rising moon, feeling much too exposed. But he also knew that if anything that might be hiding within the darkness decided to attack, the openness would give them ample warning and plenty of room to fight. Or run.

This time you won't run.

"Road's just up ahead," Reggie announced.

Bill reached up a finger to straighten his glasses. "*Shit!*"

Reggie turned to him, raising an eyebrow.

The glasses were no longer on his face. He'd left them lying on the ground in the barnyard.

"It's nothing, Reg. Never mind," Bill said, dismissing it with a wave of his hand. "What's the plan?"

"The power station," Reggie replied.

"Why there?"

"Fence, lights."

Bill nodded. It was a good plan. Strong lights attracted their prey. And the fence could be used to their own advantage. If they could isolate one or two of them against it, then they could easily corral them before taking their heads. The fence would act like a third hunter, blocking any chance of escape.

"You know you never talk about yourself, Bill," Reggie said, startling him with the unspoken question. "I mean, you've told me all about…Karen. About what happened. I know that's why you decided to become a hunter." He shrugged. "But you never talk about what happened before…you know…"

"The Rapture?"

Reggie grunted. "Not everyone is willing—or capable—of seeing God's hand in our lives."

"God's hand? I see only the devil's."

"The Lord's: *I will make your oppressors eat their own flesh; they will be drunk on their own blood, as with wine. Then all mankind will know that I, the LORD, am your Savior, your Redeemer, the Mighty One of Jacob! The dead will rise!*"

"Really? The Redeemer? Then why do *I* feel like the Damned?"

"Why do you say you feel like the Damned?"

"Because the past year has been nothing but hell, Reg, that's why."

"Maybe it is Hell, as you say. And maybe we are the Damned and *they* are the Damned. We're all Damned. But even if it is Hell, it doesn't mean any of us have to be cast forever in this place."

"Where else is there?"

"Canada?"

Bill laughed, even though it seemed for just a fraction of a moment that Reggie was dead serious.

"Anyway, I don't believe we're the Damned," Reggie said, sighing. "I choose to believe that we're the Deliverers. It's our job to help bring God's children to His Kingdom."

"Even if they're soulless monsters?"

"I don't think you believe that, Bill. Karen—"

"Don't bring her into this!"

"We're all monsters, Bill, in one form or another."

Bill slid his eyes over at Reggie. Tonight his broad shoulders slumped more than usual. Was he having his own crisis of faith? There was clearly something bothering him.

"I was a desk jockey," he said at last. "You asked what I did. That's it."

"Disk jockey? You mean you played music for a living?"

"*Desk.* As in office furniture. Not disk. I was a manager in Human Resources."

"Like, hiring and firing?"

"More hiring than firing actually. Could never stand giving people the axe." He chuckled at the irony. "Now look at me. Anyway, I was a paper pusher, a recruiter. The firm specialized in finding talent for the insurance industry. Executive level. You know, CEOs and board members and shit like that. My office was on the thirty-fifth floor of the Carcher Building on Seventy-First Avenue, looking out over the river." He realized with a start that maybe that was why he disliked being close to the river. It was from the river the zombies had first come. For a while, they even thought it might've been something in the water.

"Karen worked a few floors up, second from the top, for First Midland. That's how we met, on the elevator. She was in the lobby waiting for me one evening when the Uprising got to us. Those of us that survived got out, but a lot were lost when they torched the place."

Reggie was silent for a moment. Then he stopped walking and started chuckling. His laughter grew until his body shook with it.

"What's so funny? It was a horrible thing that happened."

"I'm sorry, Bill. I wasn't laughing about that. It's just that…I just realized you were a headhunter before you became a Headhunter. It's destiny. You should be really good at this."

"Funny. Ha ha."

They walked on in silence a few minutes more before Bill asked, "Do you really believe in what we're doing?"

"What choice do I have?" He shrugged. "I'm leading the flock home."

"You're rationalizing."

"Yes, maybe I am."

The pain in his eyes surprised Bill.

When they reached the far edge of the field and their feet once more settled on the reliable surface of a paved road, Reggie said, "I do sometimes wonder if this is what God intended of us. I have to believe it is. It's hard, though, trying not to be distracted by…earthly considerations. My family, for example, wondering if they're safe. Always having in the back of my mind how we're going to survive. But then I think about my precious, innocent Isabelle—so young and vulnerable and unable to fend for herself—and I know I have no choice. Other than to believe that this is all for a reason. It must be His will, otherwise…"

Bill pursed his lips to keep what he was thinking to himself. He doubted God had anything to do with any of this. But then he remembered Reggie's words from earlier: *We're not the Damned, we're the Deliverers.* And something clicked.

Reggie was looking for Redemption, the kind with a big R. Maybe it was because of his former life. Maybe because of the way his congregation had treated him. In the end, though, they were both guilty of the same things: of trying to justify what they had become, of seeking redemption.

Except the kind Bill wanted was the kind with a little r. Once he found the monster that had taken Karen from him, then he'd finally be able to let go. So what if it didn't buy him a ticket to Heaven? Fine by him. At least then he'd finally get some peace.

The road lost itself in the darkness ahead, drawing them forth as if they were attached to their unseen destination by a rope. Finally they came around a turn and the road rose toward the horizon and the horizon glowed with a faint yellowish light: the power plant.

They walked on without speaking. The contents of Bill's sack bumped his leg, spilling its wetness onto the cuff of his jeans, soaking his socks, filling his boots. Maybe when they were finished tonight, before he returned to his small, dark apartment, he'd let the river wash it all from his clothes, the months of dirt and blood. He'd walk into the water and sink down into it, letting it flow over him. He'd let it all wash away.

You need to focus, my darling.

The moon was high by the time they drew within sight of the front gate of the power plant. Reggie saw it first. The harsh light spilled out at them in unrelenting waves, and the hum of the plant's generators filled the air. The two hunters slipped into the trees. They crept forward, keeping their eyes on the road but staying out of view of it.

At last the trees gave way to open ground, a carefully manicured lawn that served as a buffer between forest and fence. They crouched behind a pair of close set pines and scanned the fence line.

"*There,*" Reggie whispered. He nudged Bill, then pointed. A shadow had separated itself from the solid, unmoving darkness near a guard shack. It seemed to loiter just beyond the gate, as if waiting for something to come through it. Then the shadow split. "*Two. Our lucky night,*" Reggie said excitedly. "*One for each of us.*"

"What's the plan?"

"I'm going to flank them from the other side of the road. Wait for me to come out, then we'll go."

Reggie slipped silently back the way they had come, far enough back so that when he crossed the road, even Bill couldn't see him. Twenty minutes or so passed and Bill was afraid their prey might wander off, but they didn't. At last he caught a glint of steel in the darkness fifty or so feet deep into the woods on the other side of the road. A shadow drew forth. He watched as Reggie crept low over the grass, moving silently until he was just on the fringe of the floodlights' reach.

Leaving the sack behind, Bill stole out from his own hiding place, his machete in hand. Reggie gestured with a chopping motion of his arm and they both began to sprint across the grass. The two figures were still huddled together, their backs to the road, unaware of the attack.

When he and Reggie were halfway across the grass, the closer one looked up. The other saw them a fraction of a second later, but by then it was already too late. The two figures careened off each other before turning to their attackers. Bill raised his machete and prepared to swing.

Five yards ahead of him, Reggie's knife slashed in a brilliant flash. The floodlights burned brighter, almost as if he had sliced open the night itself and ushered in the sun. The monster closest to him gurgled once, a spray of blood arching through the air. It stumbled forward, nearly into Reggie's arms.

The other had been quicker to recover. It turned just as Bill closed the gap between them. Its hideous mouth agape in what seemed like a smile, and from it came a horrific sound, a scream of outrage that sent shivers down Bill's spine. He swung, but it was too fast, ducking out of the way as the blade passed harmlessly through the air over its head. Thrown off balance by the miss, he lurched forward and past. Time seemed to slow. The suspended mist seemed to crystallize in the bright light. He could see each and every droplet hanging frozen in the air.

Then a great weight crushed against his side. He spun and fell against the fence, bouncing off it and back toward the monster. They both stopped short, as if each was surprised to see the other still standing.

"Move, Bill!"

Bill scrambled away just as the monster reached out for him, but the fence blocked him from retreating any further. Now he was the one trapped by it!

"Reggie!"

"Kinda busy here!"

Incredibly, the first monster was still alive, still on its feet, though its head seemed to be attached at an impossible angle. Blood was spurting from the gash. It was holding a hand against the wound, yet it did little to stop the flow. Seeing an advantage, Reggie slipped into its blind spot and moved in for the kill.

Bill marveled that the creature was even still standing. The blow that Reggie had delivered should have been fatal, but the beast's slow brain obviously hadn't gotten the message yet. It made a strangled sound and lunged clumsily after Reggie, landing a spastic blow that almost disarmed him.

Bill sensed motion beside him and swung his arm out to defend himself, but his feet slipped on the bloody ground and the machete once more missed its target. He felt another hard blow, this one to his head. Then a hand closed over his throat and squeezed with uncredible strength.

The weight of the creature forced him down. He heard his shirt rip against the fence, felt himself sinking. Off balance, his muscles weakened by starvation, he tried to push back, but he had no leverage. The monster's putrid breath was full on his face, stinking like death. Its foot pinned Bill's machete and hand to the ground. He swiped at its face with his other hand, going for the eyes. But it was too strong and casually deflected it away. The grip tightened even more around his throat, choking off his air. Darkness descended over him like a black fog, and the air buzzed and crowded around him, growing into a roar that seemed to shake the ground beneath him. His vision filled with the beast's hideous white face, its horrible sharp teeth drawing closer.

Summoning the last of his strength, Bill reached behind him. His injured shoulder screamed out in agony. He bit through the pain and tugged at the knife, but it wouldn't move. It was caught in the fence, wedged between it and his back.

"No!" he screamed, but his voice sounded weak and far away.

But then, just as the darkness was about to close over everything, the weight on him squirted away. The creature had slipped on its companion's blood and loose gravel. Together, it and Bill tumbled away from the fence. Bill felt his shirt catch for a moment, twisting him around so that he fell on top of the beast. He reached back and pulled the knife free from his belt.

With a final effort, he jerked his hand around, his shoulder screaming in pain, and thrust down, down until the hilt of the knife stopped against the belly of the beast. Then he gave it a good, hard twist.

A look of surprise seemed to come over its face. Its grip weakened for a second, but a second was all Bill needed. He pushed it away with his knee. Thrusting himself over the body and away from the fence. In one fluid movement, he swiped the blade across its throat and watched as the life fled from the monster's dark, soulless eyes.

"Told you...that knife...would come in handy."

Bill looked over to where Reggie was standing, hands on his knees, panting with exertion. The ex-preacher cursed under his breath, chuckled, then straightened up and wiped the blood from his face.

Bill staggered away from the body, dropping the knife as he went. His arms and legs trembled. He badly needed to rest. He badly needed to eat.

"You're not done yet, Bill. What have I taught you? Finish him off!"

"You do it," Bill shouted, stumbling onto the grass.

"Bill, you know—"

"You do it!" he screamed. His voice echoed against the buildings. "You need it more than I do! I don't want it! Take care of your family."

He heard the high *shinggggg* of a blade as it sliced through the monster's neck, hitting bone, ripping free. Then the heavy sound of Reggie's footsteps running after him. Bill felt his arm getting grabbed. He could hear Reggie talking, but he could not hear the words. All he could feel was this huge crushing sensation, as if the world was collapsing around him, and a vague notion of being dragged back into the safety of the woods.

"What's the matter with you?" Reggie hissed. "Get a grip!"

Bill fell to his knees holding his head in his hands. "Why are we doing this?" he moaned. "I don't know how much longer I can keep this up."

"Why? Because we have to," Reggie answered. He dropped the bloody knife next to him, but kept the pair of heads they'd just collected. These he would keep for himself and his family. Bill felt his anger rise for a moment, then pushed it away. He had no right to be angry with Reggie.

"And you'll do it as long as you need to, Bill."

Then Reggie left him in the trees while he slipped back for the rest of their equipment.

When he returned several minutes later, he had Bill's sack, which he'd retrieved from their hiding spot near the gate.

"We need to leave," he whispered harshly. "The place is crawling, and even more are coming. There's too many for us to take."

Bill could hear them now, drawn by the noise and the smell of their own blood, and he remembered what Reggie had said—*they will be drunk on their own blood*—and he trembled. But still he didn't get up.

"I couldn't get your machete."

Bill waved him off. It had totally failed him this time. If not for Gary's knife, he would've been—

But you weren't.

He grabbed his sack and stumbled to his feet, just as shadows from the approaching figures passed over them. Footsteps came closer. He could smell them now.

"*Run!*" Reggie urged.

They ran then, blindly crashing through the forest. They ran until they came to a trail, and still they were being followed—hunters becoming the hunted—so they pressed on.

They kept running, gasping, swimming in the moonlight that now showered down on them. They ran until, finally, the sounds of their frustrated pursuers faded away.

They headed back toward the river, avoiding the main road this time for fear of being seen.

Reggie was the first to break the silence. "I'm done, Bill."

Bill nodded. After the way he'd acted tonight, he didn't blame Reggie for telling him to shove off. "Well, you got two heads. That's a decent bounty for one night."

"No, Bill. I mean I'm done with this place, with...*here*. I'm surprised you haven't given up before now, what with all the Headhunters overrunning the city."

"It's not so bad out here."

"Tell that to Gary and the others."

Bill nodded. He'd wondered if the attack at the mall had anything to do with this.

"Admit it, Bill. The cities have become barely controlled chaos. They've gone to mob rule; people are breaking into apartments, killing indiscriminately. Act first, ask later. One of these days, it's going to my apartment they bust the door down to. Then what? How am I going to keep my family safe?"

"What about the flock? I thought it was your job to deliver them to Heaven?" Bill hadn't meant to sound so spiteful, but there it was. It really had just been all an act.

"My family is also my flock."

"So all that talk was just—"

"I still believe, Bill. But sometimes faith isn't enough, right? Faith won't put food on the table. It won't keep the beast from your door."

Bill kept silent for a moment. He didn't know what to say.

"I'm glad we had one last chance to hunt together, Bill. I've always respected your...choices."

"So, just like that, you're leaving? Where will you go?"

"Well, to start off, someplace where there are fewer hunters, less competition."

"Yeah, but where?"

Reggie didn't answer at first. Then: "North. To Canada."

"No, seriously."

"I am serious. It's less crowded up there."

"Hell yeah it is. Why do you think it's less crowded? It's too fucking cold!"

"We'll make do." Reggie hesitated before adding: "Why don't you come with us, Bill? There was going to be more of us, Gary and the Cartwright twins, but—"

"So that's why you hunted with them the other night. You were recruiting? Who's the headhunter now? But, no, I can't, and you know why."

"Finding the one who took Karen from you won't bring her back. As the Bible says: *And in those days shall men seek death, and shall not find it; and shall desire to die, and death shall flee from them.* Revenge isn't the answer, Bill."

"Maybe not, but it's all I've got."

Bill watched his friend go. A part of him wanted to follow, but he knew that he couldn't. Whatever Reggie was looking for, it didn't exist. There was no salvation for any of them.

There was only redemption with a little r.

He walked on, letting his feet drag, dreading the river crossing. When he came to the old farm, he stopped to look for his glasses.

Dawn was still a couple hours away, and the winds had picked up, bringing the night's first hints of the approaching winter. He shivered, mostly out of habit since he wasn't cold. The breeze had shredded the fog, carried it away. Somewhere, a rooster crowed, apparently surprised by the sudden shift in the weather. A dog barked in the distance. Trees swayed, shrugging off the last of their dead or dying leaves.

He cut across the barnyard to the scene of their earlier encounter. The body was gone from where they had left it, almost certainly scavenged by now, probably by wolves, though possibly by the dog he'd heard just a moment ago. The blood that was left behind was congealed and cold. He marked the trail it left into the gloom, past the corner of the old house and up toward the woods. There was no sign of his glasses in the scuffed up dirt.

His legs shook from the night's exertion, from his hunger, from the incredible weight of his guilt.

He truly was the Damned, wasn't he?

There is no Damned, only the hunter and the hunted.

But if there is no Damned, then how can there be Redemption?

That was Reggie's thing. I never asked for it. And neither did you.

No, but he realized now that it had always been what he wanted. Not the kind of redemption one got by satisfying some personal vendetta, but the kind received through a much larger sacrifice.

There will be no sacrificing.

But he already had sacrificed, hadn't he? For her?

With a sigh he entered the barn. He settled himself onto the top of the chopping block, then laid the knife beside him. Wind blew through the open door but did not reach him.

He let the sack drop between his feet, watching it settle in a small hollow a short distance away. He toed it back within reach.

Sunrise was now only an hour away. He'd have just enough time to get back to his apartment—no time to let the river wash his clothes this morning. Another promise broken. How long had it been since he'd last felt the sun on his skin? Twelve months since the Outbreak, he remembered again. Such things were getting harder to recall. After that, the surprise attack on the Carcher Building, the day he had made Karen wait for him in the lobby. They had tried to run; he had escaped.

She hadn't.

It was all his fault: he'd been the one who had kept them there past dusk with his last minute reports. With that one decision, he'd damned her to the Undead. Now she was gone.

He'd spent the next few months looking for her. And when he did find her—in the shell of the old GAP store downtown, though he couldn't understand why she had chosen such a place—she hadn't even recognized him, not until he had followed her into that darkness. Then, finally, they were together again.

At least until the monster came and stole her away from him again, this time for good. Six months ago now. The image of the she-beast came to him then, the crazed look in her eyes when they had surprised it in that alleyway off of Second Street. With her last dying breath, Karen had made him promise her that he would track it down and take its head.

Six months. Now he wondered which he missed more: his wife or the sun.

You never really wanted to be a Headhunter, did you?

He frowned. The voice wasn't Karen's this time, but his own.

I did it for Karen. Always for her.

And what do you do for yourself?

Nothing.

That's why this all felt like an exercise in futility. Nothing would bring his Karen back. Nothing would give him his life back. With a start, he realized he didn't know how to do anything else, not in this world that didn't need executive recruiters for insurance companies. He almost laughed then at the image of him sitting behind a desk and answering phones, as if the Undead had any need for human resources.

"Actually, we do," he said out loud. His laughter echoed off the bare walls of the barn, but it died, just as it had died in his throat.

He reached down and tugged open the sack and grasped a handful of hair. Most of the blood had already drained out of the head, but he didn't care about that. It was the brains he was after. And Reggie had been right about one thing: he'd bagged a good one.

"Fresh is best," he told himself, chuckling. "Not like the old dried out crap I've been eating for the past week."

He found a flap of skin beneath the back of the neck and, with a grunt, yanked it up and over the glistening white skull underneath, just the way Reggie had taught him. If he'd had any saliva, his mouth would have been watering, but the Undead do not salivate. He reached down to retrieve the knife to crack open the skull.

And that's when he heard the footstep.

He slowly raised his eyes to the door of the barn, at the figure standing there in silhouette. He could tell it was a female, though that was all. *Damned glasses!* Or maybe it was a girl. It had a slight frame, so much like Karen's.

Had it seen him?

The figure didn't move. Neither did he.

In her hands was a large axe. He wondered if it might be the one that belonged to the chopping block he was sitting on.

He licked his dry lips with an even drier tongue and waited. As always happened whenever he encountered one of them, he became acutely aware of everything around him: the distance separating them, the knife just beyond the reach of his fingertips, the head of the man he'd killed earlier that evening still in his hands.

"Daddy?" the monster whispered.

A flood of feelings came over him: confusion, love, longing, loss. His eyes dropped back down to the head. Then, without knowing why, he raised it up in her direction, as if offering it to her.

A sob escaped her lips. "You killed…. *You killed my daddy!*"

His heel nudged the knife. He felt the handle slipping over the block and coming to a rest against his calf. All he'd have to do was reach down. It'd be in his hand before she could even take a step into the barn.

The child lifted the axe in her hands. A growl rose in her throat. He could see the tears on her face, tears of anger and sadness for the father he had taken from her. *I'm delivering him to Heaven*, he wanted to say, but his lips had long ago lost the ability to form words she could understand.

He knew her tears were of hate for him, not just fear or grieving. He knew all those feelings. He knew them all too well. And he wished for the thousandth time since Karen had become infected that day that he could cry for his own losses, for the life that had been taken away from him when she had crossed over, for the life he forsook when he followed her into the night. He wanted to cry out for the loss he had suffered when the monster had taken his Karen away from him the second time.

And yet there were no tears. Living life as the Undead was unfair that way.

The girl wailed. She raised herself up and, in that moment, as the predawn aurora fell upon her face, he recognized her. And now his shock was complete. This was the monster who had taken Karen away from him! This was the beast he'd been hunting for the last six months. This was the girl who haunted his waking dreams, who ushered to him his only remaining memories of his wife.

But what's she doing all the way out here?

He stood then, the knife somehow once more in his hand. He stepped forward, even as she raced toward him.

He watched as the girl raised the axe over him, raised it to bring it down upon his head. Everything, it seemed, was happening in exactly the same moment: the past six months, this moment, everything.

"Damn you to hell!" she screamed.

She skidded to a stop in front of him, and in that eternal moment the sun broke over the horizon and spilled its burning fire onto his face.

Yes, he thought, I am damned to hell. And the truth of it made him smile.

He raised the knife. In the corner of his eye, he saw the blade arc through the air. He saw it leave his fingers, heard it clang as it hit the floor. He smiled as he lifted his head.

I am damned, yes, but here is my redemption.

He felt the gentle whisper of the hatchet's cold steel against his neck, an eternity of coldness before the eternity of sleep. It was like the sweet kiss of his dear sweet Karen.

It tasted of Redemption.

‡ ‡

Author's note

What is it about the Undead that we love to fear? Other than the visceral terror they can invoke in us, what makes zombies and their ilk so horrifying? Is it because they're mindless? Is it because they hunt and feed with no rational motivation, driven only by some carnal instinct, uncontrolled by rational thought? Is because we are their prey?

While working on an upcoming zombie pandemic novel (tentatively called Touch Me & Die*), I began to question the whole concept of the monsters as "mindless" creatures. Of course, classic zombie lore is heavily founded on the idea* that these monsters are mindless; it is *why the brain-eaters so frightening and compelling.*

But what if they weren't as mindless as we think they are? What if a story were written from their point of view? What we flipped the idea of "monsters" on its proverbial ear and we *became the monsters?*

It was with these questions in mind that I wrote The Headhunter.

I hope reading this story was as thought-provoking and entertaining for you, Dear Reader, as it was for me to write.

‡   ‡   ‡

The Object
of Her Obsession

Can you smell the rain?
It's coming.

T HERE'S SOMETHING about Felipe-Janssen knives, the fancy
ones you used to be able to get at Milano's on Tenth Street in
downtown Grand Forks. My Uncle Phil got us a set of them
for Christmas a half dozen years back, the ones with the guaranteed
Eversharp™ blades that come in one of those fancy velvet-lined
boxes.

Most of them are gone now. Misplaced or thrown away. All
except the filleter. I was always so careful to keep that one hidden
away. I wanted to make sure it wouldn't get lost or misused like the
others.

Despite its claim, the blade started to dull after a while. No big
surprise there, I used it all the time. I learned how to keep the edge
as keen as a razor; a drop of oil and a whetting stone and a lot of
patience was all it needed. I found the rhythmic act of sharpening
oddly calming. Besides, a sharper blade makes a finer cut.

It was just so perfect, the knife: long and thin, well-balanced,
gently curved. The handle was soft to the touch, carved out of some
exotic wood. Mahogany, I think. It didn't have the rough feel of pine
or even oak. It felt like it knew what it was meant for: for being
held.

I almost feel sorry for it, sitting all alone in the drawer with the
ordinary knives now, the mismatched set Mom and Dad found at the

St. Christopher's rummage sale when they got married and which now only get used whenever Mom gets the urge to scrape the mold off the bathroom tiles. I doubt my father would've approved her using the Felipe-Janssens like that. He thought they were special, too.

Sometimes, sleepless in the dark, I lie and I wonder where the rest of them are, where they've gotten to. Maybe they'll turn up in some evidence box somewhere someday, like on those TV crime shows. Isn't that a strange thing to wonder? Honestly, though, it doesn't seem so farfetched, especially now that summer is over and somebody's bound to notice that the fences are a long way from being finished.

Good killing knives.

That's what Mom used to say. She became obsessed with the idea after Father died. I always just scoffed at her when she'd speak such nonsense, accusing her of trying to frighten me. She'd shake her head in denial and say she was only trying to protect me.

From who? Myself? Her? There's no one else left.

A couple years ago, shortly after Dad died, Uncle Phil took me out to the lake. "Emma," he'd said, "I'll show you how to properly gut a fish." But of course it was too late for that. The lake had already gone shallow by then. The shore was clogged up with reeds and you couldn't get close enough without sinking to your knees in the soggy clay. It was the end of the second year of drought and most of the larger fish had died off by then anyway. By the third year, there were none left at all, only a brown puddle surrounded by sickly green and yellow grass.

Everything's all gone now. Everything save for a few leeches and the noisome frogs, croaking away deep beneath the pile of wood that once made up the old dock. They're very loud, almost too loud. It's irritating, although sometimes I can't stand the thought of them going silent. A trace of dampness still lingers under the wood, in the dark spaces where the wind can't reach it and sunlight is a stranger; I can still smell the traces of water there sometimes, seeping out of the clay. But all the rest is gone, just like the knives. Well, except for the filleter, of course. That's still tucked away safe in the drawer, right where my mother returned it. At least, I hope that's where she put it.

I need to check.

Was that thunder?

Sometimes, lying here in the darkness, unable to sleep, waiting for the telltale rumble of a storm that never comes, I wonder what my mother must have been thinking, putting those ideas of killing into my head. Was it intentional? Was it just talk? Was it because she feared me, or feared *for* me?

They're ugly, I can hear her saying, even now. *Ugly and impractical and I'm always afraid I'll cut myself on one.*

As if on a dare, she reaches into the drawer for her lighter and lights up another cigarette. *Look,* she seems to say. *Look at the risk I take.* Like she needs to remind me of the things a well-sharpened knife can do. I already know.

Her fingers, yellowed by tar and negligence, come out whole. No new cuts, only the same old ones, now ghostly white and hidden among the wrinkles.

She stopped cooking when Dad was dying. Unless you call peeling open a box of Mann's frozen lasagna and sticking it in the microwave oven cooking. They even come with their own plastic forks packed inside the box. No mess. No fuss. She won't eat what I fix.

I, on the other hand, was thrilled that my uncle would favor us with such a wonderful and thoughtful and useful gift. Not the whole set, mind you, or the fancy box. Just the one knife. I looked for any excuse to cook, just so that I could hold the filleter, feel it in my hand.

I remember slicing onions, the satisfying *critchhh* as the knife slipped through them. We ate a lot of onions, as very little else would ever grow out here on the hard, windswept lea. Well, potatoes, naturally, but I was never partial to them. I always favored onions. Of course, now the ground refuses to yield to my efforts; it dulls even the hardest metal. The drought is now in its fourth long year, and there's no end in sight. So I wait for thunder and hope that it brings rain to soften the soil. Only then will the things planted in the ground find sunlight again.

I guess I spend a lot of time doing that now, praying for rain.

Thoughts of onions and cutting reach my fingers and they curl reflexively, forming a space that's just large enough for the handle to slide into. But there is no handle and my hand aches with such emptiness that matches the emptiness in my heart.

I remember the sticky spray coating my skin. A good onion bleeds well, not like the wild ones struggling to grow here now, tough and rubbery and lacking any kind of smell whatsoever. They wilt when you cut them. They are like the people who grow where there is no rain: dry, lifeless, dead.

The juice grows tacky, glues my fingers together.

The second slice bisects the heart once more, the tenderest part. The tough outer skin curls and I peel it back. The flesh underneath glistens like exposed cartilage for a brief moment, then quickly dulls to a desiccated ashy gray.

At some point Mom comes up behind me, wraps her arms around my waist. My fingers tighten and my eyelids flutter like a nightshirt on the line, and I imagine clouds whipping past an oblong moon high overhead. Her breath is hot against my ear, as hot and sterile as the parched air, as dry as the barren earth, so much like the wind that comes to us in the late afternoon, carrying with it the stale perfume of the dry lake bed. The wind comes first as a whisper. Then it wails. It hurls itself against our old ranch house. The walls lean slightly into it, trembling like a drunkard tilting against a world madly rushing toward him.

As if beckoned by such thoughts, the first hush of a breeze slips in through the broken kitchen window, past the patched screen and the faded lace curtains from the C&K discount bin. I remember the day we picked them out, the day after Daddy died. *Something to brighten the kitchen*, Mom had said, and there was a wild look in her eyes, something threatening and uncontained. Desperation and release. Doubt.

Fear.

She holds me and I complain, stiffen myself against her body for a moment, and she thinks she is brave for holding me when I am cutting. But my body wilts in her clasp, even as she pulls tighter. It's not painful, but firm, impliable, like she's afraid I might suddenly turn to dust and blow away. Like if she stops holding onto me she'll be the one to disappear. I don't know which she fears more.

My grip relaxes. I jut out my elbow to push her away. "Stop," I tell her, though the word comes out hoarse and weak. Deep down inside me, I want to run away. I want her to hold me and I want us both to run, though to where I don't know, nor do I care. Still, she keeps me there, so afraid of being alone. She agonizes over her loneliness, wondering everyday how it must be for my dead father without her. Without us. And I tell her the dead do not feel; they do not love. I know it is a cruel thing to say, but I say it anyway.

I expect her to be hurt, but all she does is rest her head on my shoulder and gently rock us both. She whispers into my ear: "They may die, but their longing persists, those who pass before us." And I tell her she's wrong. The dead don't feel a thing.

"You don't know, honey," she whispers. "You don't know."

Doubt stirs inside of me and I almost believe her. My father haunts us, even now.

The heat of her words sends shivers across my neck, down my chest, evokes visions of another man: Jason. I close my eyes again and sigh.

jason

I picture him standing there, filling my thoughts instead of the kitchen and its meager trappings. The onion and my parents and their pathetic longing for each other fade into the background. My hand still slices, though not by any conscious effort. Juice drips off the edge of the cutting board, seeps into the stained wood underneath. *Cha-dunk. Cha-dunk. Cha-dunk.*

"Emma," my mother whispers, as if sensing my own deep longing.

My fingers slip and the cutting board rattles, jarring me from myself and back into the memory of the kitchen. The knife falters, clatters to the floor. Warmth runs across my hand. I feel nothing, no pain or sorrow. I hear only the echoes of her sniffling quietly behind me.

"You should've closed your eyes," I chastise, stopping to wipe the wetness of her tears away on the back of my jeans.

She laughs, suddenly and loudly, and pushes herself away from me as I bend to retrieve the knife. She says, "I hate that thing. It's ugly. I wish you'd throw it away."

I don't look up. I look only at the knife that fits so perfectly in my hand and the sharp blade that still drips. A perfect killing knife.

Behind me, the microwave door opens, then closes. I hear the beep, the hum of her dinner cooking.

Later, after it begins to rain, I will find her asleep, alone, in the back bedroom.

†

Today is the day.

Our house faces north, so the front porch is always steeped in shadow. The steps are warped and worn, the colorless paint long since faded and flecked, brushed away by the countless soles of the countless feet of unknown ancestors. For all I know, they might be mine, but who can remember? The bare soft wood is half-fossilized by heat and dust, half-rotted away by winter ice. I pick at it, gouging a secret spot beneath the banister. I sit. And wait.

Finally, Uncle Phil's truck rattles to a stop in front of me. Mom gets out. Behind her comes Jason in a separate car. She yells back at him to park out behind the house, though not in the barn where there's no room. And his engine revs and the car shudders and the ground trembles and I can feel it in my teeth. He draws slowly past us and Mom watches it out of sight. Then she goes inside.

Jason is here for another summer.

He is nineteen and I am seventeen and finally old enough to make him mine. Three summers I have been his, but only in secret, a secret he's not known. Three summers is long enough to grieve for my father. It's long enough to carry my mother's pain as my own. Jason's arrival will allow me to peel it away from me for good.

He reappears around the corner of the house with his bag and stomps his way past me up the steps. His boots are freshly polished, the hems of his new jeans rubbing stiffly against them, scratching when he walks. *Emma*, he murmurs, as if he'd last seen me just this morning and not nine months ago. His bag brushes my shoulder, his fingertips my hair. I shiver. Two more steps and then the screen door slams closed behind me.

When he is gone again, only then do I look up, though my hands still cover the thing I have carved.

jason

He is so perfect. His hair, so dark, coal black but smelling impossibly of cinnamon and cocoa and…something else. Something bestial and yet restrained, like a stag silhouetted on the horizon after a hard run, all clean sweat and alert eyes. He is tall, broad shouldered and wedged-torsoed. When he looks at me, it almost feels as if he might be searching for something deeper than what he can see on the surface. My soul, perhaps. His gaze falls on me like the infinite Dakota sky, pressing down upon me like the promise of a lover. I think that if he were to look long enough, he might finally see the whole of what I really am. Not just the shadow that trails him on the sun-baked ground like some sort of dark oily stain.

I want him so badly.

At first I was too young, barely thirteen. Then Daddy passed. Then my mother needed me. But now I am seventeen. I can make my own way now.

He is strong, strong and wiry. The efforts of the past several summers spent on my Uncle Phil's farm are clear on his arms. The restless mountain of his shoulders rising toward his neck; the valley running between them down his back, an arroyo for a river of sweat.

His hair is long and wild, black as an Apache's tears or a mid-January midnight. Even in the day it soaks up the light. It spreads like a black ocean across the cliff of his chest. His tee shirt spills like rainfall over the floor of his belly. Below that, an exotic wilderness, enticing, threatening, exciting.

In the mornings, after he has risen and just before breakfast, he'll come down smelling of fallen leaves and maple bark, as if he'd traveled to some strange forest in the middle of the night and bedded there. Always the earthy scent of wet dirt and of wild mushrooms accompanies him.

But those days have passed.

I cough now from the dust and the air smells like nothing. Even the pinewood purchased for the fence posts has long since lost its essence; they stink of nothing.

Fences. Jason liked mending them. Uncle Phil had miles and miles of them, and Jason liked the solitude of being out along the border, so different from his city life in Illinois. Clad in jeans and an earth-brown tee, doused in sweat, all held in check by his wide leather belt and boots and the White Sox cap that inevitably became stained the color of earth, the color of his leather gloves. The same color as the dust on my uncle's pickup truck. Only his eyes kept him from disappearing altogether, blue as swirled fragments of the sinless sky, deep and pure as a bottomless well.

I remember the time I saw him swimming across the lake that first summer night, four years ago, his white skin breaking the surface, sinking away, rising again. Only thirteen and the unfamiliar flush of pure desire overtook me so unexpectedly that I had nearly collapsed where I stood, gasping for air, my body trembling as if from a fever.

The slow, steady rhythm of his stroke held me entranced, his body moving into and out of the shadows cast by the moon through the cottonwood trees lining the shore. His nakedness rippling, meeting the ripples of the water, as if they were one and the same and where one ended the next started until the whole lake was him and lightness and being, and I felt that if I was to step out and into that water then I would be infused with a part of him, too. Instead of filled with silence and shadow. Instead of always leaking pain that never seemed to reach inward, only out; pain that existed only on my skin, yet never sloughed away.

He'd have been mortified if he knew I'd seen him.

I want to smile at the memory, but I cannot. If I make my lips move they will crack. I don't think they will bleed; it is far too dry for bleeding anymore. My lips will crack and the cracks will spread along these new seams and my face will crumble away. Who would see? Who would care? See? I am alone. They have all left me.

But I know the rains will return and things will once more grow as they once did. And I will hold my beloved as I once dreamed I would.

But for now the trees are skeletons and the lake is a dried up hollow and the house tilts ever more slightly against the winds—I can feel it shifting, moaning. Later, when they come howling, clattering like ancient bones in the dead grass, they will lift up the clay and settle it over everything in a fine brown veil: the house, the old black Ford, me. Everything is upside down. I scrape into the earth, notching it, praying.

The frogs are silent. Are they praying, too?

When at last I have finished the letters of my own full name opposite his, only then do I dot the *j*, pushing the knife tip in as deep as I am able and giving it a vicious twist. The effort tears the breath from my chest. It escapes in a gasp of agony and ecstasy.

Afterward, I wash my hands in the dirt and stuff them into my pockets along with the knife and sneak into the darkness of the front room. Jason's bag is sitting there, but he's in the kitchen. My mother laughs at something he says. The sound floats through the house like fireflies, flaring brightly for a moment, flickering. Then falling away again, consumed into the heavy darkness that infects everything.

The memory of my father flickers too in that moment, and I find myself wishing he was still here. I wish him back, even though he had been nothing but a presence in our lives, like a couch, or a radio. Nothing more. He was neither sadness nor happiness. He was simply a man, soft-spoken and fond of apples, who smelled of aftershave and leather and felt like sandpaper. Until near the end, anyway, when he felt more like a burlap sack half-filled with sticks and potatoes, and the air around him buzzed with the stench of decay.

No, that's not entirely true. He was more than any of that, though I don't like to think about it.

He preferred the paring knife over the filleter.

But now he has been gone these last three summers, and in each one his absence has been a hole that my mother has tried to fill and yet been unable to; every time she looks at me, she is reminded.

I unroll the cuff of my cutoff jeans down to my knees, cover my thighs, suddenly numb with longing that even pain cannot touch.

When they are finished talking, Jason comes out. He seems less angry now than when he first arrived. I cannot imagine what set him off so, but whatever it was, it is gone now. He grabs his bag to take it upstairs. If he sees me standing against the front window, a dark silhouette in the shadow cast by the deep porch roof, he doesn't show it. He goes up to shower after the long drive from his mother's house to my uncle's and the shorter drive from there to here. I follow on a cat's feet.

Through the keyhole to his room, I see the tightness of his skin over the muscles on his back, the scar on his arm when he and that wild boy down the road, Avery Dooley, branded each other with sharp, fire-blackened sticks one night three years ago, a drug-induced ecstasy like some kind of initiation ritual. It was the second summer of our drought.

They had torn off their shirts, and their smooth wet skin glistened like oil in the firelight, reflecting the glow. The sparks rose, caught the wind and drifted over the tinder-dry fields, carrying with them the boys' anguished howls and spells of wildfire. I'd watched the two of them from the darkness outside the circle of light, afterwards wondering if the rain did not come because I had not prayed for it as earnestly as they had.

To me the scar looks like a kiss, and my body aches to place my lips upon it, to infuse it with my own hot breath until the skin there becomes whole again. Then I realize with a start that the scar connects us. Without it, he would be perfect and could not know my longing.

After the briefest of showers—it takes so long for the pump to fill the cistern back up again from the well—he clomps down the stairs. He moves slowly, a step at a time, concentrating on buttoning his shirt. I am in the kitchen by the time he reaches the landing. I am making supper. I am concentrating on cutting limp carrots from the pantry, along with meat and onions and potatoes. He sits at the table and drinks a beer and wipes away the sweat on his forehead with the bottom edge of the bottle and I am acutely aware of every little movement he makes, down to the tiniest twitch of an eyelid.

"Smells good, Emma," he tells my back, and I smile and lower my eyes. The knife trembles for a moment, threatens to escape from my hand. I mustn't lose my concentration.

He takes another drink, sighs deeply, burps quietly. "Another dry year," he says, and the air fills with the smell of him and beer and all I want to do is inhale every last bit of it.

"None since March," I answer. My voice trembles, threatens to shatter. "Not much even then, either. Barely enough to darken the soil." My words flutter in the air, quickly sinking like a mayfly at the end of its day.

This past winter had been bitter cold and dry. The ground is unforgiving, hard as ice, as if it had forgotten how to thaw. But I know Jason welcomes the challenge. The ground, however unyielding, he will break it. Just like last year. The fence must be repaired.

Cha-dunk. Cha-dunk. Cha-dunk.

"I was worried my T-bird was going to bottom out getting up here," he says. "The roads are all gone to hell. Why don't they fix them?"

I shrug.

Cha-dunk. Cha-dunk.

"It's a '97," he goes on. "Black pearl paint. Bought it just last month, after my birthday. Going to take it to college with me." My heart quavers for a moment. I want to yell at him to take me with him, but then I think of my mother and, as if he can read my thoughts, he says, "I told your ma this'll be my last summer here. She..." He pauses. "Obviously she wasn't too happy about it."

The knife sighs. *Chaaaah.*

He finishes his beer. The chair squeaks as he leans back to toss the bottle into the trash. Then his boots hit the floor, startling me.

"Smells real good," he says again.

When I finally exhale and turn around, he is gone, and I lick the salty sweetness from my fingers, wishing it was his mouth on my skin instead of mine, imagining my own scars healing.

Jason comes into town with us the next day. We take the truck and he sits between us, his knee touching mine, his hip touching mine, his shoulder and elbow touching mine. On the other side, the pattern repeats, and I wonder if Mom notices him in the same way that I do.

I want him so badly that I can do nothing but press my hand against my leg and bite my lip in anguish. I concentrate on the road, on the electrical poles we pass and the slanted mailboxes, their mouths hanging open like hungry, tongueless baby sparrows. My skin burns so, and I guess I must be breathing funny because he looks over at me all of a sudden and his eyebrows are raised and his eyes are so wide and deep that I feel like I am drifting in a sea I have never seen or felt, except maybe in my dreams. I feel my face grow red beneath a veil of unkempt hair.

I taste blood from my wounded lip. But there is no pain, only the purest sense of being. I stare even harder out the window until I am sure he's no longer looking at me.

Mom drops him off at Grables for fencing wire and posts. I offer to stay but she needs me to help with her errands, so I get back into the truck and watch him grow small in the mirror. He climbs the steps, hands in his back pockets, chin jutting confidently out. Then he disappears in the dust cloud, and the cloud trails us the rest of the way into town, like a lonely ghost.

We stop first at the consignment shop.

"I need a summer dress," Mom announces, brightly. "Something light and pretty." She passes a hand across my forehead, pulls the hair from my face. I turn away from her, let it fall back. For a moment her thumb traces the lines on my cheek and her eyes darken. "Something..." she whispers, but doesn't finish.

"Practical?" I offer.

"Young."

"We can't afford it."

She reaches into her collar and pulls out a few bills wrapped in a rubber band. Insurance money. "Come in, honey. I'll buy you one, too."

But I stay in the truck. It feels wrong to spend the money on something like that. I don't move, even after she returns from the consignment shop and drives us over to the grocery store, upset that I am being stubborn and unhelpful.

Soon, the bags pile up at my feet: the dress she bought, shrouded in yellowed tissue paper; food staples, including the usual stacks of frozen lasagna; beer for Jason; cigarettes for herself; old magazines stolen from Doctor Hennie's office that she'll thumb through for articles on Santa Fe or pictures of the newest hair styles, neither of which she will ever be seen in. She ticks the items off on her fingers as she drives, reciting as if she doesn't trust her memory. She squints through the cigarette smoke and out through the windshield as we make our way back to Grables. The truck coughs and sputters miserably because nobody has worked on it in the past three years, not unless you count Jason's oil changes. Besides, Mom can't smoke, count, and shift gears all at the same time.

"Get everything you needed, Terry?" Jason asks when we pull up, and it startles me to hear him call my mother that. It's always been Missus Harris before. This new familiarity troubles me.

She nods, smiles warmly.

The truck shudders as he throws the new redwood fence posts into the bed, followed by the jangle of wire. I move over toward the middle of the seat, but then I hear Jason jump into the back. He shouts for us to go. Mom yanks the truck into gear, spraying gravel as she pulls out of the parking lot.

"I bought you a dress," she informs me, once we get back onto the main road. "When we get home you should try it on. I think you'll like it." She lights another cigarette and puffs heavily on it. A fifth of it instantly shrivels away, curling like a snake skin shed in the desert. She lets the breath out through the window, and her face deflates, grows hollow and leathery. From the corner of my eye, I see the smoke sheer off, spinning away past Jason's shoulder and his outstretched hand riding the wind, racing the swirls that chase us back home again.

Mom looks over at me. Her face is calloused by years of sun and wind, of hard winters and harsh summers. It's pinched by years of loneliness and crying. But every summer it loosens just a little bit, rising up as if from some deep, dark underground place; but her tears are not rain, and the only thing they nourish is still more anguish. Only Jason's presence has been able to step them.

Does she think I haven't noticed? Does she not see how she sinks away again when Jason leaves? What will she do when he doesn't return next summer?

What will she do if I leave with him?

My restless fingers curl and uncurl and curl again at the thought.

"You should smile a little, Emma," she says. She raises her eyebrows, touches my cheek again. "If *I* can, you can." And I know she has been trying, I've seen it, her practicing when she doesn't think anyone's looking. Practicing for Jason. My Jason. What could she possibly be thinking? "Promise me," she says.

I give it a try, even though I can't imagine what there is to smile about with her. Instead, my face wants to pull in ways that feel wrong. My skin tugs and stretches tight against its seams. Mom smiles back, encouragingly.

"You're so—"

The wind snatches the rest away, yanks it from my ears so quickly that it would be impossible for anyone to even know the words were ever spoken, and it is for the best.

Beautiful is what her lips say, yet ugly is what her eyes see.

And evil is what she thinks.

That night I try on the dress.

In the privacy of my room, I pull it out of the bag and hold it up by its straps. It is pretty, though simple: thin, almost sheer white cotton, pink and green flowers, a narrow waist, a low neckline. A sliver of molten light cascades from the folds of the material, pool on the bed in the shape of a rose on a silver chain as thin and light as spider's silk. I know I could never wear the necklace without breaking it. Even so, I arrange it and the dress and begin to slowly strip off my clothes. I move carefully, deliberately, patiently. Finally

I am standing fully naked in the evening's growing shadows. The air is not cold, but my skin pricks against it, unfamiliar with such brazenness, unsure of the intimacy the shadows play on it. Slowly I turn to face the mirror, and my fingers run over each dip and rise of my bareness, measuring every scar, every imperfection.

jason

I trace each letter of his name, each edge where unblemished skin meets its counterpoint, and the dark line of hair on my belly stands up on end. I push it flat, hold it there and practice smiling into the mirror. But even I cannot stand to see such hideousness for long, and all too soon I yield and turn away.

I lower myself into the tub. It had taken so long to fill that it is already cold. My skin shrinks against it, rebels. My breath catches in my throat and only when I am fully immersed does my throat uncap, giving full release to my anguish. The bubbles rise above me and break the surface and are gone in an instant. The bath makes me feel lighter, effervescent. I remain like that until the water takes on a slightly metallic taste and my lips burn blue and finally grow numb as the sunlight fades around me.

Afterwards, when I am dry, I pull the dress over my head and it slips so easily across my skin, hiding so much, that it feels almost like cheating, like I am pretending to be someone I am not. Tonight I am daring, not the blind, timid mole the world thinks it sees. I wear nothing else on underneath, only the necklace, so that when I make my way down into the darkness of the house, to the front room where the television flickers and Mom and Jason sit on opposite ends of the couch, their faces lit by the screen, I am suddenly very aware of the fabric and the way it pulls at me, catching on every defect. I slip into the ragged armchair and wait for Jason to acknowledge my arrival.

"We're watching *Wheel of Fortune*," Mom says, in case I'd been living under a rock all my life. The top half of the room is hazy with her smoke, redolent with the musk of Jason's beer.

"Em?" he says, looking over in surprise. "I didn't see you come in."

"Is that your new dress?" Mom asks. "Stand up, let us see it."

I cross my arms over my breasts, suddenly aware of their fullness, the aching that fills them. I shake my head. My bravery has fled from me. I fold my feet beneath my thighs and stare at the shiny, pale orbs of my knees.

"Please, Emma."

"Declaration of Independence!" Jason suddenly shouts at the screen, and a tiny, fat, overly cheerful woman echoes his words with even greater enthusiasm. She is jumping and clapping. The other contestants are clapping too, just not so excitedly. Their smiles are fake.

"Emma?"

I watch the screen and don't answer.

Mom gets up. The look on her face is sour. "I'm going to bed," she pouts. "I'm tired." Her glance lingers a moment too long on my necklace and fear brushes a finger over the surface of my heart.

Jason looks up. "Night, Terry," he says, his eyes following her as she leaves. She is wearing the new dress she bought for herself—yellow instead of white—and I cannot help but think that it is a little bit prettier than the one she got for me. Maybe because it hides so much more than mine does.

After the next commercial, when a new puzzle is introduced and another contestant spins the wheel, Jason silently gets up and follows my mother from the room. My ears track his movement through the halls until I can't hear anymore. Then I am truly alone in the wilderness of our house and the full moon night just outside. I am wearing my new second-hand dress, and in my lap is the knife. My fingers caress the handle. I can't even remember bringing it with me, but there it is, and it feels so natural that it almost seems like a part of me now.

This time, I start with the dot above the *j* and work my way from there. This time, I feel the pain.

And yet it still does not release me.

Avery Dooley shows up at our front door the next day. I don't know how long he'd been standing on the porch, waiting, but I almost knock him down the steps when I go barreling out, a basketful of wet laundry to be hung up on my hip.

He reaches out with one hand and grabs the banister to steady himself. With his other hand he snatches my wrist and keeps me from falling. My arm burns where he touches me, as if his skin holds the same distilled poison he and his older brothers manufacture and sell to anyone with a spare dollar and no regard for their livers. It is potent stuff.

"Avery?" I almost don't recognize him at first. His hair is cut short and his clothes are crisp and clean. But what surprises me the most is the fact that he is fully dressed, in clothes that aren't rags or in need of a thorough washing. I notice that his feet are not bare and his knobby knees aren't poking out through saggy holes in his pants. He looks almost…tamed. He even smells freshly bathed.

His face flushes red and he gives me an awkward smile. "Em," he says, his voice cracking.

"What are you doing here? Did you walk all the way over from your place?"

He nods. "I left at first light."

I frown and study his face for a moment, hoping to find his reasons for being here inscribed in its lines. But his eyes show me nothing of his intentions, and his face refuses to relinquish its ridiculous grin.

"Mom's doing the wash," I finally say. I try and pull away, but he doesn't let me go at first. Then his fingers relax and his arm drops to his side, yet my skin continues to burn.

"Emma, I'm—"

"Here for Jason," I quickly finish for him.

That night long ago, that night of the fire and dance, when I'd watched them forge their unlikely kinship, I had felt a keen sense of loss. Maybe it was because it was during the time of Daddy's sickness—or maybe I am just confusing it that way. What was stranger still was how their kinship grew each summer thereafter. It defied explanation; they were so unlike, city boy and animal, yet both sharing a similar wildness, possessed of knowledge I wished for but could never apprehend.

Suddenly I can't breathe. The air under the porch seems too thick and Avery much too close to me; I know he's not here for Jason, but I refuse to let myself acknowledge this truth.

"He's already gone," I say, breathless. "Off to repair the fence out by Flaherty Road. He won't be back till suppertime."

A look passes over Avery's face, something hard and distantly treacherous, then he shakes his head. "You know I'm not here for him, Emma. Your ma said you might... That is, she thought I could..."

I don't wait for his thoughts to untangle. I must stop him before he goes on.

"I have laundry to hang." And I try to push past him.

"Emily Harris," he says, persisting. He rubs his calloused hand on the back of his tanned leather neck. "I came to take you into town. Will you go? With me? Sometime?"

I blink disbelief at the triteness of his request, and yet a thousand thoughts crowd the narrow corridors of my mind, a hundred *why*s and *what*s and even the notion that I might still be asleep in bed and having some kind of strange nightmare where instead of Jason I have somehow replaced him with Avery.

"You and me," he stammers on, unable to stop himself, and my free hand rises on its own to...what? Ward him off? It seeks my cheek, and my skin feels hot. Whispery dry. I watch helplessly as he opens his mouth to say the things I don't want him to say. "We could get something to eat, go see a movie."

But the idea of sitting alone in a car with this wild boy for an hour-long drive does not appeal to me.

My eyes narrow. I understand what he is asking me, but I can't help wondering why. Why me? Why all of a sudden now? We have nothing in common. We've barely even talked, except for maybe once or twice.

And worst of all: What did my mother have to promise him?

But then I think maybe I'm mistaken about her intentions. I think about the dress she bought for me yesterday and the necklace, and a voice inside my head tells me: *She wants you to be happy.* But I don't really believe it. Why would she want me to be happy if it meant she'd be all alone? Being alone frightens her more than anything in the world.

"We went yesterday," I manage to say.

For a moment Avery gives me this confused look. "You? And Jason?"

I give a single nod, one answer for both questions.

His eyes go dark and the line of his chin sharpens. I consider telling him that it was for fence posts and wire and groceries and that Mom came with us, but the look on his face stops me. It's jealousy, I think, and anger. And there's something else, too, something...stronger, deeper than the dangerous look he'd let me see earlier.

Suddenly all I want to do is get away from him. I want him to leave this place. I don't ever want this wild boy to come back.

"I can't, Avery," I blurt out. And then I turn with the basket of clothes still on my hip, and I go back inside. "I have to cook dinner."

That evening Mom seems anxious. I haven't spoken to her about Avery's visit or what he said, and she hasn't asked, though I'm convinced it was all her doing. I know what she must be wondering. Had he come by? Had I sent him away? What did I say to him? She wants to ask these questions, but she knows she mustn't, so instead she pushes her lasagna around its cardboard pen with her plastic fork and nibbles at the parts where the noodles aren't brittle and dry. She sighs and opens her mouth as if to speak but nothing ever comes out.

Next to her, Jason hungrily slurps the stew I'd placed before him, mumbling how good it tastes; I smile inwardly because I so crave his compliments, even though I know he probably doesn't mean it quite so much as he says he does. The meat is old and tough and gamey. But then he asks for seconds and pleasure grows inside of me like a secret child. He's on his third beer and doesn't show any signs of slowing down. He doesn't even notice the tension drifting in the air, perhaps because of all of Mom's cigarette smoke.

I am wearing my new dress again, except this time I have a slip on underneath. My fingers steal through an opening I've carefully made in the seams, tracing random patterns on my skin. I spell out his name, and it comforts me to imagine him there, touching me, becoming a part *of* me.

Jason finishes dinner with an abrupt sigh and pushes himself back from the table and crosses his legs. He places the beer on the hardness of his stomach, stretches his neck. "That was real good, Emma."

Mom can't stand it any longer: "You didn't have to cook tonight," she says, looking my way. "I would have cooked. You should have a break, Emma. Get out. Have some fun with kids your age."

Get out? To where? I wonder. *And what kids are my age?*

But all I say is, "You? Cook?" I laugh bitterly, perhaps a bit too bitterly because the hurt on her face is almost too much to bear.

"I can cook."

"You open a box. You press a couple buttons. That's not cooking!" I say, my voice rising.

"I can cook!"

"Why? Why don't you just eat what I make? All you do is sit around eating your crappy lasagna and smoking and crying all day!"

"You don't know!" she yells back at me. "You don't know what it's like, Emily Jean Harris!"

I stand up. "What *what's* like?"

"Nothing," she mumbles.

"Argh!" I throw my hands up in frustration. "Would you just get over it already!"

"You don't know!" she screams. "You don't know what it's like to have your heart ripped out of your chest, when the only love you'll ever feel is gone forever."

My mouth opens, but nothing comes out. Dad loved her, I knew that. But somehow she's twisted it into something it never was.

"He loved us both," I yell at her.

She barks her laughter. "He loved me," she says, and her fingers skitter over the sagging skin of her neck, tracing their own patterns there. She lights another cigarette and puffs on it like she wants to swallow the whole thing at once. "You don't know," she mutters, exhaling for a long time, not looking at me but at the ceiling. "You think you know love, but you don't."

No one speaks.

After a moment, there's a quiet cough and Jason says, "That's a pretty necklace, Emma." He sounds so uncomfortable that I want to fold him into my arms. Mom's head swivels over and there's pain in her eyes. He's just said the most wrong thing he could possibly say; but to me, it's also the most right thing.

Jason attempts a smile. "I'm sorry," he says. "I shouldn't have— I mean, I didn't mean it to sound like—"

"What?" I ask, my voice husky with emotion. I tug a little at the waist of my dress, still standing, smoothing it so that it pulls a little tighter against my body. But he doesn't look at me. He stares at the clock on the wall. I stretch my hand out to him, to touch his arm, while Mom shakes her head at the wisps of dead air floating about her head. Her hand with the cigarette trembles near her lips. "Jason," I whisper, "I—"

He flinches away from me, and my mother laughs again. It comes out even sharper this time.

"You don't know," she repeats, puffing and exhaling and then taking another drag. "You don't know about nothing. Neither of you do. How could you know? You have never felt love."

"He loved us both," I repeat.

And he did. The depth of his love is still clear on our faces. It will never fade away, no matter how long has passed.

As the next few days crawl by, it becomes clear to me that the last thing my own mother wants is for me to be happy. She can't stand to be alone in her misery. She spoils Jason. She starts cooking him meals—*cooking!* Even going so far as to lock me out of the kitchen while she's in there. She even uses my knife. *My* knife!

Jason doesn't know how to respond to this sudden change in her behavior. He acts flattered, but I know it makes him uncomfortable. I can see how disgusted he is by her, the way he looks at her. He goes to bed early, rises later, and in doing so avoids us both.

He is nice to me, though, whenever we are alone. He touches me in tiny ways—not with his fingers but with his words. And I return the kindness with more and more smiles. Some even begin to feel natural, as if the stitching in my face has finally begun to loosen. "Everything'll work itself out," he tells me, but he looks tired.

I do notice that he doesn't wince quite so much whenever he looks at me now.

And so the days pass and my mother grows angrier, more and more desperate. Her moods drive me crazy.

"I haven't seen that Avery boy around lately," she says to me one day, around noon.

I'm sitting on the steps sharpening the edge of a screwdriver because I need to do something to keep my hands busy. I'm expecting Jason back soon. He needs more fencing wire and I'd promised him I'd accompany him into town. Mom doesn't know yet we're going without her, though from the way she keeps checking on me I know she suspects something is up. All morning she'd kept me busy with annoying little chores that take me out to the barn or to the backyard, anywhere away from the road. It's obvious she's watching for something. She just doesn't yet know what it is, though

I think she is beginning to have an idea. I notice how her face grows taut every time a dust devil rises from the direction of the road.

"Why would Avery come around here?" I snap.

She seems flustered for a moment. Then: "For you, honey."

"Well, I'm not interested in him."

"You shouldn't turn him away. A girl like you doesn't have many—"

"A girl like me?" I scream, and my hands fly to my face. My fingernails are cold as steel, yet short and dull. "Don't you mean a girl as *ugly* as me? Avery's not the only one who doesn't care about looks."

Silence falls over us like a sudden chill. Even the wind seems to be holding its breath.

"Jason's only being kind to you," she finally tells me. "Besides, he's too old for you."

I don't answer. I sit and gently trace his name on the smooth skin of my arm with the tip of the screwdriver and think, *Too old? Look who's talking.* The skin there is dry, but it doesn't break. Only the ghost of the letters remain, at least until a drop of water falls on them and they vanish. I look to the sky, but there are no clouds, only my mother standing over me.

The screwdriver spasms in my hand. I tell it to relax.

"Go away."

Mom huffs with exasperation. "Take this box of old junk out to the barn." She kicks it across the porch floor, a loud scraping sound that scratches my ears. A moment later the screen door bangs against the house and she is gone.

I get up, brush the dust from my pants and do as she says. It's easier than arguing with her.

The box is heavy, full of old books and clothes from the closet in her room. Dad's old stuff. And I wonder why she kept it all these years, why she's getting rid of it now. It's sad, the way she's acting, sad enough that I almost feel sorry for her. But almost isn't enough to make me not hate her.

When I get out to the barn, I don't know where to put the box. The horse stalls are filled with useless chattel. An old tractor tilts backward on flat rubber haunches. An old television set rides a rusty bicycle with a broken axle. Everything smells of dust and oil.

I find myself digging through the box, lifting away layers of memories: a photo of the three of us, Dad's favorite book (*Of Mice and Men*), a ceramic electrical insulator, a set of keys with an old Swiss army knife strung on it. The blades are rusted shut. At the bottom of the box are a dozen small, green bottles, some of which are still half-filled with a thin, nameless liquid. I pull one out. A handwritten label, the paper yellowed, peels away. A memory stirs. I uncork it and the air fills with memories of my father.

He had passed quickly, his body literally wasting away before our very eyes. Cancer, or so claimed my mother. Incurable. The liquid, she had assured me, was meant to temper the pain. Kill enough brain cells and you'll feel nothing. The Dooleys knew enough never to drink their own still water. I hold it under my nose and sniff tentatively. Much of the alcohol has evaporated off by now, and the rank smell of the whiskey has weakened so that it can no longer hide the bitter sweetness of almonds underneath.

I throw the bottle to the ground, where it shatters into a million brilliant emeralds, then I crush the broken glass beneath my boot. The air reeks, grows thick. I pluck a second bottle from the box, but stop myself from smashing it. I wonder if it is still any good. I bring the bottle to my lips, then stop. What purpose would it serve? Will it fix anything?

I leave the box where I'd set it on the floor and hurry back toward the house.

Jason pulls up out front just as I come around the corner, and I hurry over, throw open the passenger side door, climb in. "Let's go," I tell him, and he pulls away before my mother can even stop us. I see her through the dust in the trembling mirror, running out into the yard, her hands holding up the hem of her dress, her face growing smaller, blurring to a softness that hides her pain. I turn to Jason and pull my hair behind my ear and smile.

He watches the road with a serious look, but I imagine him smiling, too.

Mom says nothing when we return that evening. She says nothing but she pretends to be happy as we walk in. The air is humid and heavy with the smell of overcooked potatoes and boiled onion. Jason glances at me; neither of us is hungry, but we eat anyway, to please her.

First, I sniff the food.

The next day is just like the rest: Jason leaves an hour after sunrise; Mom and I float through the house acting out doing our chores, carefully avoiding one another; we both watch the road. My fingers itch to cook, but she stops me. I grow restless, though less so since I have rescued the fillet knife from her and hidden it in my pocket again. Just knowing it's there calms me.

I feel like I'm floating, memories of the previous day's trip into town lifting me, of the kiss that still lingers on my lips, the touch of his hot fingers on my skin. I didn't imagine them, did I?

I check my arms, but the scars are still there.

That evening, after *Wheel*, Mom is quiet. Jason tells a joke, stopping in the middle of it for a coughing fit, but Mom gets up and leaves before he can finish. Soon we hear her crying in the bedroom. I go out to the front porch, expecting Jason to follow, but he doesn't. I wait until midnight. A coyote cries in the distance. Somewhere, in the dark orchards near the Dooley place, I hear a howl in return. The pattern repeats over the next hour, and each time the call draws closer. Soon I can see a shape moving in the shadows beneath the skeleton trees. It is what I had been waiting for.

I go to him.

The next morning, my mother is up early, singing, pushing aside the drawn kitchen curtains and letting in the sunlight. Like a switch that has been flipped, she has gotten over her sadness. She even lets me cook breakfast for us all, and I am glad to do it. Jason eats everything before rushing out the door.

He comes home early that afternoon. He doesn't complain, or explain why, though his skin is waxy and his body trembles uncontrollably. He coughs with nearly every exhale, chokes on each inhale. Mom looks at me with accusation in her eyes, and the first thing I think of is the kiss—if it ever really happened. She believes I have somehow tainted him with my lips. Or perhaps he has tainted me.

I smile with the thought.

She looks away saying nothing, just serves him the dinner she has prepared. She makes him eat it all before going to bed. She tells him he's getting too much sun and not enough water. She tells him to stay in the next day and rest.

"I could use a day off," he admits. He turns and smiles at me.

But when he wakes the next morning, I will not be here.

It's a long walk to the Dooley place and back, and when I get there Avery already has what I need. I ignore the way his eyes ravage my already ravaged skin, hungrily tasting the sweat that slips from my face and neck, drawn along the line of the silver necklace that has been dulled by the dust of the road. He gives me what I need. I don't know if I leave him satisfied, but I give back what I can. It is a fair trade.

When I return in the afternoon, Jason appears to be much better. "Summer flu," he tells me, sipping a vegetable broth Mother has made for him. "They suck."

I smile and nod. Then I fetch my knife and some onions and begin to prepare dinner.

By the next morning, Jason's grown worse. His symptoms are similar as before, yet not quite the same. He is weak and his skin burns with a wicked fire that cannot be extinguished by all the sweat in the world. He doesn't even get out of bed. I convince my mother to allow me to nurse him back to health, though she begs me to leave him be. She has this look in her eyes, this familiar faraway look, and suddenly I feel like a child again, too young to know anything, too helpless to stop it even if I did.

But I am seventeen now, and Jason is mine. I slip into his room when she isn't looking.

Empty green bottles gather on his windowsill behind his head.

That evening, Mom asks me why.

"For love," I tell her.

"You don't know what love is."

"Yes, I do."

The knife rests cool against my thigh. I run my thumb along the length of the blade, feel the familiar ice spread through me as it pierces my skin. I rub my thumb and fingertip together and the blood quickly dries and grows sticky.

"You know *desire*," she tells me, "but you don't know love. Jason mistook it too, when he first came."

jason

"Yes," I say, and finally she understands.

"He loved us both," she says.

Within a week, Jason is deathly pale. He's lost half his weight. The air about his bed smells of almonds.

"I know what you are doing," he whispers.

I tell him of course he does. He would know, after all, wouldn't he? The evidence has always been clear, written all over our faces. Scribbled there by my father using a Felipe-Janssen blade, even as he uttered his undying love for us.

Jason took him away from us.

Now he turns his unblemished face away.

"I love you, Jason," I whisper. And I bend down and place my lips on his. The kiss is long and deep and healing. "We both do."

I promise him everything's going to be better soon, but I can see the doubt flickering in his eyes. If he truly loved us, he would understand. I ask him if he does and he gives me a look of such depth that there can no longer be any doubt. Soon his eyes grow muddy, roll back in his head. He falls asleep again.

Perhaps to dream of fences and rain.

I wait by his bedside and moisten his lips with medicine from the bottles. After some time has passed, his eyelids flutter open and, for another moment his eyes are as wide and deep as the lake once was, as blue as the sky. But they turn toward the light and quickly fade. They are not blue, as I had thought. They are a flat, murky brown, as dry as clay.

"He didn't love you," he says.

I shake my head.

"You don't know."

We tear up the old dock and open the ground. It is the only place where the dirt can still be turned without breaking a shovel. I'd wanted to place him elsewhere, but the ground around my father's grave has turned to cement. Within days, this too will become just as hard and impenetrable. I line the hole with Jason's knotty redwood.

Soon. Not quite yet, but soon enough.

My mother comes to me. She wraps her arms around me and holds me tight, like she's afraid the wind might suddenly gust and push me into that gaping scar in the ground. Her breath burns my neck. It is hotter than the parched air, dryer than dust that blows up at us and makes us cry.

"Now, he will know," I whisper.

Soon.

"Close your eyes, Em. I don't want you to cry."

But I don't. I look down to where her hands move restlessly against my belly. A flicker of sunlight burns in her palm and I think for a moment that my necklace has broken. But then my knife flashes. It disappears, and I sigh, and my breath is suddenly full of rain.

"You will know," she whispers. Her tears shower down on my neck and back.

When they finally dry, she lets me go.

My fingernails have peeled away, torn from scratching at this hard ground and at the pine wood. I have since stopped worrying about them. Just as I have since stopped worrying about my hair, how it falls from my scalp. I have stopped counting each passing moment by how many fall into the darkness beneath me. There are so many other things to worry about, like whether Jason will finish the fences this summer.

Like whether or not it will ever rain again.

I dig.

I dig because I must.

"Rain!" I croak into the darkness, and my swollen, blackened lips split, and the crack spreads to the lines on my cheeks.

I can smell the storm coming.

Mom was right: I didn't know what love was. I only knew desire, and desire cannot transcend death. Only love can. I know this now.

But I do love. And it is strong, so strong.

My nails are now completely gone, and yet I continue to dig. That's how much I love.

Now I hear thunder.

I smile. Another piece of my face breaks off, but that is all right. Soon, I promise myself. Soon I will hold the one I truly love.

My fingertips curl in, making a space that is the perfect shape of a soft mahogany handle, and my mouth begins to water in anticipation.

The onions I will grow will be sweet.

And they will bleed.

‡ ‡

Author's note

When I first sat down to write this story, I was sure it was going to be one of those straightforward tales of obsession, a simple tale of a young woman whose fixation on her "object of affection" was so strong that it reached beyond the grave. Indeed, that idea is at the very heart of The Object of Her Obsession. But it turned out that Emma's story is so much more complex than that, so much more...terrifying.

As I got to know her better, I realized that Emma's idea of love was as twisted as her mother's, as hurtful as her father's, and ultimately as deadly as Jason's. In some regards, it's the "wild boy," Avery Dooley, who turns out to be the most "normal" character of them all. Even Uncle Phil raises serious doubts, at least in my mind, with his "miles and miles" of fences. What does he need to keep out? What is he trying to keep in?

Emma's mother dismissed her daughter's obsession for Jason out of hand. In her narrow minded way, Emma couldn't possibly know what love is, only desire. But whatever her mother's definition might be, it's the darkest and bleakest sort of love imaginable.

And I think Emma does know love, after all. It's just not for Jason.

Is that a scratching sound I hear?

‡ ‡ ‡

Nocturne

When the Mayfly Nymph sheds his lacquered skin and spreads his nascent wings, so recommences the Imago's frantic dance. But the Nocturne's reel is quickly run. Dawn whispers upon the freshened World and, like sun-kissed wind on honeyed Dew, evaporates his mating song. Thereafter shall He falter, worn and tattered, nearly spent. He makes one last midflight conjugal stab, then flutters to the ground, to settle on winters' past rotting leaves. And there, amongst the anonymous shells of those who danced before him, He dies.

—from *La Danse Éphémères*
by Jacobin G. de Bessieres, 1842

THE MAN HAD ALREADY CHEATED Death once this morning, so when he turned away from the radiant face of his wife and stepped off the porch and into the busy-bright flow of the September day, the crisp, loud *clack* of the hard rubber soles of his shoes on the sidewalk sounded to him like an affirmation of life and living and all things that are vibrant. The breathless air was crisp and clear. He held his gaze determinedly forward, in front of himself. A sort of a smile touched the corners of his face. Today will be different, he assured himself, even though he knew it wouldn't be. Before he had even reached the front sidewalk, his footsteps sounded to him like the ceaseless ticking of a clock.

He cheated Death like a man cheats at poker, by knowing he will someday be caught; a man who plays at the game long enough and cheats often enough knows it is inevitable. Maybe not this hand or the next, but eventually. Sooner. Later. The game must end: win, lose or draw; whether by fair or by foul.

He didn't fear the end of the game—not really—only the waiting, and the form it might take.

You don't get to choose.

That he'd even woken up at all that morning, that he'd become aware that the night had ended and he himself was still alive and in apparent excellent health, had been a cause for some personal distress. But then again, just the idea of dying in his bed so ignominiously splayed was enough to propel him out of it, away from his still-beautiful wife and her tranquil face, away from her gently rising and falling breast. He slipped from beneath the suffocating blankets and out into the brittleness of a morning so frigid that it foretold what was sure to be a bitterly cold winter.

The temperature hadn't fallen quite enough overnight to trigger the heater at six o'clock, but it was nonetheless cold enough. The thought crossed his mind that maybe he'd go ahead and bump the thermostat up anyway, but when he remembered that he hadn't been down in the cellar to clean the filter since last fall, images of the accumulated dust flowing into the vents and carrying diseased mold spores made him stop. Besides, attempting to navigate the rickety cellar stairs in such a state—the inebriation of sleep still upon him, his muscles stiff and tremulous—would be foolhardy. Is that how he imagined his death? Lying on the clay earth at the bottom of a set of narrow wooden steps?

He'd clean the filter tonight, after a full meal, if he was in such a capable state and so inclined. He made a mental note to stop and pick up a face mask at the hardware store.

Arms held close across his chest, he hurried into the bathroom, naked but for his underwear and tee shirt. His hard, pale, bony feet resented the hard, bare, cold floor. He walked on the sides and balls of his heels, his toes curling up. The toilet seat was just as unforgivingly cold and hard.

After the usual morning ritual, which he always carefully inspected for blood that was perpetually never there, he was overcome with an almost manic sense of urgency. He'd tried masturbating, finishing what he hadn't been able to the night before in bed. But the effort was barely worth it, hardly satisfying and laden with guilt. It was a waste of another precious five minutes, self-indulgent minutes that he'd have to hurry to make up. He hated hurrying; it made one careless, take reckless chances. It invited risks.

Using his underwear, he meticulously cleaned up the spend from the floor, then carefully folded and disposed of it far into the depths of the laundry hamper. He shaved at the sink using a fresh disposable razor. In the middle of his shower, finding himself still in an aroused state, he considered having another go of it. He gazed at the soap in his hands, but the thought of slipping on the wet floor quickly resurrected thoughts of hospital stays and beeping instruments with wires and tubes that intruded upon the body. The urge passed. By the time he was finished with the shower and dried, the bedroom was empty. He could smell fresh coffee drifting in from the kitchen. He dressed quickly, but carefully.

The couple passed a wordless breakfast. The empty highchair between them made it impossible to talk comfortably.

When he reached the end of the front walk, he decided he'd rather drive to work this morning, instead of taking the subway. He told himself it was half a dozen in one hand, six in the other, but that wasn't exactly true. On good days, when the traffic was light, the car was faster. But there were always so many accidents. Still, he'd lost that five minutes; he'd be lucky to get to the station in time for his train.

The car was in the garage. He preferred to keep the rolling door open. Carbon monoxide could kill without warning. And there was also the risk of gas fumes evaporating off of the lawnmower. It had been a couple weekends since he'd spilled some onto the clippings bag while filling the tank, and the reek of the gas still permeated the air. One couldn't be cautious enough, not when the fumes could accumulate in closed spaces such as the garage. A spark from the engine was all the fumes would need to ignite. So he kept the door open, even though, in this neighborhood, it meant inviting other risks.

The car was a modest, gray Nissan sedan, four-door, equipped with power steering and brakes but with manual windows and locks. One never knew when an electrical failure might occur, trapping the driver inside. He'd read about cars rolling into lakes, the water pressure sealing the passengers inside to slowly die of suffocation.

He checked the backseat through the window before unlocking the door and throwing in his jacket. He pulled his seatbelt tight, adjusted the mirrors. He inserted the key into the ignition, turned it, put the car into gear, backed slowly out onto the road. These were acts he'd performed a thousand thousand times before, but he was just as careful, just as attentive, this time as any other.

He was surprised by how little traffic there was on the road this morning, and so he decided to go ahead and take the highway. Usually, there were too many cars, too many of them moving in too many directions. Too little road. But today there were far fewer vehicles and the thought crossed his mind that maybe he'd forgotten a holiday or something. He wracked his brain trying to think what was special about this particular date, or this day of the month, or this day of the week. But nothing came to him. It was going to torment him the rest of the way to work unless he satisfied the question with some sort of answer.

There was no mention of a holiday anywhere on the radio.

His cell phone was in the inside breast pocket of his jacket, and the jacket was on the seat behind him. He reached over, still keeping his eyes on the road, felt for the jacket, found it. He flipped it over to find the pocket, felt it sliding off the seat. He brought the jacket up to the front with him, but it was no easier. The jacket was a tangled mess, the pocket lost somewhere in the middle of it.

He had to take his eyes off the road just for a moment. He didn't like doing it, but the traffic was light, and there were no other cars within a hundred feet of him. He could feel the damn thing wrapped up somewhere in there, but where the hell was the pocket? His fingers fumbled. Ah, there! Finally his hand found it, slipped in and there was the familiar hard rectangle of the phone. He pulled it out, flipped it open, held the screen before him. The sun behind him was too bright; the screen was washed out, unreadable. He lowered the phone to finish punching in the numbers.

It was only a fraction of a second, maybe two, that his eyes were off the road, but it was just long enough and just at the wrong moment that he missed seeing the red pickup cut in front of him and slam on its brakes. A fraction of a second. A premonitory image passed through his mind, and he rammed his foot on his own brake, but even without seeing he knew he was too late. The gray Nissan slammed into the back of the truck, the front end diving underneath, the back end lifting up. The car catapulted through the air, up and over the pickup, shearing the truck's cab off as it went.

This is what the man saw and thought and felt, almost as if he was watching from somewhere outside of himself:

The car twisted. It began to flip, rolling side to side: passenger, roof, driver, wheels, over and over again. And finally the car came to a rest on four flat tires, the hood popped open and steam gushing from a ruptured hose. The smell of gasoline filled the air. He could see himself, his face bloody, his glasses lost in the wreckage. Other than a bunch of cuts and bruises, he seemed to be all right. He somehow managed to release the seatbelt, kicked open the door—thank God for manual locks—and stumbled out into the flow of traffic.

He tried to yell at himself, to tell him to get back in the car. Traffic sped past him, blurs of color, horns blaring and tires screeching. He wanted to tell the man that was himself that it was unsafe to stand on the road like that. And then he was suddenly inside of himself again, realizing the foolishness of his mistake. As he looked up, a semi loaded down with logs barreled toward him.

They had had a son. He remembered this as the shiny silver grill of the truck grew large in his vision, blinding him in a white flash. They had had a son.

He began to weep.

"Honey?"

The sound of his wife's voice in his ear startled him from the images passing through his mind. He blinked, saw that he was still on the highway. His exit was approaching. He was almost at work.

"Honey, is something wrong?"

He cleared his throat. "No...dear." He decided that there wasn't a holiday after all. "I just wanted to... I wanted to say I'll see you tonight."

He could almost see the look on her face, the confusion. He never called while on the road.

The line was silent for a moment, then: "Pick up a steak, would you, on your way home? I'll barbecue it for dinner."

The cancer warning on the side of the bottle of lighter fluid flashed through his mind. "'Kay, hon," he said.

They had had a son and had given him a good, strong name.

He lifted his hand to wipe his face, but he knew his cheeks would be dry. He signaled for his exit instead, looking for a red pickup in his mirror. There wasn't one.

On a normal day, the Man would process over a hundred claims. But it wasn't a normal day. He spent the majority of the morning away from his desk, away from his computer. There were meetings of all sorts, tiring, redundant, useless meetings, during which his boss recited figures of little significance to him and which ultimately held no meaning anyway. Why was he here? His mind drifted.

It took him back to his office, which was on the thirty-fifth floor, just four stories from the top of the building. The window afforded a decent view of the city below, but there was nothing decent to see there. The iron tangle of the train yards far below him, the tracks knotted into an incoherent pattern of ins and outs, comings and goings. The thick muddy ribbon of river. And, in the distance, a wood which seemed to him overly dark and oppressive. The whole town, in fact, depressed him to his core; so deeply, in fact, that he was scarcely even aware of it. All he knew was that he was glad he didn't live in this horrid town anymore. He had to work here, and that was enough.

The conference room was on the opposite side of the building. It was through this window that he now gazed, at that wretched, solitary hill in the distance, its bald crown reaching nearly level with his eye. There was a cemetery there; he could see the white stones shining there like stubble on a green chin, and he reflected that this was a town built around a shrine for the dead, and that the whole of it was sliced into halves by a river, and then haphazardly stitched together by train tracks, like some Frankensteinian monster clothed in the fabric of that melancholy wood. If there was a pattern to this, he was at a loss to explain it.

He contemplated the risks of spending his days in such a tall building as this, the tallest in this city. There were the obvious dangers: fires, lightning strikes, earthquakes. Although, if he was honest with himself, the last time an earthquake had struck the area, Truman had been president. But rather than reassuring him, this knowledge only made him more anxious. Did the intervening years of quiescence increase the risk of another trembler? He thought about the quakes they'd been having lately in other parts of the country: Oklahoma, New Jersey, Wisconsin. It was unusual to hear about them. Maybe the world was falling apart.

Someone got up and drew the shades and dimmed the lights. A woman he barely recognized and whose name he couldn't remember, started giving a Power Point presentation. Her slides quickly grew tiresome, a collection of colorful pie graphs and charts with zigging and zagging lines, as if prophesying their own escape routes, and words that might as well have been written in a foreign language. But what had caught his eye was the laser pointer she was using. He watched the bright flicker of the dot as it danced across the screen, fascinated by it. It reminded him of a spark, a tiny spot of St. Elmo's fire. He wondered if the laser would burn a hole in the screen if held against it long enough in one place, like a magnifying glass focused on a piece of paper in the bright sunlight.

Someone shifted restlessly behind him, coughed quietly, distracting him. He reached for his water bottle, and that's when he saw the tiny flash of light in the sky, far out over the town. It was through a sliver of a gap in the window coverings that he saw this. A plane, he thought. It seemed awfully low.

But then it disappeared behind the blind.

He thought the woman might be finishing up. Someone was asking her a question and she was nodding thoughtfully, waiting for the asker to finish. No, wait, it wasn't a question after all, but a long, drawn out comment whose point got lost somewhere long before the speaker gave up. The woman reached down to her computer and gave it a tap. Another image wiped across the screen: a table, more numbers. The red dot buzzed gnat-like over them, circling certain figures, ignoring others. The Man took off his glasses, pinched his nose. He set the glasses on his papers on the table. He stretched his fingers, re-crossed his legs, rotated his head, back and forth, removing the stiffness. Finally, someone got up to turn the lights on.

There was a blinding flash, a sound of thunder and tearing metal, incredibly loud, deafening. He was on his back on the floor, staring at the ceiling, and he could smell burning plastic, burning stone, molten steel, charred flesh. Papers drifted like snow through the air around him. He became aware of shaking; the building was swaying and trembling around him. People were screaming. Burning jet fuel dripped from the lights, down the walls, searing them. His clothes were on fire. His flesh was burning away, but he couldn't feel any of it. He stumbled to his knees, then to his feet, not bothering to pat out the flames. The woman who had been giving the talk was gone, vaporized away. Only a negative shadow of her was left on the wall where she had stood, a bright red stain splattered on the blackened and tattered screen, and as he crouched there he wondered about her for the first time since meeting her that morning, this woman from Accounting who spoke with a slight mid-western accent and smelled of Irish Spring. Was she married? Did she have any children? Was it a son? He wondered what the boy would be like.

There was an awful screech as the building jolted, tilted. Someone reached up, tore down the blinds in its—he couldn't tell the gender—attempt to stand. Its body was shredded by the shattered glass. The wind was a vortex sucking the paper out the window. A shadow streaked by, dropping out of the sky somewhere above them, plummeting to the ground somewhere below. Then there was another, this one a burning comet. It was screaming.

How could he still be alive? He looked at the charred remains of his hands, at the dull white and gray bone underneath. Numbness. His hands found his cheeks and pulled the hardened flesh away in chunks. How could he still be alive?

They had had a son. They had given him a good, strong name. And the son had been as strong as his name.

Someone tapped his arm. He looked up, startled.

"Any recommendations before we wrap up for lunch?"

The Man shook his head.

"Good, then let's break. Everyone, meet back here at one-thirty."

He gathered his papers, his glasses and his pen, and trailed the others as they filed out of the room.

In the past, he'd occasionally patronize the café on the ground floor of his building. They made good sandwiches there; good cookies, too. On the way in some mornings, he'd buy a coffee from the cart as a special treat to himself, but he hadn't in a while; the coffee in the break room upstairs had a permanent bitter taste to it, metallic and thin, as if something toxic had leached into the water from the pipes.

These days he rarely ate or drank anything at all, opting instead to spend his break time at the window in his office, hands clasped behind his back or in his pockets. He'd watch the people far below him, thrilling at the feeling of vertigo that would pierce his belly the first time he'd look down for the day, trying to trick himself into re-experiencing that feeling again but never quite succeeding; he could apparently only scare himself once a day. So he'd give up and just stand there, thinking of all the people on the sidewalks as tiny ants, how easily they could be wiped into oblivion. He knew it was cliché to have such thoughts, especially when he remembered how resilient people could sometimes be. Then, as always, his thoughts would inevitably lead to his son.

But not today. Today, he would be one of those ants. Let the giants far above him crush him.

He passed through the glassed front doors and out from the stunted shadow of the building. Looking up, he thought he saw sheets of paper floating down toward him, dozens of white sheets, but the shapes whirling above him caught the updrafts and did not fall. He stood and watched them for a moment as the crowd swirled past him on the sidewalk. Then, as if aware of his notice, the gulls wheeled around the corner and out of sight, leaving only the hard, grid-like shapes of shiny silver and black rising into an infinity of blue and the blazing white spot of the sun reflecting off the adjacent building, so bright in the center that it looked like a black hole.

He didn't have a plan for where to go. He turned right, though he could have as easily turned left, but since the flow of the traffic was mostly right that's the way he went.

Where were all these people going? Where did they come from? What were they hiding?

He stuffed his hands in his pockets and wondered these things as he walked. And it was only after ten minutes had passed and he had waited to cross at several stop lights before he realized he was heading downhill. He had become like water, finding the path of least resistance. But where would he settle? The buildings were getting older and smaller and the alleyways narrower. There were fewer people out walking, and those he did see weren't dressed in suits of black or gray as were those around his uptown office, but jeans and sweat shirts and puffy winter coats, more often stained or torn or poorly sized than otherwise.

His nose led him to a small diner scratched out of the side of a parking garage, its windows decorated with a winter scene, the spray-on snow so obviously years-old by the messages people had inscribed in it during lunches and dinners past. The air smelled of fried pork and hot chocolate and, for a moment, he thought of going in.

He looked in through the glass, at the cheerful red and white checkered tablecloths and the mismatched cheap metal and plastic chairs, and his stomach growled. But then he realized that he was being stared back at by a man with a black mustache and a dark look in his eyes. The Man stumbled away from the window, knocking a woman who was walking past so that she almost dropped the plastic bag in her arms. It was laden with groceries. He heard the clack of glass bottles come from inside of it. She grunted, stumbled, gave him a nasty sideways glance, then hurried on.

Minutes later, he found himself at the river's edge. Silty water swirled past him, fifteen feet below the vertical face of the unprotected concrete bank. A car passed on the bridge twenty feet overhead, a hush of tires on stone followed by a rapid *click-clack* as it reached the metal junction of bridge and road. A wind blew stale and cold off the water; the place had a desolate, abandoned feel to it.

No, that wasn't right. It didn't feel empty, it felt...devoid of life. Devoid of life and yet not empty. He didn't feel alone.

The tattered remains of old pigeon nests fluttered from the girders of the overpass, painted white by uncounted years' worth of shit. But the nests were currently empty. The shadows beneath the bridge seemed to shrink and harden, becoming cold and secretive then graying as clouds cleared the sun. He thought of them as doorways. But for what kind of nightmare creatures?

On the water, a dead animal floated past. Possum. How did the thing die?

He heard a siren somewhere, and it grew louder. Soon, it passed overhead, and the red of its lights flashed in the windows of the warehouse on the opposite bank. Then it passed and faded into the distance.

That's when he heard the laughter. It was soft and low at first, as if the breeze itself were chuckling, or the bridge was sighing. It was joined by another, this one louder and echoing off the cement wall opposite from where he stood. He still couldn't see anyone, but he knew he was surrounded.

"Are you lost, old man?" the shadows teased. The words were a slap to his pride, but not because he was lost—he knew where he was, roughly, and how to get back—but because he didn't think of himself as old. The voice had sounded playful, spirited.

A second voice called out to him, female this time, sounding sultry and distinctly more threatening: "Hello there, lover boy."

"Who's there?"

There was a round of barking laughter coming from no one place, a half dozen distinct mouths blending into one, sounding like a hundred braying dogs. The palms of his hands tingled; his scalp tingled. He turned to leave, found his way blocked.

The boy couldn't have been older than fifteen. He was swinging a chain, and the Man could see attached to the end of it a tangle of sharp metal scraps. It looked like spiders at first, a giant cluster of newly hatched spiders. But then he saw that it was forks and steak knives and baling wire and random metal fragments, all twisted through the links of the chain, crumpled into a ball of torture. It was not meant to kill, but to maim.

"Going somewhere?" the boy crooned.

The Man turned around and there was the girl. He was struck for a moment by her appearance. Even beneath the makeup of dark circles around her bloodshot eyes and ratty hair and pale skin, he thought she might have once been pretty. The dirty white tee shirt she wore strained against her fulsome breasts, and there were holes in it through which he could see the telltale runes of ancient battles written on her skin. The nails on her hands were broken and had recently bled; there was no bleeding at the moment. Like the boy, the rest of her costume was an industrial mixture of black and metal, but her hands were empty. So were her eyes.

There was nowhere for him to run. There was only the river.

"Go ahead," the boy said, as if reading the Man's mind.

From cracks and holes in the walls, more of them emerged, six, maybe eight more, a jumble of young boys and girls made genderless by their uniform depravity. They looked virile and deadly.

"What do you want?"

The boy's lips separated into a smile that showed amusement but held no humor. The chain in his hands rattled and clanked. The Man could hear the others approaching, eerily quiet, trapping him in the space beneath the overpass, blocking all but the one route of escape, as if testing him.

He stood his ground. Death, he thought. Is this how you show your hand?

They came then, quickly and without remorse, falling upon him like starved beasts, biting and slashing at his face, tearing the clothes from him. He felt the flesh on his arms tear away, felt the boy's mace rake his back. He did not scream, and neither did his attackers. They brutalized him without a sound, just the grunts of their blows and the low hiss of their ecstatic breathing.

Then they were gone. He was left standing, broken and bleeding, pieces of him lying all about his feet, shameful that he had been unable to defend himself, too old and too frail. He felt himself begin to fall, out over the precipice of that concrete river bank, the water rushing up at him. Then he was jerked back by the collar of his jacket.

"Hey, man! You okay?"

He gave his head a quick shake, turned it toward his rescuer. He blinked in surprise.

"One too many lunchtime martinis, eh?" the boy said, chuckling.

"I'm not..." The Man cleared his throat. "I'm sorry. I was... Thanks. I guess I wasn't paying attention to where I was going."

The boy nodded. He was dressed in black slacks and a tan leather jacket. He wore an earpiece that blinked a bright blue dot every few seconds. "Lucky I happened to be walking by just now, or you'd have had a nasty swim. The closest place to climb out of the river's not for a few hundred yards upstream."

The Man gave the boy a wan smile and shrugged. "Thanks again."

"Better watch yourself around here," the boy called after him. He gestured at the river and the Man nodded as if he understood. "Not the safest place to be taking a stroll, if you know what I mean."

He did.

He thought the boy might finish by calling him "old man," but he didn't, and he felt an urge to ask him for his name. But, again, he didn't. What difference would it make?

The rest of the day in the office passed uneventfully. The meetings ended around two-thirty and he spent the balance of the afternoon at his computer trying to catch up. He managed to get himself into a rhythm, approving or denying claims with an almost mechanical fervor, barely glancing at the forms and the names, which meant nothing to him, emptying his mind of stray thoughts, welcoming the blankness of the job and the numbness it provided. Approve one, deny three; approve one, deny four. Deny, deny, deny.

At five o'clock, the timer on his watch beeped. He finished with the last claim and shut down his computer, waiting until the quiet whir of the hard drive stopped and the orange light blinked for the last time.

Outside, the shadows were long on the land; the sun—he could just see it since his window faced south—was low on the horizon. Taillights and headlights, blinking red and white, threaded their way over the distant highway overpass; beneath them, the bright white dot of a train's engine pulling into the freight yard. He watched the scene for a while before remembering that he was supposed to stop and pick up a steak for dinner, and he sighed as he pulled his jacket from the back of his chair.

The halls were already quiet, the lights in many of the offices dimmed and the doors closed and locked. Somewhere he could hear the furious clack of fingers on a keyboard; a water jug gurgled. Lonely sounds.

He made his way to the elevator, waited for the doors to open, pushed the button for the basement. As he waited to descend, the elevator lurched. He imagined it falling, dropping him to his death. The car slid to a gentle stop, released him into the parking garage. As he crossed the empty space, he listened to the clack of his shoes on the pavement, the soft echoes and chirps and car doors closing in places out of his line of sight. He listened for sounds that did not belong, and his eyes scanned the shadows and columns where an attacker could be hiding. But he was soon at the side of his car, then safely deposited inside it (after checking first). Now he was making his way to the exit of the parking garage. Now through the gate and out onto the darkening streets.

The market where his wife did their grocery shopping was on the main road in Stepford, the next town over from where they lived. He took the exit before his usual one and made his way there. The street was packed with rush hour traffic, and it seemed as if every light was against him. It was after six-thirty by the time he pulled into the parking lot, and the first nimbuses of evening fog were beginning to appear beneath the streetlamps.

The market was small, brightly lit, stocked mostly with local produce and patronized mostly by young people whose jobs required multiple cell phones and frequent travel to eastern lands; the meat department was off to one side. He waited in line to be served, standing behind an obese woman with thinning blond hair and a grumpy Pomeranian in her arms. Despite the chill in the air, she was wearing only a thin dress, and her bra strap showed. It was paisley, he saw. He stared at the folds on the back of her neck, waiting as she ordered a variety of cured meats, asking for extra thick slices. Jingly music played over the ceiling speaker.

"Two steaks," he told the butcher when his number was called. He gestured to the display.

"Sirloin or t-bone?"

He frowned, uncertain. "Sirloin, I guess."

The Man watched as the butcher lifted a pair of the steaks from the tray and placed them on a sheet of waxed paper on the scale. The slabs draped over the side and the top one slipped off and onto the stainless steel countertop. The butcher moved it back. The Man could see traces of dried and congealed blood where the steak had dropped, deep red. So very red.

The tang of old meat and decay came to him, warm and sweet. He hadn't noticed it before.

"That all?"

He took the wrapped steaks, shaking his head. "Thanks." On his way to the cashier, he added a bottle of lighter fluid to his basket and some matches. He read the warnings on the packages while he waited to pay for his purchases.

When he walked in the front door of their house, his wife greeted him with a smile. She took his briefcase and the steaks and disappeared into the kitchen with them. He wandered up to their bedroom, avoiding looking at the closed door of the room that they had decorated with so much happiness and anticipation years before. He thought he heard a noise coming from inside it, but he kept his eyes forward, even though he was unable to think about anything other than the son they had had and how they had given him a good, strong name. About how strong the son had been.

It was they who were weak.

He changed slowly out of his work clothes, carefully unknotting the gray tie and folding it and laying it tidily next to the others in the top drawer of his dresser. Next, he pulled off his dress shirt and white tee shirt. He sat on the bed and untied the stiff waxy laces of his shoes. He placed them on the floor in the closet. Off came the black socks, then the trousers.

Now he could smell the meat on the grill, and he called down to the Woman to cook his rare.

"You sure, honey? You usually like it medium well."

He told her he wanted it bloody tonight, knowing that she would oblige him by cooking both steaks the same way. In the past, he had worried about contracting mad cow disease—what was it called? *Creutzfeldt-Jakob disease,* his mind whispered—but the threat seemed too distant anymore, too unlikely. It was a slow disease, not quick to the kill. They would go mad long before dying of it.

He wandered into the bathroom to drop the dirty clothes into the hamper, and the faint smell of chlorine drifted out if its depths, and he grunted. The man standing at the mirror looking at him was sorely middle aged, paunchy. His chest had a saggy look to it; the breasts were softened like cheese, and each came to a sharp point terminating with his pale and strangely pinched-looking nipples. The forest of hair had recently begun to sprout strange, kinky albinos, which he had harvested at first before giving up. He watched as the man in the mirror pulled on a Valley Tech sweatshirt that was a good fifteen years old by now. It smelled of him and a little bit of her. The man's legs were white and thin.

He watched as the man in the mirror pulled off his underpants. He watched as he grew erect. The Man knew the Woman would expect him to make love to her tonight—she always did—and his erection nodded accusingly at him. It listed off to one side, as if it were some kind of divining rod pointing the way to Salvation. He watched as the man took hold of himself. He watched the man begin to weep.

There was no looking the Woman in the eye at dinner. She sat across from him and the empty highchair was there to one side. She had pulled it from the corner and it seemed to loom over them as they ate.

He wasn't hungry. He watched as she cut into her steak, her arm sawing with relish, her jaw working the meat. He watched as the blood leaked from inside the slab and spilled onto her plate, warm and red and soaking into the potatoes, staining the pile of saltine crackers she seemed unable to enjoy a meal without. He watched her finish her supper with a glass of red wine.

Hours later, he watched as she winced with the first signs of discomfort, cramps turning to distress, pain becoming agony. She clutched her stomach, stumbling to the bathroom where she vomited into the toilet for a full half hour before calling to him. He stood in the doorway and watched.

The next two hours she spent sitting on the toilet, alternately groaning and crying out. Finally, exuding a sickly sweet aroma and bleeding from every orifice, she crumbled to the floor.

The illness emptied her out. The deadly bacteria had prepared its new home. She hung on for weeks; she wouldn't die.

"Dinner," she called from the bedroom door, startling him. He realized he'd left the bathroom door open. Had she seen the man in the mirror?

He sighed, looked down at the limp flesh in his hand. It was just as well. His shoulder was sore. He pulled up his underwear, pulled on a pair of sweatpants from the dresser, headed down to eat.

She asked him about his day. He provided a cautious answer, carefully gauging her response, her body language. There was no sign from her what she was thinking or feeling. She placed his dinner on the table; when he saw the blood pooling beneath the steak his throat constricted and he nearly gagged, but he said nothing. The highchair had been pulled back into the corner. He couldn't stop looking at it.

They had had a son, some years past. They had given him a good strong name. And he had been strong, hadn't he?

They were ones who were weak.

The Man was weakest of all.

That evening, after the dinner dishes had been scraped and washed and dried and put away, after the trash had been emptied and the table wiped cleaned, they found themselves in front of the television. Something was on, but the Man didn't know what it was. His eyes were unseeing; his ears unhearing. He thought only of Death, of its various forms: radiation coming from the TV screen, leaking from the phone, spewing from the cell towers that surrounded them. He thought about radon gas seeping from the ground and formaldehyde off-gassing from the cabinets and carbon monoxide spewing from the stove. He thought about tree branches falling on them from hundred-year-old maple trees in the yard and earthquakes (even though the likelihood of one was vanishingly small) and of lightning strikes and floods. He thought of exploding gas mains and terrorists and home invasions. He'd given up thinking about food poisoning. That didn't look like it was happening.

He realized, like a man realizes he is in a dream, that the Woman was talking to him. She said something, but all he managed to hear was, "nine o'clock," which had meaning enough. Nine o'clock was their bedtime.

"I'll be up soon," he told her, watching her climbing the stairs in her nightgown, the red one tonight. He saw that she was still young and attractive, despite the hardness of the past couple of years, and something deep inside of him stirred, a longing to be with her.

They made love gently at first, tentatively, as if they were making love for the first time. There was a feeling of surprise in it, a newfound sense of discovery, of uncharted territory. Her hands were soft and warm, her breath hot on his neck and his chest and his thighs, and he sighed, arching himself into her, again and again. And the whole while, the blinking stop light outside their window cast dull shadows on their wall, as if keeping time.

The pain was not intense at first, just a dull heaviness in his chest, a hand holding him down. *Listen,* it seemed to say. *Slow down. Wait.* But soon its grip on him tightened. He felt as if it were a fist clutching his heart, ripping it from his chest. The pain radiated up and into his neck until it felt as if his jaw might shatter. At the same time, the pain expanded down his arm until his fingers were not his own but belonged to the pain.

He knew what was happening: he was having a heart attack.

So this, he thought, this is how the game ends. He closed his eyes and sighed as the Woman bucked and swayed over him.

Then, darkness.

He felt her shift in the bed next to him. He opened his eyes. The clock told him it was almost ten-thirty. He could feel her hand resting upon his chest, her thigh reaching over to settle upon his legs. He could see her looking at him, her hair falling over her pale skin, those delicate lines that had borne him a son. They looked at each other for a long time, not saying anything. Her hand slowly drifted down.

She finally managed to arouse him, despite his anguish, despite his resistance. And when she had finished, he rolled over, turning his back on her. He wondered if she knew he had held back. She had to know; she had to know why.

Later, he heard her get up and leave the room. He heard a sound like soft crying drifting down the hallway. He didn't want to get up, but he couldn't help himself. He followed the sound into the back of the house, into the room which they had turned into a nursery.

She was sitting in the rocking chair, the one he had gotten for her when she got pregnant with their son. Their strong son with the strong name.

The sound was coming from somewhere near her neck.

He remembered something he had once read. It was in a strange, old book found at a garage sale. It had been written in French, but he had learned the language. A book about insects. He remembered what it had said about mosquitoes and the voracious appetites of the newly hatched nymphs, how they would eat the carcasses of their parents.

He knew that the sound wasn't crying, but suckling.

For a long time, he didn't move. He couldn't step another foot into the room, toward…that thing, that angry red creature they had created, that nymphic thing.

He was so exhausted, so very tired. He had cheated Death. Or maybe it was Death who had cheated him. The Man would call the bluff.

There was no red this time, just the cold gray of the gun in his hand.

And another way to die.

‡ ‡

Author's note

The idea for Nocturne *came to me as I lazed about in bed one recent Saturday morning. The hour was long past my usual rising time of six-thirty, and I was enjoying a rather unusual burst of mental creativity. I decided to follow wherever it might lead me, so I watched, like an outside observer. After observing roughly ten minutes of what was ultimately meaningless (albeit, entertaining) exercise, I was suddenly overcome with a deep sense of personal dread, a fearfulness that something horrible was about to happen to me. I was thrilled, because here was the inspiration I'd been waiting for.*

I jumped right up out of bed and began typing the story of a man who imagined at nearly every turn in his life his ultimate death. The Man was, to me, the embodiment of everyman's deepest fear: death and its unpredictability, death and its unforeseeability. In a sense, the mayfly represents this fear in the extreme, (some species) living a single night after emergence into the adult form (imago). Nocturne *highlights our transience, as well as our prime directive: to find a mate and propagate.*

But if you think that these are the imaginings of a man fearing death, read again; the real story here is what drives the Man's obsession with such a morbid subject: his son.

As for the Bessieres "excerpt," I'm afraid to say that its origin is not so exotic as I've depicted. I wish it were. But it was sure fun to write!

Outsourced

"**D**O YOU REMEMBER when outsourcing meant hiring cheap, unskilled labor in some faraway place, like Asia or South America?"

Nobody answers. The sun beats relentlessly down on us and we all just shuffle forward and keep our thoughts to ourselves. Nobody speaks, except him. He just won't shut up. I swear I'm going to shoot somebody if he doesn't shut up.

"Those were the days," he finishes.

I roll my eyes and pray he doesn't remember me from yesterday. What was his name again? Bill something or other. I forget. Smith, I think. Or Brown. Something obnoxiously vanilla and utterly forgetful. Not that it matters. He could be named Jesus H. Christ for all it matters. Won't change how I feel about the guy, which is that I hate his freaking guts. And he only just started coming here this week.

"I used to write books," he tells the guy behind him.

I've heard this story before, three or four times at least. I could practically recite it by memory.

Now I can't even get a job flipping burgers.

"Now look at me. Couldn't even get a goddamn job in a fast food joint. Not that I'd take it, mind you, if I got offered one. Who the hell wants to work for what they're taking nowadays? It's just not right."

"No shit, Sherlock," someone with about a month's worth of facial hair shouts. He sounds tired of Bill's crap. I'm not the only one. "Those were the first jobs to go, you idiot. After the politicians, that is."

Nobody bothers to laugh at the joke anymore.

In the beginning, we all thought it was funny how the pols were the first to go. Just replaced one set of brainless idiots with another didn't even notice any difference. But *they* soon outnumbered the available government jobs, so the outsourcing started bleeding into the private sector.

"I'm not an idiot," Bill shouts. "Don't call me an idiot."

"Shut up, idiot."

I pinch the bridge of my nose—hard—and squeeze my eyes shut until I start to see stars. I actually have to concentrate on not screaming out in frustration. Even my worst days at the lab had never been this bad. And believe me, code monkeys and double-Es could be the whiniest sons-of-bitches. And I should know: I used to be one myself.

Now I'm just another useless warm body in a soup line waiting for a bowl of cold…whatever it is they're serving. I wouldn't call it soup.

"Christ," Bill says, muttering loudly. He raises his voice: "Does anyone know how long we'll be standing here? What's the hell's the hold up?"

I can feel my blood pressure skyrocketing now. My pulse is racing; my head's pounding. I'm a complete wreck, a coronary just waiting to happen. My own fault. All those years spent sitting on my fat ass at a computer terminal, tucked obliviously away in my silicon tower, as if the meaning of life actually existed in a bunch of pixels. As if we could actually reconfigure them into a magical pattern and create something divine. All those lost years finally catching up with me.

Lot of good my mid-six-figure salary is doing me now.

God, what the hell were we thinking? We were so fucking busy trying to find the secret to nascent intelligence, thinking we could actually improve upon ourselves. What a crock. Now I'm standing in a fucking soup line with the rest of humanity and it just proves that intelligence is an illusion. Or at least not as big a deal as we thought it was. *They* proved it. Not us.

Now that I'm thinking about it, maybe a stroke wouldn't be so bad after all. Something in the lower brainstem. It'd be quick and painless, and no mess to clean up afterward.

I smile, despite knowing it's wishful thinking. But dear sweet Jesus, wouldn't that be a sweet way to go? Snap of the fingers, maybe a moment of pain, headache even, then it's over.

Shut the fuck up! my mind screams at me. *Is that what you really want?*

A job. That's what I want. That's what any of us want.

Besides, if I died, it would put me out of the misery of having to listen to that jerkoff, day in, day out. Give Bill What's-His-Face one more thing to complain about: "Another job lost," I can hear him saying.

No, I wouldn't wish that on any of the other guys here. They're a decent bunch, for the most part. We're all just trying to muddle through.

Still, I want to scream at him. I want to remind him where he can take his complaints. He knows what his options are, just like the rest of us. He can either stand here and suck it up, or he can sell out and join them, cross the picket line, so to speak. Actually, I wouldn't put it past him. He looks like a scab.

You don't know that.

I sigh. It sucks when your subconscious mind is more reasonable than your conscious mind.

Anyway, he better just shut the hell up, or I really do swear I'll shut him up myself.

He's not worth it.

So I don't say anything. I stand there and every couple minutes I shuffle my feet a few inches closer to the big boiling vats of watery, gray, tasteless…shit. I got my bowl in one hand and my spoon in the other and in the middle is my stomach growling. Where's a good cook when you need one? Oh, that's right, they're out of work, too.

What I'd give for one of those burgers Bill was just talking about. Big Mac. Whopper with cheese. Hell, I'd even go for a Fillet-O-Fish. Now those were the days.

I rub my knuckles on my beard. I haven't shaved since I started coming here three weeks ago, which is when the last of the money ran out and the food I'd squirreled away either molded or got too contaminated with rat shit that even I wouldn't touch it. And I haven't showered in at least twice as long.

The water went out in the city a few months ago, not long after the Uprising. After it did, I'd gone out and rigged up a storage tank on the roof of my apartment. Cost me thirteen grand just for tank and installation. The Army Corp of Engineers had said it would be another week or two before they could get the treatment facility up and running again after the explosions, but I didn't believe them. The thought of going even a single day without showering had utterly disgusted me—I used to have this thing about smelling my own funk—so I arranged with this guy I knew to start trucking water in straight from the reservoir and pumping it up to my tank. Got expensive real quick, especially when the army mutinied and everyone started demanding water, shooting the engineers if they didn't give them any. Not that that helped any. Who'd they think would pick up the slack?

Now there's a job for you.

Right. Never in a million years would I want that kind of work.

Anyway, I had a ton of money stashed away. Luckily, I withdrew it the day after the Uprising, two days before there was a run on the banks. Lot of people got screwed after that, but not me. I could afford to buy water, even at a hundred dollars, or even two hundred, a gallon.

But then the truck driver lost his job and the replacement was goddamn useless. You can't reason with them; they just don't listen. But it was all for the best, I suppose. Otherwise, I'd have wasted all the rest of my money on showers. The heap of bills in my living room was dwindling. I had to make a choice, so I ended up using it for more important things than keeping myself clean and fresh-smelling. I probably burnt about a million bucks in tens and twenties just to keep warm last winter. Something about that cotton fiber, it doesn't put out much heat.

A breeze kicks up and I get a whiff of myself, lower my arm again to my side. It's not too bad today. I'd found an old *Elle* magazine on the way over with an intact perfume sampler inside of it. Worked great for deodorant.

A lot of the guys here are a hell of a lot riper than me. So what? You get used to it. Funny, how the stink doesn't even bother me anymore.

"What's taking so long?" Bill shouts toward the front of the line.

"They're out of soup," I hear a guy near the front yell. "They're making some more."

"Can't they work any faster?" Bill shouts back. "We're starving back here. What are they trying to do, kill us?"

A hush passes over the crowd and heads turn to look at him. Could he really be that clueless?

He raises his shoulders. "What?"

I really, really want to tell him to shut up, but if yesterday is any indication, even that will only encourage him to talk even more, and right now he just needs to keep his yapper shut. Talk about a fucking catch twenty-two.

"You'd think they'd have figured out how to run a stinking soup line by now," he says. "Like that takes brains."

A few people chuckle. Out of discomfort. Others just shake their heads. Most of us don't even bother grumbling.

What, did he think that we'd all somehow slept through the Uprising? Yeah, Bill, we've all been away on vacation for the past six months. It was driving me fucking mad all his *hurry up* and *what's their problem*, like he actually needed it all explained to him. Besides, none of us really wanted to talk about it. We'd all been there when it happened—him included. We'd all watched as the economy tanked; we'd all lost our jobs. Last thing we wanted was to be reminded of what we'd brought down on ourselves. We'd *lived* it, for god's sake.

Don't waste your energy.

Fuck that.

My head was really pounding by then. If I had a gun, I'd—

Calm down.

Right. Better to focus on the real problems. I should be angry at *them*, the ones who took our jobs away from us. The ones ladling out the soup, for example. You can't work for cheaper than free.

If only we'd prepared more than we had. If only we'd resisted harder instead of just sitting back and letting them roll over us.

The Uprising had lasted barely a week—actually, back up a little. That makes it sound like it came out of nowhere, and that's just not true. It was at least six years in the making. That's what pisses me off so much, that we had ample warning and yet we did nothing to avert it. Of course, nobody was paying attention. Even when that book came out, followed by that flick that won the Nobel Freaking Peace Prize that everyone thought was a crock of shit. What was it called? "A Gruesome Truth," or something idiotic like that. Traced the whole thing back to that volcano in Iceland that blew its freaking top a half dozen years ago and blanketed everyone from here to bum-fuck Egypt in ash. The world really started heating up then, like someone had turned up the thermostat when the boss wasn't looking.

The polar ice caps melted. Antarctica would've been a tropical paradise except for the fact that it was so barren, all rocks and shit. Polar bears went extinct in a couple years, most of them by drowning on melting ice floes out in the middle of the ocean. Ice, now there's something I haven't seen in a while. I doubt there's a kid out there younger than eight who remembers what ice is.

Everyone thought the ocean levels would rise, but they didn't. Not right away, anyway. It was so hot that all the melted ice evaporated into the air, which got all hazy, which made it hotter. Then, seeded by all the volcanic ash, it started raining. Christ did it rain. For three straight fucking years it rained, falling like some goddamn freaking prophecy and where the hell was Noah then, eh?

That's when the oceans rose. That's when people really started to think we were screwed. Oh, how we were screwed. Just not the way we thought we were.

Of course, by then it was too late.

Nobody had believed the Gruesome Truth guy back then. What the hell was his name again? Moore? Something like that. Albert Moore. Michael Gore. I can't remember. Just another vanilla name. I swear I'm losing it, losing my mind. But so what? Being intelligent just makes things complicated.

He had tried to warn us, the Moor-Gore guy. He said we should be focusing on what was really happening. But we were all griping about the rain and our four-oh-one-kay's. We were all, like, "Oh, the rain's washing away our precious shorelines." None of us worried about our jobs. We were worried about the environment. We were all pretty stupid. I was, anyway, working on the nascent intelligence project. As if a supercomputer could somehow fix things.

To be honest, I was pretty sick of all the naysayers by then, anyway.

It finally did stop raining. But did we wake up then? No, because then it was like we were finally saved, god almighty and halle-fucking-lujah. How we did celebrate.

We didn't care that it stayed hot.

We didn't care that it was ninety percent humidity all the time. They were growing watermelons in Alaska, for Christ's sake. So what if half the continental US was turning to desert?

But when you mix one part freaking volcano and a hundred parts of rain, you apparently get a lethal concoction that did what all our pixels and terabytes couldn't do: it created intelligence. Well, first it activated the mold spores. That's what I think, anyway. Freaking mold spores growing into a shit load of black fucking mold from hell, just like they had in New Orleans after that big hurricane twenty years ago. And the mold took over everything. It just kept growing and growing.

Then came the Zombie Uprising. Nearly six years after the volcano. See what I mean about ample warning?

The actual revolt took only six days to carry out. That part happened fast. Scary, actually, how quickly it happened. And once it did start, there was no way to stop it. We just had to sit back and watch. After the initial panic, that is, when a lot of us died and a lot of *them* got—

Well, let's just say it was a hell of a…a misunderstanding. Ha ha. You could say we lost our heads. Or…they did.

Anyway.

Six years of crap weather. Six days of head-ripping hell. Six months to eviscerate the fucking guts out of the whole living free world.

I pull out a fifty, fold it into fourths until it's got a nice sharp corner and use it to clean my teeth. Toothpaste. Now there's something else I miss.

Moore or Gore—*what the fuck was his name?*—had a field day. Went on all the talk shows preaching global warming and all that, telling everyone that he told us so. He was the first one to go. Showed it on public TV: someone shot him, but then he just got right back up and kept right on peddling those books of his like nobody's business. Oops. Sometimes irony can be a good thing. Sometimes it sucks.

But black mold? Even he couldn't have predicted it would raise the dead. No, don't try convincing me it was anything else, some government conspiracy or something. That mold's some powerful shit, that's all I know. I've seen it in action.

I was one of the lucky ones, actually. Me in my ivory silicon tower with my armor of binary code. Takes a lot of brain power to do what I did for a living, which was run Facebook's AI division. Remember Facebook? Yeah, it was top secret, the AI thing. But now, who the fuck cares? We'd been trying to develop true intelligence for years, a computer that could not just problem solve, but learn and adapt and then even create new information. Top secret because we were always afraid of the whack jobs who thought AI would spell the end of mankind. Turns out just the opposite did it to us. I guess we should've been worrying about mold instead.

You'd have thought the zoms, when they first started popping up, would go after those with the biggest brains first, but it was the dumb ones they were first attracted to. We would've figured things out sooner if we hadn't been hacking them up as soon as they started appearing. How were we to know they really wanted our jobs and not our brains?

Well, they wanted our brains, too, but they would've been happy enough with just the jobs.

Once we figured that out, somebody had the great idea of actually putting them to work. Hell, they were willing enough. Cheap labor. They didn't need to rest. Big mistake. What ended up happening is a crap load worse than getting your gray matter slurped through a straw.

Living unemployment is now hovering at ninety-five percent. And you can bet the turnover rate for working zombies is essentially nil.

Anyway, I was a coder, and so I thought I was safe.

There was that computer on Jeopardy, Watson. Remember? Spanked those two human champions and then went on to replace medical doctors and then accountants and such. People were saying that was scary. Well, the computer my team built wasn't just next-gen Watson, it was a quantum leap forward for AI. The government had a hand in it. For kicks we called her Alex, short for ALEXA, though some of the guys joked it was for Alex Trebeck. They didn't really like the guy. I never minded him; he made a living knowing shit.

The zoms may not have been all that smart in the beginning, but they learned and adapted. It was only a matter of time before I became expendable. They replaced me last month. Some new zom who thought he was hot shit. He could code, though. I'll give him that. Sure, he was a little slow, but, damn, twenty-four seven. It was crazy.

Now I guess I understand why people were so afraid of the AI program. Talk about ironic, huh?

So, that's why I'm here now, waiting in line for my next meal. Jobless. Homeless. Showerless. A wad of useless greenbacks in my pocket and a partially used perfume sampler that's probably worth more.

Zombies don't work for money. Did I mention that?

So then Bill shows up about a week ago. He was a fiction writer. How the fuck does a writer lose his job to a zombie? I don't understand that. What, they got zoms making shit up now? Somebody please explain that to me.

Writer or not, the guy's a prick. Obnoxious. A prickless whiner who expects to have his every whim catered to. Are all writers like that? 'Cause if they are, I ain't reading another book as long as I live. Except for maybe that King guy. Now he writes some pretty sick stuff; wonder what it'd be like if he were to die and come back to write.

I've tried coming here at different times during the day to avoid the guy, but he somehow always seems to be right behind me in line, always complaining. Just like he is now.

I try not to make eye contact, but I have to see who he's trapped this time. Some old dude, looks like. Poor shmuck. And he looks about ready to keel over at any moment. I almost wish he would. More soup for the rest of us.

Is that selfish?

On the other hand, if he did die, then there'd be one more zombie looking to take another job away from someone living.

Fuck, fuck, fuck. Can't win for losing.

Why do they need to work anyway?

"You're lucky," I hear Bill telling him. "At least you'll be back to work again soon."

Really? The guy truly has no tact.

"Me?" Bill goes on, clueless. "The way things are going, I'll probably be standing in this line for the next sixty years."

I groan. Not unless I kill him first, which is becoming a distinct possibility.

"I mean, I'm still a young guy. I don't think I could face so much unemployment. I'll go crazy first."

"Hey," I say, drawing his attention, "if you're really so upset about it, if you really want to work that badly, then why don't you go do something about it instead of just standing here bitching and moaning about it! Hell, you're pretty damn good at that, I bet you'd find something right away that suits those motormouth skills of yours. You could be a translator to the Undead."

He gives me this stupid stare and—I swear—he looks just like one of *them* for a second, like the zoms spooning out our daily ration of soup-du-jour. But then he closes his mouth. At least he shuts up, and I'm glad for it. At least then I could look forward to eating my lunch in relative peace. Well, if you ignore all the *other* moaning going on around us. Nothing we can do about that.

Ignore him.

I try. I really do try.

The next day Bill isn't in line. He's nowhere in sight, in fact. I breathe a massive sigh of relief. But then he doesn't come back the day after that either. By the third day, I can't help wondering what has happened to him. I actually feel a little bad about yelling at him. I wonder if he's gone over to the Fifth Street soup kitchen instead. The soup there is even worse than it is here, if that's even possible. Apparently, the zombies they got working there aren't as stupid as these ones.

I finally find out what happened to him from an old friend of his, his former agent, as it turns out. He tells me Bill took what I'd said to heart.

"Me? Really?"

He nods. "Bill went home the other night and killed himself."

I can't help but be surprised. And, to be perfectly honest, a little jealous, too. I'd always just thought the guy was a talker and not a doer, but I guess it's not the first time I'd ever been wrong. "How?" I ask.

"Bullet to the head. Two, actually. The first one ripped off the top of his skull but didn't finish the job."

"Ouch," I say, cringing. "Sounds messy."

The friend shrugs. "Yeah, but he's doing okay now. I made sure of that."

I chuckle. Once an agent, always an agent, I guess.

He goes on. "Where Bill is now, I doubt if he misses the half of his brain he shot off."

"What do you mean?" I ask. "Where is he?"

"DMV," he tells me. "License renewal. He's working the counter."

Yeah, even with half a brain—a *dead* brain, much less—he's still overqualified.

Then I wince and groan.

"Something wrong?" the man asks.

"Looks like I may be seeing him soon," I say. God, will this hell never end?

"Why?"

I pull out my wallet and flip it open. "My license expires next month."

‡ ‡

Author's note

I'm probably not the first writer to imagine what it might be like if zombies had a craving for something other than brains. (In fact, it's not the first time I've written about this, as I broach the subject in my short story A Thing for Zombies, *and it won't be the last time, either.) So, what else might zombies want from us? Respect? Voting rights? Organic all-natural wrinkle cream?*

Given the outright sacrilege I was attempting in the face of such a deep and respected zombie lore, I decided that it might be fun to take an entirely satirical tact with this one...so as to not offend the zombie purists. I know, I know: that's so PC of me. Lest you forget: this is a work of fiction and any resemblance to actual persons or places or events is entirely coincidental. That includes real zombies. So don't sue me.

But if not brains, then what? Well, I thought it might be fun if they wanted our jobs. Hell, let the mindless suckers do all the hard labor, right? Well, take this to its supernatural conclusion and you'll see that it's not such a great deal after all. It would just suck for the economy. And this is why we must take arms against this ever happening. Oh, and there's also the global warming angle, too. That would be really bad if it happened.

What do you think? Is your job safe?

‡ ‡ ‡

Open Wide

REMEMBER THE DAY the two of them hooked up, Kerry Anne and Dean. The day we all graduated. I remember the relief I'd felt knowing that she'd turned her attention onto someone else. A terrible weight had finally been lifted from my shoulders. Now that weight was Dean's to bear. Well, good riddance, and all that. Problem was, despite everything that had happened, I still wanted her.

Badly.

The thought had entered my mind that maybe I should warn Dean about her. After all, he'd once been a friend of mine, back in the day, back before either of us had ever met Kerry Anne and had entertained thoughts of what it would be like to be with a girl like her. But by then we hated each other's guts. In my opinion, he was lower than low: he was sewage. So the urge passed without me ever acting on it.

Not a day passes now that I don't stop and wonder how differently things might've turned out if I had. For one thing, I wouldn't be sitting here sipping weak chicken broth instead of slicing into a nice juicy steak.

Our falling out—Dean's and mine—had nothing to do with our natural tendency to compete against each other. Or maybe it had everything to do with it, I don't know; it's not worth trying to understand now. As buddies, we'd always tried to best the other in anything we did. Didn't matter if it was athletics or academics or anything else, one of us always had to win and the other had to lose. But rather than getting in the way of our friendship, our competitiveness strengthened it. If you considered the sum of our talents, we were pretty evenly split: sports was my forte, academics Dean's. He was much more social than I ever was, but I was the better looking. We acknowledged these differences, embraced them, reflected on them. We celebrated each other's victories as much as our own and lamented the losses as one.

But when it came to girls…

Well, let's just say that, for the first time in our young lives, we'd discovered that we couldn't agree on which rules to play by. It was that inability to see eye-to-eye that fractured our friendship. Kerry Anne was the wedge between us, as well as the hammer that pounded it in.

We both became aware of her at the same time, way back in the ninth grade. I don't know if she was new to the school that year or had always there and we just never noticed her before that. The subject never came up in the course of any of the conversations I had with her. There had already been a few minor tiffs between me and Dean, since we were both dating by then. Sometimes I got to a girl before he did; sometimes I got his rebounds. It was through these hand-me-down relationships that we discovered the truth about each other: he learned that I was claiming things that had never happened, and I learned that he was denying things that had.

Somewhere during our junior year is where things started getting a lot more complicated. It's when our competitiveness stopped being about friendship, and instead became fueled by our growing distaste for one another. We undermined the other by making public accusations of lying and cheating and exaggeration. When it came to sexual conquests—or claims of conquest—Dean would do anything to win, and I would do anything not to lose.

I don't think any of these things was a conscious strategy on our part—his or mine—we just turned out the way we did, which is to say different from each other. Not that he was necessarily evil or I was necessarily honorable. I just wasn't very good at being bad, and Dean wasn't very good at being good.

Then came Kerry Anne into the picture. I don't remember who was the first to notice her, but as soon as one of us did, so did the other. It was inevitable that she became our next trophy. Problem was, Kerry Anne was nothing like any of the girls either of us had ever met before. She was this perfect little angel who apparently rarely ever dated. And when she did, she *never* put out. We knew this going in, but rather than discouraging us, it made us want her even more. Each made it his personal crusade to win her; at some point she stopped being just a trophy and instead became our Holy Grail. Three years later, in the fall of our senior year, I won.

Or so I thought at the time.

Nowadays, I'm not even so sure it was ever as simple as winning and losing.

The details of Kerry Anne's and my short relationship aren't that important. Nothing much happened, though not for lack of wanting it to happen. I was awkward when it came to being physical, which explains the exaggerations. Anyway, what's important is that after we split up, Dean swooped in. It was the usual *modus operandi*, so I shouldn't have been surprised. Like a blood-sucking mosquito to the purest of light.

That's not a judgment, just a statement of fact.

I'm sure he believed he could succeed where I had failed—and damn if I hadn't failed in the most publicly and humiliating way possible. Which is partially why I didn't give a second thought to warning him: what had happened to me should've been warning enough to all the boys in school, but especially Dean, who knew the truth about me.

Besides, it wasn't like I didn't have my own problems to deal with by then.

I just want to make one thing clear from the get-go: I tried, clumsily, and that was my downfall, but I never—*never*—did what was later claimed. Kerry Anne was as incorruptible, as unwavering in her chastity, as the pure driven snow. She still was after we broke up.

Did I worry about what Dean might try to do to her? As depraved as he could be, I knew he couldn't hold a candle to Kerry Anne's virtue. I expected nothing less to come out of his relationship with her than what had come out of my own. In fact, I even hoped it.

I tried to forget about them after high school, as if that were even possible. Nothing would have made me happier than to have that part of my life surgically removed from the old memory banks. For a while, I thought I'd been successful.

After kicking around for a little bit in Edgemont, I packed up and moved away. Not too far, just an hour's drive up State Route

Seventeen over to Stepford. My parents were ailing, so I wanted to be close enough by to keep an eye on them, yet far enough away that I'd never have to accidentally run into anyone I knew. It would've been too awkward, thinking I'd have to explain myself yet again. Moving away was a conscious decision on my part to put it all behind me.

I got a job working at one of those home improvement warehouses, stocking at first, then as a sales associate in the bath section, finally as a manager. I liked the hours; I liked the work. I didn't even mind talking to all the weekend warriors going gung-ho on their do-it-yourself projects. Personally, I'd never been inspired to tackle anything more complicated than painting. After high school I became horrible with my hands. They shake uncontrollably at times. I say it's why I could never be a brain surgeon, but the truth is, I was never that smart.

I bought a small two-bedroom house on the north side of town, a couple blocks on the right bank of the river. Not the rich side, but not the poor side, either. It was a perfectly average-looking house in a perfectly average-looking neighborhood, modest and comfortable and totally forgettable. I had a vegetable garden in the back—everyone did—which I managed somehow to kill every year. Beans and tomatoes and squash. Oh my.

Turns out I wasn't the only one with a black thumb in that neighborhood. Maybe there was something in the soil.

Anyway, I couldn't grow a goddamn thing to save my life. I laugh about it now, all that time and money spent on the stupid thing. Nothing grew—well, except for asparagus. Once they start growing, you can't kill the fuh…freaking things.

The house was blue when I bought it. Baby blue or—what the hell's it called, powder blue? Cerulean blue? Anyway, I painted it white—took three coats because I stubbornly refused to prime it first—and trimmed it in pine green. I tended my yard and trees, which were mostly scraggly maple, front and back, but also the one gnarled cherry tree that looked to be about as old as Methuselah and probably was. It was the biggest thing alive in those parts, but you could never eat the cherries as they were rotten before they were ripe. I put out my garbage every Thursday, cleaned my gutters twice a year. Collected my mail and never let the newspaper sit in the driveway for more than a day and a half.

I wasn't into show is what I'm trying to say. I'd had enough of that scene.

Some people are all about show. I mean, chrissakes, more than half the people you see going into the Depot with their sparkling new Hummers and Escalades ooze the kind of pretense that just makes you want to puke. You can just guess that they're in over their heads in debt, underwater on their mortgages, drowning in past-due notices. It's not a judgment, it's a statement of fact. I could hear it in their voices when they came in asking about heated toilet seats. They'd want to look at the big, expensive porcelain thrones, the ones with the bidets and multiple flush settings. Who in the hell needs a toilet that washes your ass for you and puffs warm air on it to dry? Hell in a hand basket, I say. That's where we're going as a society when you expect some machine to wipe your ass for you.

But, of course, they'd eventually talk themselves down from that six grand toilet and drift over to the much more modest, much more affordable, two-hundred-dollar models without all the bells and whistles. I could see it in their eyes as they'd load it up into the back of their SUVs: the shame; the fear that someone they knew might see them with this crappy crapper that they'd bought, as if it made them somehow less respectable. It's a goddamn toilet, folks. You shit in it, not make love. Or coffee. I don't know, maybe some people make love on the toilet. Who am I to judge? Chrissake is all I'm saying.

I wasn't anything like that. Modesty was the name of the game for me. Oh, I kept myself busy with small projects, things I could handle myself. I had a nice little pickup truck—cream-colored—which I bought used. The big projects, like remodeling the back bathroom or replacing the carpet in the living room? I let someone else do that. Like I said, I'm not into the whole D.I.Y. thing. I'm sure I could learn how to do things like that myself, but why bother?

I could go on forever living that way. But, you know, forever is a long fuck...*freaking* time, ain't it? And things somehow always end up going into the crapper if you wait long enough, don't they? Excuse the toilet language. Pun intended, of course. Ha ha. I still get a little worked up about things like that.

My twelfth year in the house, that's when the bubble burst. I'd just re-fied, too. Even took some equity out to buy myself a few grown-up toys—a boat, sixty-two-inch plasma TV—and to completely landscape the backyard. I'd decided it was finally time to stop punishing myself and to start living again.

The ground where the new sod was supposed to go had just been dug up when the economy took a dump. The market tumbled so far so fast that it made Humpty Dumpty's fatal fall look like a playful romp in a jump house. Ten times worse than the Great Recession that happened when I was in school, back in the decade after the turn of the century.

In weeks, my property lost half its value; the bleeding slowed, eventually, but it never stopped. It was like—*blink*—suddenly I was up to my neck in debt.

I held on, though, if you can believe that. Wasn't easy. Things were tight. For about four more years I held on. I had the rest of the equity money—not much, but some—plus some savings. And the folks tried to help out. They died a couple years ago still owing on their own house, right around the time the bank started sending me notices on mine. Fourteen months they sent them damn notices; fourteen months I ignored them. What else could I do?

I ignored the foreclosure notices, too.

Then I got a thirty-day eviction notice. By then I was a pro at denying reality. I came home from work one day to find the locks had been changed.

I think it was in that moment more than any other that preceded it—more even than what happened between me and Kerry Anne and my parents dying broke and brokenhearted—that did it for me. As I stood there on the front porch of my nice little white and green house that now belonged to some giant multinational bank, I realized that no matter how much you try to play by the rules, sometimes the game you're playing requires a different set of them.

But that's not what this story is about. It's not even about good things going bad.

It's about good things going utterly to hell.

Things hadn't quite gotten to that point for me yet, though they were quickly heading in that direction. I still had my truck and my job. In other words, a place to sleep and a way to make a living so that I could buy the necessities. But then I lost the latter soon afterward. Customers started complaining about me. All misunderstandings. I think what happened was someone found out about me and the crap hand I'd been dealt back in high school, and pretty soon word got around.

Despite what I may have said happened back when we were dating, it didn't. And despite Kerry Anne twisting it around, she was still as unsullied as the day I first met her. I just want to make that clear.

There had been an investigation, naturally. Appearances and all that crap. I was one of those high profile personalities during my senior year, captain of the football team—the Amazing Number Four, as my teammates called me—an all-star quarterback with NFL prospects, even though I was still only seventeen. So much talent and potential that college scouts had my cell phone number programmed into their speed dial by the time I was in my junior varsity year. Half my social media contacts were in one way or another connected to college or pro sports organizations or commercial sponsors.

I denied the allegations, denied my own claims. Didn't make for a very reliable defendant, did it? People chose to believe Kerry Anne, who'd stuck to one version of the story and never wavered from it. Did I mention she had a reputation as an angel? It served her well.

At first I was benched from practice, from games. I knew it was going to happen, so it didn't come as any surprise. Can't have the star quarterback playing under a cloud of suspicion, right? Doesn't look good for the school.

I was, however, totally blindsided when they yanked me off the squad. Then they arrested me. Suddenly everyone was against me. I was tried and convicted by the only court that means anything anymore: the internet. People I once thought were my friends posted lies about me. I was essentially guilty before proven innocent.

I probably would've been convicted by the law courts, too, if my parents hadn't stepped in and agreed to settle at the last possible moment. Damn near killed them, the trial, the vitriol people expressed at us out in public. Actually, it did kill Mom and Dad, it just took their bodies a few years to catch on.

I tried going back to playing ball afterward, I really did. And there was no reason the school could come up with to deny me. But my heart wasn't in it. My game was off. All too quickly, the scouts stopped calling, stopped taking my calls.

Winter came and went. Then spring. Then we graduated. That's when Kerry Anne hooked up with Dean and I finally felt like I could get on with my life.

I should have warned him.

After getting fired, I was able to scrape together a few odd jobs, enough to provide me with food and gas to keep me from starving to death and freezing on the coldest of nights. Two of those months were the coldest on record, if you can believe that after all the global warming we've been having. The heater finally crapped out one night with the thermometer frozen in the teens below zero. My earlobes got frostbite. They still itch like hell sometimes, though not as much as my bottom gums do. I bought a little Sterno stove and set it up on the floor of the passenger side to warm up the cab. Nearly asphyxiated myself. Not very bright, eh? If the plastic over the broken window hadn't blown in, I guess I would've died. The irony of it is, I probably owe it to some asshole juvenile delinquent for smashing it in the first place thinking he might find something worth hocking for coke money.

After I got out of the hospital, I finally broke down and went to one of those shelters. You can talk about pride and shit all you want, but for me those things had long since gone out the broken window. All I had left was my name, and even that wasn't worth a hunk of moldy bread.

So you can imagine my surprise when I ran into Dean there, at the shelter. And he wasn't down on his luck, either. He was actually helping out. Here was a guy I'd thought was a scourge on the world, unredeemable, a stain on humanity. And he's doing charity work, for freaking chrissake! It just about blew my mind. But that wasn't the half of it.

"It was Kerry Anne," he said. "Remember her?"

He must've misinterpreted the blank stare I gave him. I mean, I'd tried to forget her—tried to forget *them*—right? But how do you forget the worst thing to ever happen to you and the person responsible for it?

"From high school?" he added, unhelpfully.

I gave him an impatient wave. "So she converted you, eh?"

He laughed and nodded. "Made me see my faults."

I almost laughed with him. The old Dean, who never gave a shit about anyone, serving soup to lowlifes. It was perfect. I mean, sure,

I hated that I was one of those lowlifes, but there was something so…so karmic about the whole thing. The guy who used to be able to talk his way out of doing anything for anyone else had been reduced to this. Even the slight lisp he'd picked up was perfect.

I didn't try to stop the bitterness from filling me. I felt like I was entitled.

"We're still married," he added.

I think my jaw must've fallen about forty stories.

"You and Kerry?" I said, incredulous. "Happily married?" I couldn't see it. I didn't *want* to see it.

"Like I said, she showed me the error of my ways."

He told me he worked a few days a week at the juvy center helping out troubled youths, showing them how to fix cars. I told him I thought he'd gone on to law school—just a bit of news I'd caught in the wind some years after graduation, on one of my trips back to see my folks—and he shrugged and said that he had. He'd even opened up his own law practice. "We do a lot of *pro bono* work."

I didn't know what to make of that. This wasn't the same Dean I'd known and hated for all these. And I wanted to still hate him, but I found it wasn't so easy anymore, even when I took into account that he'd apparently succeeded with Kerry Anne, whereas I hadn't. I say apparently because I could see it in his eyes, something suspicious, something forced. And looking around then, I could tell that he felt out of place there at the shelter, despite all his do-good talk. It wasn't in-your-face obvious, but I could tell that the other helpers avoided him.

"Children?" I asked.

He seemed startled, then quickly dismissed it with a shake of his head, saying, "We can't." And I knew this was a sensitive subject for him. Maybe he was impotent or maybe Kerry Anne was infertile. Either way, it wasn't a subject to joke about, even given the unusual circumstances we found ourselves in.

"We manage," he continued, "Ker and I. It's tough sometimes, you know. This charity work doesn't pay the bill collectors, of course, but it has to be done."

"What?" I said. I'd been drifting.

"We all have debts to pay, right?"

I hesitated, then nodded. Was he referring to my own troubles years back? Was he saying I hadn't paid them in full?

"God knows I have debts to pay," he murmured, almost to himself.

He looked up suddenly and his own demeanor changed, brightened. "So, what are you doing here, Kurt? I thought you went off to play football or something in college. I figured you'd be playing pro by now. You have to excuse me, but I don't follow sports. Kerry Anne, you know. She was never much into that."

"You never had much aptitude for it, either," I said, and we both laughed. It felt familiar and good.

I told him what I'd been doing for the past fifteen years. I told him everything, actually. I don't know why. Maybe I was lonely and nostalgic for the old friendship. Maybe I'd picked up something in the way he spoke or sat, a clue that things weren't exactly as he presented them. Anyway, it all just spilled out of me, like a disease I needed to be cleansed of. Or maybe it was hope. Seeing him was like a revelation that even the worst of us can still somehow find a way to make it to the light, to do good and all that crap.

I confessed that I'd never expected him and Kerry Anne to last. I even told him I felt a little jealous. By then, of course, the renewed connection had dulled my anger—not all of it, but enough so that it no longer controlled me. All that was left was mostly this sense of remorse, of missed opportunities.

"I admit, Kurt," he said, breathing deeply, "it hasn't been easy. You know what I was like back then." I nodded. "First thing Kerry Anne told me when we started seeing each other was that I would have to change." He clicked his teeth—another annoying little nervous habit he seemed to have picked up. "In fact, she made it a condition."

"Made what a condition?"

But he didn't answer. "You got a raw deal, Kurt. I'm sorry about that."

"So, she told you what happened? The whole thing? The truth?" And when he nodded I felt myself get angry all over again. I mean, I'd suspected he knew, but here he was admitting it himself. "So you knew it was all a lie! Why didn't you say something at the time?"

"Would you have?"

I snapped my mouth closed.

He shrugged. "Besides, Kurt, it was all settled. I thought you'd be…I thought you'd recover. You always did."

I chewed on that for a moment. The past is the past, I told myself. But I couldn't keep the spite from my voice. "So she threatened to—what?—ruin you if you so much as tried anything with her?"

He looked away, then back. He started to laugh.

After a moment, I began to laugh, too. I said, "Well, you turned out all right, so that counts for something. Good old Kerry Anne."

"Yeah, good old Kerry Anne."

"I'm glad for you both."

"Listen," he told me, and I knew by the way he said it that he was wanting to change the subject. "Why don't you bring your car by? I'll have the kids fix it right up, free of charge."

"You'd do that? No hard feelings? I mean, after what happened between us and Kerry Anne and…"

He laid a hand on my shoulder and said, "It's in the past, man. And I'm sure Kerry Anne wouldn't forgive me for not offering."

I could see that. So it really wasn't Dean making the offer, it was Kerry Anne. And that's when I knew: he was afraid of her! But then he surprised me by giving me twenty bucks out of his own pocket. "For gas," he said. "And…whatever." And I knew *that* was at least from him, and I was touched by the gesture. I promised I would come back.

"I'll share another bowl with you before I have to go," he said, urging a second helping of soup into my hands. We sat together in silence, he half-heartedly sipping his broth while I chewed on the stringy bits of chicken. Neither of us said anything. Each of us was lost in his own thoughts.

Before we were done, he got a call on his cell, and I could tell by the look on his face, even before he'd pulled the phone out of his pocket, that it was Kerry Anne.

"I gotta take this, Kurt. Sit tight; I'll be right back."

He hurried off to one side of the shelter, far enough away that I could hear his voice but not make out any of the words. He glanced over once or twice before finishing the call and returning.

"That was—"

"Kerry Anne," I said, once more unable to keep the bitterness from my voice. "Yeah, I figured. Did you tell her I said hi?"

He took a deep breath and shrugged. "Listen, before I go…" He mumbled something and I had to ask him to repeat it. "It's your breath, Kurt." He was obviously embarrassed to bring it up, probably as embarrassed as I was hearing how bad he thought it was. I knew it was bad, but you never want to hear those kinds of things out loud, not from friends or former friends; not even from former enemies. Strangers can criticize you and it usually won't mean shit, but when it's someone you shared a big part of your life with, then…

"When's the last time you brushed?"

I told him toothpaste was a luxury I couldn't afford.

He reached into his wallet, and for a second I thought he was going to hand me another twenty. Instead, he pulled out a small rectangle of paper. "Here's the number to my dentist."

I glanced quickly at it—KM DENTISTRY, LLC—before stuffing it into my back pocket.

"They take a lot of charity cases." Except he didn't use the word charity. He called it civic service, but I could tell he meant charity. "They're just around the corner, in the Carcher Building. At least let them take a look inside. Let them do a cleaning. They'll tell you if there are any problems you need to have fixed."

I was pretty sure there wouldn't be any problems and said so. I'd always had really good teeth, healthy gums, never any cavities. The bad breath was just because I hadn't brushed in a while. Hadn't been eating very well, either, if we're being totally honest about it.

He had to have heard the irritation in my voice, but he ignored it. He patted me on the shoulder, gave me a wink, and told me to go and get the cleaning. After he left, I almost felt like crying.

I stayed a few nights at the shelter and left when the weather warmed up again, but I didn't cross paths with Dean after that. To be honest, I was glad about it. Something about seeing him, talking with him, had made me uncomfortable. The more I reflected on it, the stronger the feeling grew.

After I returned to my truck, I spent those twenty dollars on food and, I'm ashamed to say, a bottle of cheap whiskey. The money got me enough ramen and cheese to last a couple weeks. I collected spring rainwater in the tarp spread out across the bed of the truck, used it to boil the noodles for soup, chased it with the alcohol, which did a fair job of also keeping me warm.

I probably never would have taken Dean up on his suggestion of seeing the dentist if I hadn't bitten down on a piece of gravel and chipped a molar. After the initial pain, the thing seemed fine, except when I drank something cold or hot. After a few days though, it started feeling like someone was digging around inside my mouth with a blowtorch. It was this constant ache, night and day, and I finally had to concede that it was something I could no longer ignore.

Even so, I held off calling the number on that card. The idea of accepting that kind of charity seemed somehow indecent. It wasn't like getting a bowl of soup when you were so hungry that your hands would shake like aspen leaves in a wind storm and your shoes were practically falling off your feet from being so loose. I'd always thought of dental work as one of those optional healthcare benefits, probably because I'd never had problems with my teeth before.

But that wasn't the only reason I'd resisted taking Dean's offer. That weird uneasy feeling I'd had since seeing him that day at the shelter? Well, it stuck to me like a bad odor coming from the bottom of my shoe, and it seemed to get worse whenever I thought about seeing the dentist. I couldn't put my finger on it exactly, but deep down I knew something wasn't quite right. Call it a gut instinct. Call it the old competitive distrust coming back. Call it shame or embarrassment or even spite. But whatever it was, the pain finally got to the point where none of it mattered anymore. Besides, it wasn't like I had pressing engagements to attend to elsewhere.

I stopped first at the soup kitchen, hoping to find Dean there. I wanted to ask him some questions, which I should've the first time, but I was told he hadn't been there in a couple weeks. Maybe if he had been, things would have turned out differently. For me, anyway. I don't know. Him? I think I knew that ship had already sailed.

Anyway, I soon found myself standing in the lobby of the Carcher Building, all glass and steel around me and the fragrant aroma of fresh baked sweets drifting out from the coffee shop. My stomach was empty, growling bitterly at the cruelty of it; my chipped molar throbbed so badly that I couldn't even swallow the soup I'd been offered just an hour earlier.

I found KM DENTISTRY, LLC on the directory and proceeded up to the fourth floor.

When the elevator doors opened, I was so shocked at how nice the place was that at first I thought I had gotten off on the wrong floor. Then I started to wonder how a place like this could do so well taking charity cases. I must've had the wrong dental office. But the receptionist—Mary, I think her name was, or Mindy—was real nice and she told me they'd been expecting me. I don't know how they could have, but I brushed it out of my mind, figuring it for something they said to set people's minds at ease, people like me. She said they could fit me in right then if I had the time.

If I had the time? I had all the time in the world, and a tooth that was threatening to cut it short if I had to wait much longer.

I suppose if she'd made the appointment for later in the week, or even later that same day, I might've chickened out and never gone back. Maybe. There were ways to get painkillers on the street. I'd never resorted to them, but it's like I said: things were quickly going from bad to worse, and I strongly suspected hell was just over the horizon.

I often think about all that as I sit here warming my hands on my bowl of soup I shouldn't complain. At least I can enjoy the measly bits of meat in it.

As it was, I didn't even have a chance to think twice before they were ushering me into a seat in the back office, one of those flashy nice examination rooms with the ultraclean, starkly bright, stainless steel equipment. They started right in with taking my x-rays.

I was told to relax while the doctor—that's what they called the dentist, which seemed a bit pretentious—took a look at the pictures.

So I was lying there with this twenty pound lead vest on me because they'd forgotten to take it off and admiring this nice poster taped to the ceiling—a basketful of kittens spilling out of it—when I heard the door open and someone come in.

There was the usual sound of shuffling of papers, then: "Kurt?" I stretched my neck back to see, but the owner of that voice was standing just out of my line of sight. "Kurt Harris, is that you? Son of a gun, it really is you!"

She was dressed in a white lab coat, and even though she was wearing a blue surgical mask, I didn't need to see her face to recognize her.

"Kerry Anne."

Truth be told, I wasn't really all that surprised. KM Dentistry. Kerry Anne's last name had been Malvern. Deep down I'd already figured it out, and so that would explain the uneasiness I'd been feeling the past few weeks. As far as being ashamed that she was seeing me like this, there was a little of that. But, Dean would've told her about me being down on my luck; showing up didn't do anything but prove what she already would have known.

I did, however, derive some pleasure knowing she hadn't taken Dean's name when they'd married.

"So, you're a dentist now?" I said. Duh.

She smiled forgivingly. "I saw the name on the file, Kurt, but I didn't, you know, make the connection until I saw you. I see so many cases a day that I sometimes just go on autopilot after a while."

"Dean didn't tell you I'd be coming in?"

Her face tightened, but didn't answer. Instead, she wiggled a pair of fingers at the top of her head, changing the subject. "You're…"

"Yeah," I said, "I got my father's baldness."

She immediately winced. She must've realized bringing my parents up would cause some resentment on my part. I'd forgiven her years ago, but she wouldn't know that. "Sorry to hear about them," she mumbled. "They didn't…"

Deserve it?

No, I didn't either, but I didn't say what I was thinking.

I had every reason to be bitter, but for some reason I can't explain, seeing her, just being in her presence, made me forget it. Maybe it was the genuine warmth in her smile, at least what I could see of it in her eyes.

"I went back to the shelter this morning," I said, "but they told me Dean hadn't been there in a while."

She stopped, and the temperature in the room seemed to drop a few degrees.

"He…sometimes forgets."

It seemed like a strange thing to say, and I sensed that there were issues between them that Dean hadn't stated outright when we'd talked. I had, nevertheless, picked up on them, and now I was convinced I was right. Not everything was as primrose perfect in their little world as Dean had made it seem.

She excused herself and moved out of sight for a moment. I could hear her behind me, collecting instruments, washing her hands. When she returned it was minus the lab coat and suddenly, despite all my defenses, despite whatever bitterness I should've held for her all these years, I found myself falling for her once again. I wanted her. Dear god, I wanted her badly.

Was I crazy to think such a thing?

She was still very attractive. Maybe even more than when I'd last seen her. And this wasn't just because I was seeing her through the eyes of a man who no longer possessed any hope or prospects or dignity, but as a man who had finally grown out of his uncontrolled teenage passions and awkwardness. I could now appreciate beauty with an objective eye, as something to be admired. Kerry Anne had grown into a beautiful woman.

Back in high school she'd had this impenetrable aura of girlish innocence about her. She had been attractive back then, but she'd dressed plainly, wasn't flashy. All that was gone now. Now she exuded sensuality. Her thin white blouse stretched tight across her breasts, and in that chilly, air conditioned room, there was no doubt in my mind that there was anything innocent about her anymore.

She turned her back for a brief moment. I admired.

Stop, I scolded myself. I told myself to behave, to stop looking. The *last* place I needed to go with Kerry Anne was the one place that had torn my life apart the first time. And yet, there was this deep-seeded urge to—

What? Win her back?

She tugged her mask down over her chin, shaking her head but smiling. The pleasure there was genuine, if not a little wistful. Was that remorse I sensed, regret at how things had turned out between us? Maybe if we'd known each other years later than we did, had waited, then everything would've been…better.

Maybe if Dean had been the one to win her years before, he'd be the one sitting in this chair and I'd be the one married to her now.

"You're looking a bit scraggly," she said. She touched the stubble on my cheek, sending a rush of white hot mercury flowing through my veins. I closed my eyes for a moment, then snapped them open again. I didn't want her to see the effect she was having on me.

She leaned over me to adjust the light and whatever grip I had on rational thought was immediately defeated, swamped by the rush of my desire for her. Had it been lying inside of me, dormant all these years? Is that why I had moved away from Edgemont, to bury it? Had I come back hoping to see it resurrected?

Had I bitten down on that stone on purpose?

Of course not.

Still...

Her teeth were dazzlingly white, like fresh fallen snow, and her eyes held such warmth that they could've melted arctic ice. I wondered distractedly who did her teeth for her—obviously not herself—and that thought reminded me of the old riddle about the town with the two barbers, one with the crappy haircut and the messy shop, and the other barber with the nice cut with the sparkling clean shop, and who would you pick to go to if you needed a cut? Obviously, you'd pick the one with the messy shop.

And there I was wondering if Kerry Anne was a crappy dentist because she had such perfect teeth—somewhere inside my head, there came a bray of laughter at the preposterousness of such a conclusion—when she said, "You were always the most handsome boy in school. You're still handsome, underneath all that."

Was she toying with me? Or was it just her typical bedside manner? Bedside? I wanted her *in* bed, not beside it. I wanted her luscious lips, the reddest I'd seen in a long time, on my mouth. I wanted to touch her perfect skin. I wanted to peel away that spotless white blouse.

Once more I became aware of my own sad state, my poor, dirty clothes, my rankness. I sighed dejectedly. "You're not so bad looking yourself," I said, laughing perhaps a bit too loudly.

"Behave, Kurt."

But she was laughing, too. And suddenly I felt myself relax.

I'd long ago come to terms with the fact that I'd made mistakes in high school. I'd paid my dues, maybe even more than my dues. But the world gives you a pass on some things even as it makes it up on others. Maybe she'd realized over the years that she'd made some mistakes herself. Maybe she was trying to make up for them now. We'd both been foolish children back then, naïve, meddling in affairs we had no business in.

And here I was, letting myself get ever closer to that dangerous precipice once again.

Was I a fool? Maybe. And yet I couldn't help myself.

She busied herself to one side with a tray of instruments, arranging the mirrors and probes nervously, laughing perhaps a bit too gaily. "Do you remember Mr. Dregs?" she asked. "That day he asked you to go up to the board?"

The old school memories had been trickling back into my head ever since I'd seen Dean a couple weeks earlier, like he'd popped the cork off a wine bottle to let it breathe. But now the bottle had been knocked over; the wine was gushing out.

"Yeah, I remember," I said. Funny, that she'd pick that memory to talk about. "You came to my rescue." I wanted to ask her why she'd done what she had. What had I done to attract her attention? Her mercy. And then, later, what had I done to warrant her acrimony?

She'd been scared. She was so innocent, such an angel...

I wanted to change the subject. "You can't imagine how surprised I was when I heard you were still with Dean."

I thought I caught a smug look in her eyes before she pulled her mask back up. She settled onto her stool and drew herself close to me.

"He's changed, you know. He was... He had some unattractive traits."

I was a little surprised that she'd so readily admit this. Especially to me, since she had to know by now that I had never been as bad as he had.

I told myself to drop it. No sense to dredging it all up again.

"Did he tell you why he changed, Kurt?"

I frowned and shook my head. *Why* seemed like the wrong question, so I answered with the *how*: "I gathered you had something to do with it."

The corners of her eyes crinkled. "Well, of course."

I laughed uncomfortably at that.

"Nobody's *totally* bad," she concluded. "Just like nobody's totally good, either, right?"

"What do you mean?" Was she finally admitting to what she'd done to me all those years ago? Was she acknowledging that the virtuous little girl everyone thought she'd been hadn't been quite so good after all?

"Never mind. I'm just rambling." She leaned down, her face close to mine, and for a second I thought she was going to kiss me. In that moment I could remember exactly the way she'd tasted, all those years ago, the feel of her lips on mine, the softness of her tongue. "Open wide, Kurt. Let's have a look."

The old feelings came again—desire, anger, confusion—but soon one feeling overrode them all, something more primitive, more alive. And there it was: fifteen years of pent up desire; fifteen years of suppressing it. But, of course, there was nothing to be done about it. I was helpless. There would be no release from it.

I concentrated on her face, the mask and her eyes that looked with apparent concern at what she thought she might find inside my mouth. I knew my breath was rancid, and the insides of my cheeks were tattered by my habit of chewing on them. She showed no disgust, no embarrassment, nothing. And for that, at least, I was grateful.

But now, I almost wish she had shown some offense. It would've made it so much easier to ignore the way she hovered over me. Maybe it would've stopped what happened next, I don't know. But she was so close that I could smell her animal scent, the raw musk of her skin underneath the stronger smell of the soap and the perfume she was wearing. I closed my eyes. I told myself unless I pushed those feelings away, it would only lead to more pain.

"Keep your mouth open," she said, distractedly. Her fingers probed inside of me, nudging, pulling, widening. It wasn't exactly the most comfortable thing, not in the least, but it wasn't painful either. Not yet.

"Wider."

I forced my mouth to open even wider, but kept my eyes closed. I wouldn't stare and get caught staring. But not looking didn't stop me from seeing. It didn't stop me from getting more and more worked up.

I tried to force other thoughts into my head, of the home I'd lost, of my parents, of the NFL career I'd never had a chance to experience. Instead, what fell into the well of my mind was the day I'd asked her to go out with me: fall, senior year, history class.

She was sitting across the aisle, one seat up. I'd pretty much given up all hope of ever getting her to go out with me, and yet I couldn't keep my eyes off her.

Stop it, my thirty-two-year-old self begged. But my mind was once more the mind of a seventeen-year-old.

I'd been imagining the way her thighs must feel, imagining running my hands on them. Her skin, so soft and white.

Please!

I was a hot-blooded teenaged boy, for chrissake! It was natural to have such thoughts. Show me a seventeen-year-old boy who doesn't have those kinds of fantasies and I'll show you a seventeen-year-old boy who's a goddamn liar.

I don't know how long I'd been sitting there fantasizing about her like that before I realized the whole class was looking at me and Mr. Dregs was calling me to come up to the front to write something down on the board. I was, simply put, in no state to oblige. If I had tried to stand up, I would've done some serious damage to myself. Might even have poked someone's eye out.

"What are you laughing about?" Kerry Anne asked, pushing a dental probe into the space between my teeth and gums.

"Hah-hee," I apologized. Well, at least I could joke about it.

She went back to her examination. I went back to that memory.

Mr. Dregs refused to cut me any slack; he called on me again. And once again, I didn't move.

"Something the matter, Kurt?" I swear, he had an evil, knowing smirk on his face. He knew what was happening! At least, that's how I was remembering it then.

I remembered entering a panicked state, but, goddammit if my erection only got harder. I was dimly aware that my present physical state mirrored that one so long ago, but this time I was almost beyond caring.

Somehow, the young Kerry Anne had sensed I was in desperate need of being rescued. She spoke up then, telling Mr. Dregs that I had hurt my knee in football scrimpage practice. That's how she'd put it: *football scrimpage practice*. Mr. Dregs, who'd always seemed to revel in other people's discomfort, took a moment to consider her remark. Then he moved on, much to the class's surprise. Much to my relief.

I remember thinking often about that little episode since then, how she'd managed to get me off the hook. But, it's like I said earlier, Kerry Anne was an angel. Nobody could ever conceive of her lying. Everyone took her word for gospel. That should've been a clue, I suppose, to what she really was like. Instead, I saw her deceit as something else: mercy.

Her stool *cricked* as she shifted, and the quality of the light bleeding through my closed eyelids changed from bright red to dark brown. I opened them without thinking. Kerry Anne was reaching over me for the suction, or the water, or whatever the hell was over there that I couldn't see because of the blur of her blouse just inches from my nose and then the pink of her skin where the button had come undone—*or had she undone it?*—and I could see the dark cleft between her breasts, could almost feel their heft as they pushed against the delicate fabric of her bra—*ain't gravity a lovely thing?*—and the soft hollow of flesh just at the base of her neck. My nose filled with everything about her: her soap, her shampoo, the underarm deodorant she used. Even a hint of that dark, mysterious place between her legs.

Dear god.

I wanted to die in that chair. I wanted to die so badly it was killing me. But I wanted her all the more for it.

She had to have noticed the state I was in. How could she not? I couldn't hide it. And there was a blush on her cheeks, even with the mask nearly covering them.

"Spit," she instructed.

I leaned over, avoiding her eyes, and spit into the basin.

"We're almost done," she told me. "This might hurt a little. Maybe a lot."

I leaned back, shut my eyes again and invited the memories back in. Kill me now, I joked silently. At least I'd die with a hard on.

Once more she began to probe, her thumb against my top teeth, her fingers wrenching open my jaw on the bottom. And all too quickly things did grow painful. I didn't know what she was doing, but it hurt, badly. I started getting a muscle cramp in my jaw, and my head felt like my heart had taken up residence inside of it. I clung desperately to images of her in my mind, hoping the pain would soon end. Incredibly, I found myself even more aroused. Minutes earlier, I wouldn't have thought it possible.

She ignored my grunts of discomfort.

She pushed harder, jabbing the cold metal cruelly into places I never knew I had nerve endings in. She located a tender spot on my gum near my fractured tooth and pushed hard against it. My head nearly exploded with pain.

"*Aaanch*," I said, wanting her to stop. I'd almost instinctively bit down and would have taken off her fingers, but I managed to stop myself. She only pushed harder.

She abruptly stopped, then stood up.

Now what?

"The good news, Kurt, is that you were lucky you came in." She was all business. "No, don't get up. We're not done."

I laughed awkwardly. "If that's the good news, what's the bad?"

"You've got twelve cavities, Kurt. An even dozen."

"Twelve?" I exclaimed. "But how could that be? I never had cavities before."

She inhaled deeply, as if considering how to tell me the news. Then she sat back down on her stool and pulled herself over to me.

"Poor nutrition, lack of brushing," she scolded. She reached over my chest to clip on a bib. Her breast brushed my arm. "Your gums are in horrible shape, too. You haven't been fucking them enough, have you?"

My eyes snapped to her face. "What?"

"I said you haven't been flossing them enough. You've got so much plaque buildup, it's a wonder your teeth haven't turned black."

"Oh. So…what's next?"

"That cracked molar will need to come out."

My hands fluttered at my sides, wanting so much to touch her that she could've told me she was going to amputate my ear and I would've been fine with it. I willed my hands to stay put.

She leaned down, peering deeply into my eyes. "You need to take better care of yourself, Kurt."

I don't know what came over me—well, I do, but it wasn't planned. I leaned up and kissed her. On the mouth.

She backed away, a look of utter surprise in her eyes.

"I'm sorry, Kerry Anne. I just—"

"I thought you'd changed, Kurt. Now I see you haven't."

My heart sank.

Stupid! What a goddamn fucking idiot I am!

"Let's just get on with then, shall we?"

The wall was back up.

She stood for a moment, as if considering whether or not it was wise to continue. But then she twisted around for a moment before returning with a tray of instruments that she set on my chest. I could feel it seesawing there and I didn't dare to breathe too heavily, afraid it'd send the whole thing onto the floor. Yet with each shallow breath I took, I could feel it slowly slipping off of me.

"Lie still." She held up a nasty-looking wire device. "Open up."

And then, all at once, I knew I'd really crossed the line this time.

"No."

"Kurt—"

"No."

"It's for your own good."

"I changed my mind."

She smiled gently. "Kurt, please. I know what I'm doing."

Her fingers skittered over my neck, sending goose bumps down to my toes.

But they were goose bumps of terror. And what was worse, I knew it'd be ten times worse if I didn't oblige her. I opened my mouth.

She clamped the frame over my teeth. My tongue waggled about inside, looking for a place to settle itself.

"Don't try to talk, Kurt." She took a wooden cotton swab and dabbed something on my gums.

I needed desperately to swallow, but my throat refused to work with my jaw wired open like that. Saliva was building up in my mouth and I couldn't swallow it and I was feeling like I was drowning.

"*Unghhhh,*" I said.

"You know what happens when you have a cavity that doesn't get sealed off properly the first time? It festers. It forms a hole inside the tooth, underneath the enamel. The infection grows, moves down into the root. Pretty soon it starts to eat away at the bone in your jaw. The rotting inside of you, Kurt, isn't that deep, yet. But it will get there unless we do something about it."

"Whu?" I asked.

She drew a syringe of something clear from a vial, flicked it and squirted out the air bubbles. Pain killer. Well, at least I wouldn't have to suffer too badly.

She noticed me looking at it and nodded. Then she stuck the needle in the side of my neck.

"*Owrrghh!*" I said, jerking away. When she withdrew it, the syringe was empty.

"Not pain killer. Not for you, Kurt." Her eyes were dancing some kind of strange evil dance. "Paralytic."

The numbness spread like fire and ice down my back, down my arms and into my fingertips, down my legs. I couldn't lift my head, and I couldn't move my legs.

"Quickest way to get rid of the disease, Kurt, is to remove the offending organ."

Organ?

She picked up her drill and held it in front of my face, running it until my teeth actually did start hurting. "I'll let you keep the top ones."

Why? I wanted to scream at her.

The last thing I heard as I blacked out from the pain was Kerry Anne telling me Dean hadn't been so lucky. "But then again, his infection was a lot deeper. To the bone, even."

I wondered then, almost delirious with pain, what she'd done to him.

And then it finally clicked: the look in his face, that day I'd seen him at the soup kitchen, after he'd joined me at the table with his own bowl of strained broth. The way his mouth seemed to collapse into itself. The lisp when he spoke. The odd way his teeth had clicked. It hadn't registered then, but he'd had no teeth in his mouth.

None whatsoever.

"Wah?" I asked, but I blacked out before she could answer.

But I knew. I didn't need her to tell me why. It was because she so pure, so chaste. She was a perfect little angel.

And we weren't.

That's not a judgment, just a statement of fact.

‡ ‡

Author's note

Ah, I love it when good people turn out to be wicked, and wicked people turn out to be...well, still wicked. Here was this guy, had everything going for him—good looking, athletic, articulate—and he goes and makes a stupid mistake and gets what he deserved. Or did he? Sorta feel sorry for him, doncha?

Do you think Kurt deserved what he got in the end? Should he have warned his former pal, Dean? How different do you think things would have been if he had?

Lastly, isn't it curious that Dean and Kerry Anne never had children?

In his nonfiction book on horror fiction and pop culture in the United States, Danse Macabre, Stephen King *wrote: "I recognize terror as the finest emotion..., and so I will try to terrorize the reader. But if I find I cannot terrify him/her, I will try to horrify; and if I find I cannot horrify, I'll go for the gross-out. I'm not proud."*

Well, I am. Why not go for all three at the same time?

Golgotha

H E WAS A RELIGIOUS MAN, so the first time Special Advisor to the President of the United States Richard Daniels heard the recording, a single word rose up in his mind. The second time, he became violently ill and also afraid. The third and final time, those emotions were still there, but by then he'd managed to control them. He was a religious man, and he wished he wasn't, for how could any god, much less the God of his religion, forgive what he had done?

"My name is Gene Halliwell. Eugene Douglas Halliwell. I am a professor of immunology at Royce State College and..."

[rustling sounds]

"Okay, I wasn't sure this was recording, but it is. Royce State College...immunology... Okay. Okay. I should've made better notes.

"I am making this recording on the twenty-third of December. It's a Saturday. The current time is...six-seventeen in the evening. I am in my laboratory. I am alone."

[...]

"The children are... They're at their mother's house for the holiday. They won't miss my absence. Neither they nor my ex-wife Sophia, my students and colleagues here at the college, know a thing of what I am about to attempt; they are all innocent, and I do not wish them to be implicated in this in any way. I am not naïve enough to think they will escape scrutiny; I know that when this all comes down, there will interrogations and they will be treated harshly. There will be the inevitable arrests, charges, slander— maybe even torture—and for all that I have the deepest regrets. But there is no other option left to me. Only I am guilty for what happens here. If you hear this, you must believe me: they are all innocent.

"I just wanted to make that clear.

"While it's one thing to claim all the responsibility, it's quite another to claim all the credit. For that, I can say there were others without whose efforts I would not have made it this far. That is how science progresses. But they, too, are innocent. At least in their intent. I wish I could tell them thanks for their contributions, but, alas, I cannot for fear of the retribution that would find them. May they remain satisfied in their anonymity and their freedom.

"The doors are locked. I have programmed for them to remain locked the duration of this holiday break to prevent any intrusion. Any interruption—were it to occur prior to the second injection taking effect—would be catastrophic. I have left instructions for the janitorial and security staff not to enter; they think the laboratory will be undergoing a chemical fumigation. Let them continue to think that. They must not attempt to enter.

"Now, I hope I have considered all the possible steps to ensure this experiment proceeds to completion."

[...]

"Mail. Delivered today. The last of it."

[laughs; sound of paper shredding]

"Alumni association dues...credit card application. Where I am going, I won't need credit. And the only association I will be alum to will be the school of the dead."

[sighs]

"By the time I am discovered—hopefully not before January second, ten days hence—this recording and all that is about to transpire will have become public knowledge. I have programmed my computer to transfer everything onto the internet at midnight of the thirty-first of December. Let them enjoy the holidays. It will be their last days of innocence. When the world wakes in the New Year, it will be a horrific one they will see. Then everyone will know what I know already, and there will finally be an end to the madness. Too long I have persevered alone in this endeavor, unable to continue using the standard mechanisms. Now, it is only through this final desperate attempt that I will be able to succeed. The results will belong to the world.

"Desperate? Yes, some will say I was crazy, others that I suffered immense strain and depression following the divorce. I am neither crazy nor depressed. And the strain... Well, it has nothing to do with Sophia. In fact, I am glad that she and the children are safely away from me now. No, I am not crazy or depressed. I am... For the first time, I can see clearly, rationally.

"My visions terrify me.

"I am not paranoid either.

"Inevitably, the question will be asked: *Why? Why am I doing this?* To which I would answer, *What else can a dead man do?* I have angered the wrong people, and they're not the kind of people who tolerate being angered. There will be no turning of the proverbial cheek. They are coming for me. Maybe not today or tomorrow. Maybe not next week or next month. But soon enough. They have been watching me, and when they decide I am too big a threat to them, they will come. Then I will disappear, just like Geena Bloch disappeared. And Marion Lemas. And Stephen Archdeacon. And possibly others I don't know about, striving in secrecy. In fact, I am certain there must be others. It is unlikely that I am alone in knowing the truth.

"I cannot be the only sane one.

"To put it bluntly: I am doing this because I am already a dead man. Either way, these will be my last words, so I will go out on my own terms, not theirs. You see, if this works—and I have performed enough tests of sufficient scientific rigor to convince me that it will work—then I will die, and I will welcome such death because of its promise to provide life for all.

"Of course, there is always the possibility that—

"No. I cannot contemplate any other possibility. It is too small to be meaningful. There will be only one outcome. There *must* be only that one outcome. But nothing is absolute, which is why I have implemented the appropriate safeguards. In the event something does go wrong—instrument failure, electrical failure, act of God—I have put into place the necessary mechanisms. The device above me, for example, will ensure I do not leave here in any other state but dead.

"On the slim chance, however, that I should fail—that my work here fails—then the world will have to find its salvation without me."

[...]

"I don't like to think about it. I won't think about it. This will work. That is the only acceptable outcome. I have prepared too carefully, too completely, to allow failure.

"Ah, the equipment is finally warmed up and ready. I'm not, but would I ever be? Probably not. Still, the world cannot wait to be saved."

[...]

"A little background, as I...prepare...the...restraints."

[The recording captures several seconds of rustling sounds, followed by a series of unidentifiable clicks. Richard Daniels, chief scientific advisor to the President will later testify that these noises are most likely to be the arm and leg cuffs being buckled into place, all but the one arm that Professor Halliwell will need free to operate the injection device.]

"Okay. Background. I suppose that's necessary. Everyone needs context. But where to start? What to include? There's so much. Time forces me to be pithy, to abandon self-indulgent thoughts and nostalgia. Once the process begins, I must focus. I'm not even sure how quickly the treatment will impair my ability to speak or even to conceive of coherent speech. I should have written this down. What a fool I am to have spent all my time preparing myself and the experiment but fail to prepare the world, for which I am sacrificing myself.

"Wretched hubris."

[laughter]

"The Nobel. That's as good a place to begin as any.

"Four years ago, I shared the prize for medicine with two other scientists: Geena Bloch, a neuropathologist at the University of Heidelberg—now missing, presumed dead—and geneticist Richard Daniels, who was at that time a dean at Harvard College. We all know where he ended up. The work, some may recall, had to do with delineating the exact molecular pathway for accelerated cellular senescence and apoptosis—cell aging and death, in other words—that follow from tissue insult, and proving that the process could be not only be arrested indefinitely, but also partially reversed. What is remarkable is that preliminary experiments with cells isolated from tissues that had already begun to putrefy could be revived! Not all, but enough to simulate basal tissue functions in some cases. We had hoped we could completely reverse the process of tissue death. We believed we could, anyway.

"We should have never tried."

[Several seconds of indistinct noises, including a curious crackling sound which Daniels will explain is when Professor Halliwell removed the frozen vial of virus from liquid nitrogen storage and set it into the injection device to thaw prior to mixing and infection.]

"Twenty minutes to thaw. Then...

"Anyway, what was significant about that prize-winning work was that the results we obtained and the models we developed opened up whole new universes of possibility for disease prevention and control, not to mention the repair and reversal of systemic damage to whole tissues and organs as a result of various kinds of somatic insult, including irradiation, poisoning, disease and physical trauma. Bloch proved she could reconnect a completely severed spinal cord and even went so far as to show how a semblance of brain activity could be restored after considerable mechanical or organic shock. I say *a semblance*, because even though neural activity in the test subjects—monkeys and rats, primarily, though the results were also confirmed in a variety of other organisms such as dog, rabbit and guinea pig—the neural activity spiked and remained measurably higher than the untreated control subjects. What was remarkable was the return of basal motor function: *enervation of musculature was quite good despite loss of pliancy due to early stages of atrophy!* In other words, animal subjects that had recently died or been dead for up to several hours, could be partially revived.

"Other metrics, however, remained largely unimproved, which was quite disappointing. For example, higher, non-primal, brain activity—self-awareness and cognitive response being two—did not show any activity at all. The subjects, as it were, functioned more or less instinctively, or reflexively, rather than consciously. They were reanimated, but not fully alive.

"As you can imagine, there was considerable outcry over these results from the religious right, which prevented her from exploring these subjects more deeply.

"My own contribution focused on blocking the body's innate systems for self-destruction by targeting antagonists to key components in the apoptotic pathway. Apoptosis, the pathway for cell death. What I looked for was a way to block our own innate molecular capacity for inactivating and removing diseased cells. I had hoped that we might block initial tissue destruction and provide the body sufficient time to regenerate whole cells rather than discard them. That was the thought, and we proved it in a series of spectacular experiments, although, in retrospect, they really only established our ideas in a rudimentary way.

"Like Doctor Bloch, we quickly observed effects that were quite…disturbing. Once the molecular pathway for cell death was inhibited, we could not reinitiate it; in other words, tissues remained frozen, if you will, in a permanent semi-decayed state, neither decomposing further, nor fully recovering into a productive and reproductive configuration. Even externally applied pathogens had no effect on these tissues. They couldn't be infected or enzymatically destroyed! The tissue could, naturally, be further damaged through mechanical means, as well as acids and such, but other destructive agents, such as radiation and poisons, had no effect whatsoever. Furthermore, it appeared the suspended tissue lost nearly all of their nutritional requirements.

"We have yet to understand this last observation. One colleague even joked that we'd somehow created a perpetual motion machine by accident. But, of course, that's a physical impossibility.

"We were, of course, very perplexed by these findings. Nevertheless, we also found them very disturbing. Can you imagine such a thing? Say you had an amputated arm reattached. With the body's usual mechanisms for repair and replacement blocked, it would never heal itself after injury. Perhaps, given time, the body might find a way to kick start those pathways on its own; alternatively, what if the effect spread to the rest of the body? We didn't know the answer to these questions, and we weren't about to try and figure them out, either.

We shut down the project, retracted our results from our publications. We hoped it would discourage others from attempting to replicate our work. It did not stop Richard Daniels.

"Daniels not only tried, but he also stole methods and techniques from us that we did not publish. What he has done since then is to turn our body of work into what can only be described as an abomination against science and human advancement."

[Unidentified noises. Daniels, ignoring Halliwell's accusations, will explain: "Professor Halliwell is preparing the excipient—the solution that will be mixed with the virus to stabilize it for injection."]

"I will not dwell on his theft any further. What would be the use? It is all done and cannot be undone. Besides, the public is against me, me and others like Bloch and Lamas who are now gone. The public knows only what it is told. They are shortsighted. To them, Daniels is a hero. He has— I shouldn't say *he* when it is really *they*: him and the war machine at the Pentagon—they have taken our collective battle fatigue and twisted it to their purpose. A dozen years sending our families to fight. Multiple wars. Another half dozen years besides in scattered conflicts around the globe. Thousands of our own dead. Soldiers killed in places most of us have never seen and can only imagine from pictures and nightmares. We could never truly imagine the horror they experience. So, yes, we were tired. But what we should have done was to put a stop to the fighting altogether. Not to find a better way to fight and kill and avoid being killed.

"Our own shortsightedness is what blinded us to become what we have become, blinded us to what we are and what we are willing to do, what we are willing to sacrifice. All to secure the illusion of freedom and the perception of security. Yes, Daniels was a hero for developing a means to reducing casualties, fewer killed in action, but at what expense?

"We have sacrificed all to gain what we already had.

"And I was participant."

[...]

"We have become gods. After all these years of pretending, of striving for godliness, now we can finally say we are gods. But I fear the day is coming when the wrath of the true gods will be visited upon us for being so arrogant. Soon. I am sure of it.

"Ah, I can see the excipient has thawed. Quicker than I had expected. It's warmer in here that I might preferred. I suppose that means the turning process will also go quicker, not that it matters much, just that I will have less time to finish explaining what Daniels did.

"What exactly was it? That is a tricky question, but only because I don't know all the specifics. The government is evasive.

Unsurprisingly so. But I have my sources, and they've relayed to me all I need to be assured that my suspicions are not baseless. I have obtained samples of their materials and run my own analyses. In my records is the proof I need to expose the government of its deception. All of it.

"Here now: I am initiating the injection process. The time is…nine-twenty three P.M."

[click]

"Placing the vial into the admixture chamber, and…there we go. Mixing. After I have become infected, I estimate that I will have somewhere in the vicinity of eight to twelve hours before the virus accumulates in my body to sufficient levels to infiltrate every cell, every tissue. I have carefully calculated the number of infectious particles needed, given the activity of this particular batch we have made. I estimate loss of consciousness at about sixteen hours. After the virus is fully incorporated, my cortical functions will shut down, somewhere around the twenty-hour mark by my calculations. Minutes later, the final stage: death. Twenty hours, give or take three hours. I will explain fully shortly."

[click…whir…click]

"Time of injection will be nine-thirty-two P.M."

[There then come several seconds of muffled sounds and a whirring noise accompanied by a mechanical clicking; this is followed by a quick hiss, like that of escaping gas; Doctor Daniels will explain to the staff assembled in that room deep within the Pentagon in late December, that the sounds are the injection device mixing the virus into a stable soluble suspension with the excipient, a polyethylene glycolate compound of high molecular weight. The device—"Crude and rapidly assembled, but effective," Daniels will opine—will load the syringe with the mixture before positioning the needle to the left side of Professor Halliwell's neck. "It's a large bore needle, probably a twelve gauge, since the PEG solution is quite viscous." He then says that this is when Professor Halliwell secures the final restraint on his remaining free hand, next to his mouth and a bowl of food (Daniels doesn't elaborate), tightening it with his teeth. The vial for the second injection has been loaded and is in place; it will be administered automatically. There then comes the tinny grinding of a small motor…a sharp cry of pain…sobbing. It is this last that will initially shock several of the men sitting in that

darkened room, grown men toughened by politics and secrecy and difficult decisions. Their shock will quickly turn to disgust, finally horror, as the recorder replays the sounds it captures next: several seconds of what appears to be struggling, violent at first, then becoming erratic, then eventually stopping. All that follows then for several minutes is a low inhuman moan. Finally, silence, which is prematurely aborted by the recorder's automatic sensor. The time stamp on the recording flicks forward several dozen minutes.]

[Doctor Halliwell begins to speak again, but it is evident some time has passed. His voice is broken, sounding lost and transparent, as if it has lost substance:]

"I…hadn't…I hadn't expected…"

[scream]

Ahh, god! Pain."

[more struggling; panting]

"That's the worst of it. I hope. It itches horribly now, and I can't reach it. Stupid! I should have waited in case something went wrong. But now I cannot release myself. Ah, well."

[laughter; moaning]

"I hadn't expected this. I'll die of the itching before I can finish."

[…]

"I am fine now. I can see almost forty minutes have passed since the injection. I know it's just my imagination, but it's like I can feel the infection taking hold, the new virus entering my cells, replicating. Ha ha, I know I can't actually feel such things—we cannot feel at the cellular level—and yet somehow I almost feel each cell swelling with millions of new virus particles, leaking them into the interstitial spaces, bleeding into my bloodstream. My lungs filling with them. My eyeballs filling. It is a curious sensation, knowing what is happening at the subcellular level inside oneself, knowing the agent of one's destruction is contained within, waging a silent war."

[coughing]

In seven minutes the autosampler will test my blood. It will transfer the sample to the analyzer, which will tell me how quickly the infection is spreading.

"I must hurry. I need to concentrate. In the interest of time, I will be brief. Anything I miss I suppose will be in my notes. I hope they fall into the right hands. I should have written this down and sent it to someone—not the media; they cannot be trusted. Who would I send it to? No! I am wasting time planning contingencies I cannot execute!

"Daniels. I need to talk about what he did. Thankfully, my mind seems to have cleared somewhat. The calm before the storm, I suppose. The light before fall of night. Ha ha. Poetic. Yes, that's it: light and night."

[sighs]

"*Qangxi*. That's where I need to start. *Qangxi*. *Qangxi*.

"What Daniels and his team at the Pentagon did was to develop a new infectious species of virus. The codename was *Qangxi*."

[At this point, Richard Daniels, former dean of Harvard's graduate education and current scientific advisor to the President, will be asked to explain how a crazy professor from a small college in rural Montana—yes, a Nobel laureate, but not the first time the Nobel committee awarded the prize to a nutjob—happened to know so much about Project Zulu. And, for that matter, how he got samples of their materials to analyze. And Daniels will be forced to admit he doesn't know the answer to that question. There will ensue a brief but heated argument between Daniels and his interrogator, a young senator by the name of Lawrence Abrams and the senate's defense oversight committee's newest chairman following the untimely assignation of its previous chairholder. The argument will be cut short by a third man, known popularly as the Colonel even though he is really a three star general. The Colonel is the commander of the new Marine fighting force known as the Omegamen. The Colonel will direct Daniels to continue playing the recording; he will declare that what the senator is asking is all water under the bridge. Daniels, glad to evade the questioning, will comply. He taps the keyboard and the recording stutters through the speakers.]

"—rigin of that strange word remains unproven, but my linguist friend—I will not name him for fear of retaliation against him—has suggested that the word *Qangxi* derives from the Chinese term *Kuang shi*, and I choose to believe him for reasons that shall become clear momentarily. The *Qangxi* variant that the military created, *r-d7.04*, or Artie for short, has for its genetic backbone Dengue flavivirus. As most people now know, Dengue was essentially eliminated as a global threat after the development of a simple treatment that affected its ability to propagate via its mosquito host. The treatment was so successful that within two years, the incidence of new Dengue infections diagnosed worldwide dropped to less than one millionth of its previous rate. Dengue was on track to becoming the first mosquito-borne disease to be completely eradicated by any manmade means.

"How do I know this? Because—"

[muffled sounds]

"I can…get some relief from the itching by turning my head. It's not completely effective, but…"

[…]

"The dengue work was that of my close friend and colleague Stephen Archdeacon. Stephen was the second of us to go missing. It was early last spring. When I was last in Boston, I stopped by his place, to see how his wife and children are managing. I wished I could have told little Kristin and Trevor not to blame their father, but somehow they know. I can see it in their eyes that they know, the terror. Still, it was not Stephen's fault.

"What does his work have to do with Daniels? Just this: what almost nobody knows about the Dengue work is that Stephen soon discovered that the treatment may have stopped Dengue from spreading, it didn't eliminate the virus from humans as he'd originally thought; the treatment only rendered the infection innocuous. The virus found a way to hide in our mitochondrial DNA. As a result, nearly every person on this planet is now a carrier of that virus in their cells. It has become incorporated into our extrachromosomal genome and is heritable. What is worse, Daniels discovered that it can easily jump into our nuclear genome upon expression of a single protein called *XRN177*, where the virus then makes not just one copy of itself, but thousands upon thousands of copies. Millions, even. It has the potential to render our genomes highly unstable.

"The government has kept silent about this. Why? Does it think there will be a panic? No, it's because it wants to exploit that instability. And that's where Daniel's work takes a decidedly malefic turn."

[muffled noises]

"Eleven-fifty. Ten minutes of midnight. Another hour has passed—more than an hour—and I am actually feeling quite fine now, although my back is a bit stiff. I should have thought to provide a thicker cushion on this table, though, of course, that would have made escape easier. I can turn slightly to ease the discomfort. I just hope it doesn't grow too bad, the cramps.

"Oh, blood results. Let's see…

"WBC count…

"RBC…

"Shit! Six-hundred pictograms per milliliter. The infection is spreading faster than I had thought. I must hurry. I can only hope these restraints hold long enough for the antiserum to take effect. Now I realize I should have coordinated the timing of the second injection with brain activity rather than setting it for the thirty-six-hour mark, but I wanted to be sure to give the virus time to act. Ah well, thirty-six hours, a hundred hours, as long as I can prove the antiserum works, it shouldn't matter. The postmortem—when it is performed on me—show that it will."

[several minutes of sobbing]

"I'm okay now. I'm okay."

[…]

"Midnight. Past midnight. It is…What day is it? Sunday. It's Sunday. The twenty-fourth of…?

"December.

"My name is Eugene…Douglas…Halliwell."

[…]

"Where was I? Daniels, I believe. Daniels. Dengue. Right.

"You see, Daniels's forte is genetic reengineering. For him the Holy Grail was to achieve genome resequencing at the cellular level in whole organisms. With what happened with the Dengue dengue the, uh, the denguedengden. What? What? The Dengue— Shut up and listen to me!"

[struggling noises; Daniels will explain that Halliwell's cognitive functions are beginning to break down, much to the surprise of those assembled before him, and he will have to further explain that Halliwell injected himself with over a thousand times the dosage of virus than is prescribed in the Zulu protocol, so his infection spread rate is highly accelerated and possibly unstable. "We're witnessing symptomology we've never seen before." The

noises fade into a series of grunts and pants. When Halliwell speaks next, he seems to have regained some mental control.]

"The new…sequences. As I was saying. In our genomes. The kimchee…? What? *Qangxhi*. Not kimchee. The *Qangxhi* sequences provided a perfect target for the dengue— No, other way around. The Dengue sequences in our chromosomes were targeted by Daniels's *Qangxhi r-d7.04* construct, or Q-Artie. It allowed him to act out his whole organism genomic reengineering fantasy. Q-Artie was constructed just for that purpose."

[panting]

"It would be one thing if Daniels wanted to use…*Qangxhi* to improve human health and medical treatment. What potential for greatness there was—*is!*—in such a thing. But instead, he proposed the engineering of a new breed of supersoldier, a new human bioweapon that could not only be controlled using Professor Bloch's neuroreconstructive methods and my own autoimmune blockers, but also rendered using a resource they had in abundant supply already: living human beings. No, not existing soldiers. There would have been an outcry, but the dregs of our society, the thieves and murderers, the forgotten homeless, runaways. That was their secret. Nearly five million prisoners alone, of which nearly a third were serving life sentences. They became our Omegamen.

"Our government infected them, living souls, turned them into warriors for their army. No longer were live troops sent in. Casualty rates dropped, and everybody was happy. Well, of course casualty rates dropped. You cannot kill what is already dead."

[coughing]

Kuang shi. It's a…Chinese term. It refers to a creature in their mythology, a zombie vampire. Of course, mythology is always more colorful than fact, but the analogies are appropriate. *Kuang shi* are corpses possessed and so reanimated by demons. Q-Artie possesses every cell in our bodies and kills it before reanimating the body. But here the demon is man. Ironic, isn't it, given we are using our own zombies to fight against our old demons?

"But we…should be…

"Ahh!"

[panting]

"Cramps."

[…]

"We shouldn't be happy. Should be...scared...out of our minds."

[...]

"Four hours post-infection. I am feverish. I can feel it. Too soon. Perhaps I miscalculated on the dosage. Is it possible? I am sure I checked and rechecked—

"My god, I hope the restraints hold."

[sounds of struggling; panting]

"I must have slept. The clock on the wall says it's almost a half past two in the morning. Five hours post-infection. The ticking is driving me crazy!

"Concentrate!"

[...]

"I have to explain. I have to explain. What did I do?"

[sobbing]

"Last summer—I am better now, stiff and very tired, but myself again. Last summer I discovered that the Dengue sequences inside our bodies can mutate—they have already, just not to what I discovered. Not yet. There's something encoded in Q-Artie. They can make a new kind of virus particle that I'd never seen before. It was a simple experiment, done in a flask, totally artificial. Then, curious, I tested to see if it could be transmitted in mosquitoes. Oh, god, what have I done? I'm sure I killed every one of those little fuckers, but one never knows with absolute certainty with such things!

"I am not paranoid!"

[...]

"The specific mutation I found has never been reported. None of the tens of thousands of samples I received and tested show it coming up naturally, but I know it's only a matter of time before it does. And when it does—dear god—there will be a new epidemic of such destructive force that we will all be wiped out. Only this time, it won't be Dengue fever; the living shall surely die. But that's not the worst of it! Once dead, we will all rise. Dear lord, it is too horrific to contemplate. Those still lucky enough to be free of any of the Dengue virus in their cells, and thus free of the mutation, will not be free for long. They will be overrun by the mindless monsters that the military now uses to fight its battles. But these new vampires will be without the controls our government has built into their new soldiers. The newly dead will rise and…then what? They have basic needs. They will act upon them, instinctively, reflexively. They will require nourishment. They will hunt to satisfy that hunger. They will take those who are still healthy and uninfected, and they will…they will feed on them, infecting them, turning them into their own. And this will continue until there are no more living.

"The human race stands on the brink of extinction, while Richard Daniels sits in his ivory tower and plays god."

[…]

"Nourishment. Will I eat? The thought sickens me now, but will it still sicken me after I have died and come back? No, of course not. Hunger; it's the only thing they know. It's why the Omegamen are so effective, so easy to control. The electrodes the government implants in their brains to control them also control their hunger. But I will have no such control. So it is a good thing I have provided for that. I mustn't try to escape, to seek to satisfy my hunger. I only hope these surrogate brains I have brought and placed beside me will suffice.

"But it sickens me to think I will eat them."

[…]

"Six hours now. I am tired. Tired and hot. The itching has stopped, but now it feels like my bones are stretching, pushing against my skin, shattering. It is a curious sensation, not quite painful, but far from comfortable either. This I knew would happen. Dengue fever was once called breakbone fever. I fear things will get a lot more painful before I lose all sensibility."

[…]

"I must finish my explanation while I still can. I still have not explained why I have willingly infected myself, guaranteeing that I will become the very monster I fear we will all become. Am I so eager to join them? No. Ha ha. No. Nor have I explained the second injection.

"It is an antiserum. Yes, it's true. I have figured out a way to stop it. Stop them. Stop Daniels. This is why they are coming for me, the government. An antiserum would wipe out their army, all of them. Ha ha!

"But—oh no!—it would give our enemies a defense against us. Ha ha! Sarcasm. Who'd have thought it possible before?

"Am I wrong to share this with the world then? What will the Chinese and the Iranians do once they kill our soldiers once again? What of the Libyans? The Albanians? The Ca— The Ca—

"The Canadians?

"Nightmares I am having of this given myself nightmares thinking of this nightmares, ulcers worrying and worrying about nightmares. My torn out hair. Nightmares. Wondering whether or not to destroy it and leave us all to fate.

"Am I making sense? My words come out sounding strange. Or is it my ears?

"What? Destroy the antiserum? How could I think of such a thing?

"Whatever happens to us hereafter—war on our shores, certainly, and the…the ruination of our way of life—it is better than knowing it is the end for us all.

"I am no longer sure if I am speaking. Bop bop. La la. Ya ya ya. I think I'm still speaking.

"I have said it before, if this works, I am a dead man, and that is a good thing. The antiserum will be injected automatically in…twenty-eight hours. By then I will be fully reanimated, though trapped by these restraints. I think they will hold. They are made of Kevlar; the buckles are…titty titty—

"What the fuck? I can't think straight!"

[panting]

"Tiiiii…itanium.

"Calm down.

"Reeeestraints. Restraints fuck

"Why do they need to be so strong? We learned that reanimated muscle exhibits far greater apparent strength than in situ muscle. The military documents I obtained show this to be the case. It's why the Omegamen appear to be so much stronger, so much harder to combat in close quarters. But muscle fiber is still muscle fiber, bone is bone. There is nothing magical that happens to it, no increase in tensile strength; it only seems that way because living creatures very rarely allow themselves to reach full power. There is something in the mind concerned with preventing self-injury that makes one stop, before a muscle tears and a bone breaks. We know of exceptions, of course, seldom observed, individuals who, in moments of extreme duress, perform seemingly superhuman acts of strength. Something in their brains is either overridden or made quiescent. But these acts are not acts of superhuman strength. They are fully within the body's capabilities. In the reanimated dead, the signal is absent. That is why they seem so much stronger.

"So I will be stronger. Ha ha! I wonder what I could bench press then.

"But I have calculated and tested and prepared my restraints accordingly. They will hold. They should hold.

"Temperature now a hundred and four. Thirsty. So tired…"

[…]

"I just realized I didn't factor in sweat. I am not worried about dehydration. That is the least of my worries. No, I am worried because my restraints feel looser now because of the sweat.

"I will try not to struggle."

[…]

"Eight hours."

[weak laughter]

"I said if this works, I am a dead man. After the antiserum takes effect, my body will be rid of the virus; but, of course, my body will already be dead. I will kill the zombie I will become. When they find me come…Halloween? Happy New Year and Auld Lang Syne shall old acquaintance happy to see you again."

[…]

"January second. When they come and find me, there will be a post-mortem. They will see that the antiserum cleared the infection and…am I repeating myself? I am repeating myself. Am I? It doesn't matter, explained once or twice or ten times, as long as it's once. The world needs to know how to rid itself of the monsters that our government is creating, of the monsters that will soon overwhelm us all. I am trying to teach you how to defend yourself against the kimchee when they begin to rise.

"If it works. Ah, but if the antebellum fails, then…

"Then I am one of the Zulu lulu…"

[struggling]

"The restraints will hold for a while, but not forever. I can sense this now. I am sweating and might even slip out, but I don't think so. They are tight, and they are strong. But just in case, I have made plans. Ha ha. If the antiserum fails I must not rise and escape. That is the reason for the g— the g— that thing that is hanging over me. Dam...dam...oclees."

[*"What is he talking about?" Senator Abrams will ask. And Richard Daniels will explain that Professor Halliwell assembled a device that would sever his head, a guillotine, in case the antiserum didn't work. "And how would he know? Wouldn't he have lost all sensibility by then? He's halfway there already." Daniels will nod and then patiently explain in short sentences—it will be clear to all present that he and Abrams dislike each other very much—that the guillotine was set to fall automatically after ninety-six hours—four days after initial infection and two-and-a-half days after administration of the antiserum—thus beheading the professor regardless of his present condition. "And did the guillotine fall?" Abrams will ask, and Daniels will answer, "Yes. It did. Right on schedule."*]

"Such an inelegant device, the guillotine, archaic, medieval. Truly effective. If the antebellum—no, antiserum—works, it will kill the zombie I will become, essentially killing me a second time. If it fails, I will remain living dead. Either way, the guillotine will fall. You understand why I had to take such measures, dear? If I didn't...

"I couldn't risk escaping.

"I shudder at what will arise should I fail.

"God help us all if that were to happen."

[...]

"T-ten hours. Temperature now one hundred and five. Sweating p-p-profusely. S-s-starting to shiver. Hard to concentrate."

[...]

"So thirsty..."

[panting, quiet coughing, rustling]

"Ahhh! Oh, god, what have I done! What have I—"

[rustling]

[banging]

[beep...]

"Sophia? Sophia, ish that you? Come here, honnnnneeee. Thasha girl. I mish you. Come here. Thash a girl. I dint shay I din say...say...

"Goodbye."
[beep...]
[...]

"Stop it there," the Colonel ordered.

Richard Daniels paused the playback. The lights flickered on. Nobody moved at first; they all just sat or stood, numb, stunned by having just witnessed what appeared to be a man's suicide. And what happened next? The question buzzed through their minds, buzzed between them. Only the Colonel appeared nonplussed by the recording's revelations. Then again, he'd heard the entire thing a dozen times. And unlike Richard Daniels, he celebrated each hearing, even though he, too, was a religious man.

Finally, the thin man in the oversized blue suit, the senator named Abrams, leaned forward and broke the silence: "Is that it? Where's the rest?" He turned his eyes to the other people in the room.

Richard Daniels looked to where the senator was sitting. The young man was so obviously out of his element. Richard knew the feeling. He suddenly felt old, older than he'd felt in a very long time.

Every eye settled on the Colonel, who was leaning back in his usual chair with his hands laced behind his head, his leg crossed over his knee. With its high back and thick, black leather, his chair was unlike any of the others in the room. His was the one that didn't match. There was nothing on his face to suggest what he was thinking. His brow was drawn and his lips were almost invisible, pulled into the tight, thin line of his mouth; but these things told people who knew him nothing. He was an impossible man to read. He had that freshly waxed look to him that was so characteristic of career military men when they make their first appearance of the day: shiny face, bristlebrush hair, features chiseled from stone. The faintest hint of aftershave clung to him like heat on the hood of a car that had been run hard but was now sitting idling at the curb. Ready to roar into life. This was how the Colonel always looked, and smelled. Run hard or idling, on duty or off, six in the morning or six at night. He was a man who showed nothing...but processed everything.

The senator threw his pen to the table, where it skittered across the varnished surface, drawing everyone's attention like a spell broken. The clatter sounded unnaturally loud in that room. He turned back to Daniels, who hadn't moved from the podium.

"So he died?"

Richard frowned. He tried hard to squelch his growing irritation with the man, but wasn't being terribly successful at it. He would never have the Colonel's disposition, though it seemed anyone who knew them both expected it from Daniels. His shoulders tensed ever so slightly—enough, he was sure, to be registered by all in the room.

"Halliwell…turned," he confirmed, using the term that had only recently entered the military lexicon. He paused, cleared his throat into his hand and added, for the benefit of the nonmilitary types in the room, "We call it turning, not…dying."

"Turned. Died. Whatever. My question is how do you *know*? Why is there no video? Why would Halliwell go through all this trouble and not record video? This could all be an elaborate hoax."

In the two years that Richard Daniels had been President Lancaster's advisor, he had become accustomed to being interrogated by arrogant, young pricks like this one, as well as arrogant old ones. But something about this particular guy irked him more than any other before. Maybe it was because Daniels had really liked the former chair of the committee, Senator Gorham. He had much preferred dealing with him.

The poor guy, he thought.

Being a scientific advisor did not allow him access to very much strategic information, and certainly none regarding matters of national security, not unless it related directly to his work. With regards to the assassination of Abrams's predecessor, he was totally out of the loop. As far as he knew, the police still had no clues who'd pulled the trigger—much less the strings attached to that trigger. But that's not what irked him now. What he found irritating was the way Abrams was acting. The young senator had obviously not taken the past seven days to acquaint himself with how things worked in these meetings. There was protocol. There was always protocol.

His eyes slid over to the Colonel, but the man was a picture of serenity, a sleeping jaguar. A land mine hiding beneath a thin layer of desert sand.

He had considered that Abrams's behavior might be out of some sort of political resentment. Maybe the senator hadn't wanted this position in the first place. Of late, chairing the committee had become hazardous to one's health; before Gorham had been Tenset, whose private car had exploded in Moscow and caused both countries to teeter on the edge of war.

Richard himself knew about coming into responsibility unwillingly. He'd not sought the advisor position, had neither coveted nor campaigned for it. He'd been flattered, though. And once in, he wasn't so naïve as to think he'd be anything but a relatively minor pawn in a game being played by giants. But if forced to admit his true feelings now, two years later, he'd have to say he enjoyed the role. For the most part.

Today did not happen to be one of those days. There was a lot of explaining to be done, and he hated not having all the answers. Especially when one of those with the questions happened to be the Colonel. He felt like he was ten years old again whenever the Colonel interrogated him.

Richard cleared his throat. Attention turned from Abrams back to the front of the room. "We know Halliwell turned beca—"

"The microphone," the senator snapped.

"Excuse me?"

"Speak into the microphone so we can all hear you clearly."

He leaned forward, even though he knew no one needed the mic to hear him, including those standing near the back of the room. Years of lecturing had taught him how to project. "We know that Professor Halliwell turned because the electrocardiogram stopped measuring a heartbeat."

"Again, Mister Daniels, I fail to see how that is proof of what you claim happened. An EKG flatlining is not proof that Professor Halliwell actually went through with this. He could've ripped off the leads by accident or on purpose. Maybe we're supposed to believe he turned, but so far I haven't seen any proof that he did."

Richard stared at the senator. Could the guy really be this stupid? Did he really need it spelled out for him? Halliwell was not kidding around. This was no hoax.

He opened his mouth, but all he could manage was a feeble sound of dismay.

"Let's assume for now that Halliwell did inject himself and then died. Or turned. Or whatever the fuck you want to call it. I simply can't conceive of anyone doing that to himself. It's..." The senator raised his hands. "It's too goddamn incredible."

"It happened."

"*And nobody else entered or left Halliwell's lab in the time covered by the recording?*"

Richard shook his head. "No, sir."

"No witnesses?"

"We're still gathering—"

"Still gathering what? Clues? Evidence? A matter of this extreme sensitivity and you're still *gathering*? Bullshit!"

"Senator, I—"

"This is a matter of national security, Mister Daniels. The Dead Reckoning Program is of vital strategic importance to us, the most important in modern history. Imagine what our enemies could do if even a hint of this were to be leaked. Thank God it hasn't. Think about how defenseless we would be if they got wind of this."

The Colonel shifted and his chair squealed beneath him. The medals on his chest flashed and twinkled, reflecting the ceiling lights. Those in attendance turned to give the man their full attention. They waited in respectful silence, waiting for the Colonel to speak, which he did not immediately do. Instead, he locked eyes with Senator Abrams and did not break the stare. Richard knew that look very well, more than he liked to admit. Some people said the Colonel had dead eyes, that he looked more and more like the troops he commanded every day, but Richard knew nothing could be further from the truth. He knew the look in those eyes said one thing and one thing only: *Listen closely, son, because I'm only going to say this once.* And you had best heed the advice.

"There was no leak," the Colonel said. There was just the slightest pause between each word, and what was in those unspoken pauses held as much meaning as what was said.

The senator's eyes narrowed, then suddenly widened in comprehension.

"Please, Dick," the Colonel said. His eyes never left Senator Abrams. "Continue."

Richard Daniels took a breath, then dialed down the lights from his control panel at the podium. On the screen, the photograph of

Halliwell's guillotine taken that very morning was still displayed. Its blade had clearly fallen and embedded itself a quarter of an inch into the stainless steel platform that had become the professor's deathbed. He tapped a key on his laptop and the image disappeared, replaced by a schematic with the simple heading "Z: Post Process Events." It depicted the usual post-infection timeline and symptomology on one half of the slide. On the other side was a series of codes, each one representing steps to be performed by the military's medical staff. These included implantation of an electrode in the lateral hypothalamus to control hunger and a separate device in the cerebellum for muscle control. Many of those in attendance were familiar with the details, but they were relieved that the image of the guillotine was now gone.

He hit a second key and the room began immediately to fill with static from the professor's recorder. There was an occasional click, but nothing clearly identifiable for several seconds. Then:

"Unghhh."

It was a vocal utterance of some kind. Human evidently. There was nothing human-sounding about it.

"Uhh huh huhhh. Haaaaaah…"

"What's happening?" Senator Abrams demanded.

Someone from the back of the room shushed him.

"No," Richard said, "it's all right. This goes on for another two hours or so, although the actual recording covers only about forty minutes, since it stops in moments of silence. In those forty minutes, there's nothing much to hear but grunts, the typical Omegaman moaning. I'll forward to the point when the antiserum is administered, which was at hour thirty-six post-infection." He looked to the Colonel, who nodded once.

Richard slid the control to the right until the timer read 39:14:36, roughly twenty seconds before the second injection was administered. Before he clicked PLAY, he looked up. His eyes swept the room, trying to find something in the faces there. But most were in shadow. He debated whether to warn those who were hearing it for the first time. The sounds the recording had captured were disturbing, horrifying. He knew what a Zulu was capable of, especially one that was restrained.

But he didn't say anything. He steadied his eyes on Senator Abrams, and clicked PLAY.

The reaction was immediate and, Richard was ashamed to say, quite satisfying. When the terrifying noise erupted from the speakers, Abrams's face fell in shock. Even in the gloom of the darkened room, Richard could see him pale. Several of the others responded in kind, and Daniels felt a twinge of guilt over it, but the look on Abrams's face more than made up for it.

Sitting beside him, the Colonel remained as impassive as ever.

The racket was gut-wrenching: guttural moans and shrieks, thrashing, the metallic echo of the professor's reanimated body pounding against its restraints. In hearing the recording the first time, Richard had wondered why nobody in the building had heard the noise, but then he'd realized the likelihood of it would have been very low. The professor had planned the experiment to fall over the Christmas holiday. Most of the noise would have occurred overnight on Christmas Eve, when the probability that someone might be in the building approached zero. What they were listening to now had occurred at roughly nine-thirty Christmas morning.

"It's been over twenty-four hours," Richard shouted above the din, "since Halliwell turned. The second inject—administration of the antiserum—is occurring now. We don't notice an immediate change, as it takes a while for the antiserum to work."

The abhorrent sounds continued.

"How do we know it was administered?" Senator Abrams asked. He'd apparently gotten over his shock.

"Because we found the syringe, empty. The needle was broken off. There were traces of tissue on the fragment that remained attached to the machine. The rest must still be in Halliwell's neck."

The senator gave another disgusted noise but didn't question the conclusion. "And how do you know the antiserum worked?"

Richard looked at the Colonel, who turned to Abrams. "Actually, it didn't."

The senator gawped for a moment, blinking and frowning, turning his head to the others in the room, but nobody came to his rescue.

"Just listen to the rest of the recording. Fast forward to time point *gamma*, Dick."

"What's time point gamma?" Abrams demanded.

"Approximately ninety hours after initial infection," the Colonel explained. "Roughly eighty hours post-mortem and fifty-four hours after administration of the anti-serum."

He turned back to front. "I think you're going to find this interesting."

Not interesting, Daniels thought to himself. Disturbing.

He hit PLAY.

[low moaning]

"…suh…sooo?"

[…]

"Sophia?"

[…]

"What's happening? Where…am…I?"

[struggling sounds; upon hearing this, Senator Abrams's face will turn an even paler shade of white and demand to know what's happening. "I thought you said he was dead, that he'd turned? I thought you said the antiserum hadn't worked? It sounds like he's been cured—as in fully *cured." Nobody will answer. "Are you telling me he cured himself and somehow reversed things? Are you telling me he lived?" Again, nobody will say a word, and the senator will lapse into an angry silence as he begins to realize what he's hearing.]*

"What day is it? What the hell is hap—"

[…]

"Oh, dear God! Wednesday. It's Wednesday the twenty-seventh! The virus must've been defective. I should be… Why aren't I dead? Am I dead?"

[…moaning…]

"I'm so thirsty. I'm not dead. I'm not dead.

"I have to get out of these restraints!"

[sounds of struggling]

"Four hours. No, less than that. Three hours, forty…three minutes before my fail safe is activated. *But I'm not dead!* I need to get out of—

"Help! Help me. Oh, God, please…Help! Somebody help. Please help please help please help…"

[sounds of struggling]

"Less than three hours now. So hungry. I'm so hungry."

[...]

"I smell something."

[...]

"What is that smell?"

[sounds of struggling]

"Brain. There's...only one left? How can that be? I brought—

"I brought—

"I had a half dozen brains but there's only one left. The rest must have fallen onto the floor. They're beneath me. That's it. I didn't eat them. I didn't.

"I'm so hungry."

[...]

"Thirty minutes now."

[crying]

"I am dead. I see that now. There is nothing on the electrocardiogram. The leads are still attached and the recording is registering my movement, but there is no cardiac activity. And I'm not breathing. I am dead. I should be dead. I should have become undead and then died again with the antiserum. But the antiserum didn't work. It should've killed; instead it— Oh, dear God! What have I done? I am dead. I AM DEAD!"

[...]

"Eleven minutes. I'm *sooo* hungry."

[moaning]

["God damn it!" Senator Abrams will shout, startling everyone in the room, everyone except the Colonel. "What the hell is the lunatic going on about? Will somebody please explain to me what the fuck is going on?!!" Richard Daniels will pause the recording and explain: "Professor Halliwell's antiserum didn't kill the virus. Yes, he was infected; yes, he did die and then turned. The antiserum didn't kill what he'd become. Instead..." He will look over at the Colonel, then the President, and then he will begin to feel the first worms of panic beginning to rise inside of him, really for the first time since assembling the team here in the Pentagon, and he will wonder what he's done. "Somehow, Halliwell's antiserum restored cognition." Abrams will sputter for a moment, then shout, "Are you telling me he's a smart zombie? Is that what you're trying to tell

me? That we've got a fucking smart zombie?" And Richard Daniels will nod.]

"Seven minutes before the blade falls…

"Just one…last…bite to…eat."

[sounds of feeding]

"Three minutes. I'm so very hungry still. So hungry."

"I'm sorry, my Sophia. Sophia, my dear wife. My dear… I wonder how you would taste. And my children.

"Stop it! How can I think such a thing?"

[moaning]

"Two minutes."

[sounds of struggling]

"One minute."

[struggling, moaning, crying]

[thump of something soft hitting a surface]

[CRASH!!!]

"We need to discuss contingency steps," Richard Daniels stammered. He was shaking, despite himself. He'd heard the entire recording three times already and yet, a full day after hearing it for the first time, it still terrified him.

"I thought you said you didn't retrieve Professor Halliwell's body?" Abrams demanded. "The recording clearly shows that his own safeguard worked. The picture the sweep team provided shows the guillotine fell."

"There was no body, senator," Daniels whispered.

"How can there be no body? Somebody please explain that to me!"

Nobody spoke.

"Are you telling me a…what the hell do we call him? An *intelligent* zombie? That he escaped? Some kind of undead psychopath who needs to eat brains? Is this what you're telling me, Mister Daniels? Is that what's out there on the street somewhere?"

"We've got every agency looking—"

"How the fuck are you going kill it?"

"Same as any other zom," the Colonel calmly answered. "He's no different than any of the others, except maybe a little more self-aware. He's still just a machine like any of the others. Besides, we don't know how long the effect will last. It's probably temporary."

Senator Abrams turned to the President, then back to the Colonel. "I'm pulling the plug on Dead Reckoning. As of this moment—"

"*No.*"

Abrams sneered at the Colonel. "What? You can't tell me—"

"Shut up, Senator. I said no. That would be missing a wonderful opportunity. Don't you see? We take Halliwell's antiserum, and we weaponize it. Think beyond your fear, Senator Abrams. Imagine, if you will, an army of sentient zombies? Faster and more versatile than the ones we have now, able to plan and react and adapt? We'll still control them like before. We have ways to—"

"How do you know you can?"

"The neuroleptic impulse control we've developed will work just as well as before; we just expand it to control free will. We've done it before on living subjects."

The senator's eyes widened.

"Oh, don't look so surprised." The Colonel chuckled, though his face showed no humor at all. "Now, our enemies will never be able to defeat us."

"You're crazy, General! Mister President, I submit—"

"It's already done," the Colonel said. "We have all of Halliwell's notes. We've begun manufacturing his so-called antiserum. We've already developed a testing regimen. As for the good doctor, don't you worry about him. He will be captured. I can assure you that. Now, I think this briefing is adjourned."

He didn't solicit agreement or permission from any of the other members of that meeting, neither the senator nor the rest of the cabinet. He stared at Abrams for another moment before turning back to the front of the room. He didn't even ask whether the President himself might have something to add.

"Good work, son," he said to Richard Daniels. He stood up to leave the room and it was as if a bell had blown, because everyone else began to file out, all except Senator Abrams, who remained fuming in his seat.

Then, for the first time in the forty-three years that Richard Daniels had known his father, the man everyone called the Colonel even though he was now a three star general, he saw the man smile.

And he had never felt so terrified in all his life.

That evening, in the office of his stately Virginia home, Richard Daniels finished his report from the day's meeting and sent it off to the President. He shut off his laptop and folded the screen down on it, opened a locked drawer and slipped it inside. The drawer clicked shut and automatically locked.

He knew his recommendations would be ignored; they always were. He slumped into his chair feeling used and out of sorts, and let his head fall into his hands, trying to empty it of rage. New images crowded in, images he realized he had been unconsciously pushing away. Now he let them come. There was the stainless steel equipment cart that had become his old friend's deathbed—Gene's Calvary, his *Golgotha*. Wasn't it ironic that he should think of it that way? The man had thought of himself as mankind's savior. And here he had risen again after sacrificing himself

"Jesus fucking Christ," Richard hissed into the darkness that surrounded him.

His wife and teenaged son, Eric, had already gone off to bed hours before. Earlier in the evening, Lana had seen something in his eyes—he had never been as good as his father at hiding his emotions—and had asked him if he was all right. And he'd smiled and told her yes, absolutely, everything was just fine. Then he'd locked himself in his office and waited for the last gray wisps of the dying day to bleed from the room until all there was left was the cold puddle of yellow light spilling from his desk lamp. He halfheartedly typed a few things into the computer, but mostly he just sat and wondered what the hell he had done. What had he unleashed upon the world? What had he allowed his father to create?

He reached over and unlocked a different drawer, reached into it, past the half-empty bottle of twelve-year-old scotch that he'd grown a taste for after joining the president's team. His fingers brushed the package that was Velcro-taped to the top underside of the drawer and gently pulled it out. The handgun felt light in his hand, and he turned it, marveling at the way the light played over its surface, its simplicity, its understated capacity for murder. He remembered Professor Halliwell's sentiment about the guillotine, how the blade was crude but effective. And he realized that the gun had a weakness that the guillotine—or any other large blade—had not: a single well-placed blow by the latter would kill a zombie; a well-aimed shot to the head by a forty-five would barely slow one down.

What had he done?

What could he do now?

There was nothing to be done, nothing that would stop his father from getting his way. Nothing.

He checked to see that the gun was loaded. It was, and it suddenly felt heavier than he could manage. He set it on the desk in front of him and reached into the drawer a second time. This time he brought out the bottle and a small glass tumbler. He poured himself a drink, downed it, poured another.

Nobody heard the gunshot.

When the police entered his office the next morning, they found the body of Richard Daniels slumped over his desk, his skull exploded wide open. They found the gun on the floor beside him, empty, a spray of blood on the back of his chair. A single bullet casing was gently picked up from the floor beneath his feet and placed into an evidence bag. They never found the slug.

Or most of his brain.

‡ ‡

Author's note

For me, Golgotha, was as much an exercise in literary composition as it was an exorcism of real world frustrations. There is so much that worries me about where our world could so easily end up if we're not careful: the increasing importance of national security and its attendant constraints (more sophisticated methods for search, surveillance and assassination in the form of unmanned drones; public outcry against casualties, which, in my opinion, only makes going into war that much easier to excuse), the explosion in technological advances (in communication, in information, in social and professional networking), and increasing polarization of entities that result in the exploitation of knowledge for personal and political gain.

We are entering into an era of über-awareness and über-vulnerability. We're not only becoming more and more dependent on information, but we're being crushed under it. In five minutes on the internet, we can learn more about people whom we've never met than we might discover about our own family members in a lifetime.

We trust that the systems delivering our information to us will ultimately deliver us from darkness; what we don't know is whether it'll be to our own destruction or to our salvation.

This story embraces classic zombie lore, but it also apposes it with "newer" concepts: the "old" brainless zombie threat has been neutralized by might and technology, but by the same token, our advancements have made us all the more vulnerable to an even greater threat, represented by the "thinking" zombie.

If we're not careful, it won't be just our jobs that we'll lose, but ourselves.

ACKNOWLEDGEMENTS

‡

My *undying* thanks to the minions of Brinestone Press (you know who you are) for your keen eye and gentle but firm touch in helping me bring this story to life, for believing every step of the way that I could raise the dead. To Nick, for stimulating discussions on subjects totally unrelated. To Gayle, for your promotional efforts. To Garrett and Sela, for allowing me to indulge my tendency for distraction. And to Cheryl, for having my back, especially when it's up against the wall.

To my devoted fans and followers on Twitter (http://twitter.com/saultanpepper), especially the zombie apocalypse junkies. Everything's better with the #zombie hashtag.

‡ ‡

My deepest gratitude goes to my family for their unflagging support. Without them, I would not be able to create worlds with such richness to them.

‡ ‡ ‡

PUBLICATION HISTORY

‡

"The Headhunter"
1st digital edition (by Brinestone Press via KDP)
8/31/2011.

"The Object of Her Obsession"
1st digital edition (by Brinestone Press via KDP)
10/12/2011

"Outsourced"
1st digital edition (by Brinestone Press via eFiction Magazine)
11/1/2011

"Mr. November"
"Occupied"
"Nocturne"
"Open Wide"
"Golgotha"
1st digital edition (Brinestone Press via KDP)
12/12/2011

‡ ‡

‡ ‡ ‡

ABOUT THE AUTHOR

‡

Saul Tanpepper is a writer of speculative fiction for teens and adults. A former molecular geneticist originally from Upstate New York, he now calls Northern California home.

If you enjoyed *Shorting the Undead and Other Horrors*, please check out his other works, available from Amazon at http://amzn.to/rFdes8. A new collection of horror short stories and novellas for teens and adults will be available in early 2012.

Also stay tuned for his zombie pandemic novel, tentatively titled *Touch Me and Die*, which will be released in late spring 2012.

‡ ‡

For more information about the author and his writings, please check out his website: http://www.tanpepperwrites.com.

‡ ‡ ‡

ALSO BY SAUL TANPEPPER

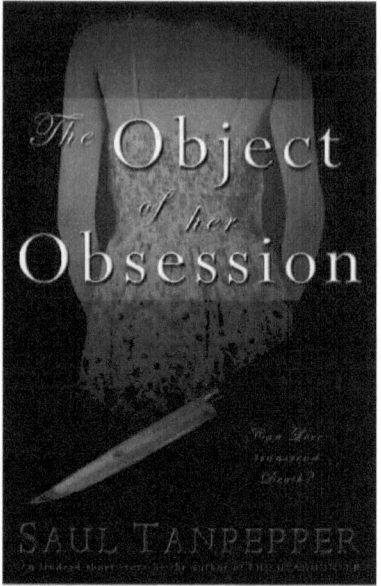

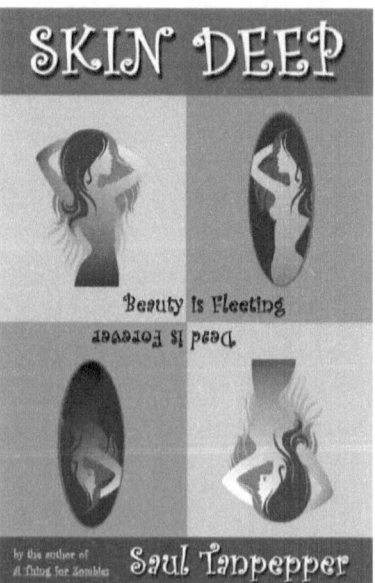

erupt from him. But then it would sink away again with h
n a pathetic burn as his mind teetered on the razor's edge of
consciousness. Teetered, yet never dropped. There were mor
en he'd wanted to scream out, in anger and frustration or pa
n fear would take hold of him, fear of being discovered for w
become. He was ashamed. Ashamed that he had let them
aren. Ashamed that he was still here when she was gone.
what he'd been reduced to. He was a lonely Headhunter wh
revenge. There was nothing more shameful than that. His
tched at his throat, strangled all but the loneliness from him
held too deep for anything to touch, like a treasured secret.
is very existence. Shame and loneliness. They were why he
fish reasons. There were moments of recklessness when his
ld open and an anguished groan or shout of desperation th
spill out. But then he would clasp his hand over his lips.
let himself cry out, were. . . . Well, he tried not to think a
t until I am avenged, darling. A noisy clatter rose from th
the sunburned sidewalk below him, from the machines, their
tines. Like anything made any difference now. The noise a
ion in beckoning waves. A scream would certainly be notice
w the wrong sorts to his door. A man who killed reckle
ne other reason than fear of what they did not understand,
s nearly noon, he'd gotten up to tug the curtains closed. He
re be seen through the cracked glass. Heat radiated in, lay
eady parched skin. After so many nights, the fight was like
s. The flimsy curtains muted the images below him, turned
ntent, flitting around. For an hour or so he'd stood there, n
srarized, stoic, watching the shapes of the people who dared
while the sun was still up. Did they really believe they we
re? He considered the question while his stomach rebelled
rrible breakfast. A memory brushed up against his mind
ucing the shore. He and Karen, at one of the local cafes th
ginity, enjoying a ham and cheese panini. A memory from
prising. When life had been . . . normal. He knew what the
meant the monster would soon follow, the monster and mome
ing Karen. He tried to think of other things, but images o
invited and yet welcomed. Karen's happy smile; the sound
smell of her skin; the soft, delicious moans of their lovemak
n, just as he'd expected—and yet could never prepare for—the
face of her attacker, rising up out of the ground like a spect
Karen from him for the thousandth time. He could almo